Raising Kane

Praise for Lorelei James's
Raising Kane

"...the sex is hot. It's graphic. But most of all, it's done with love and care...I don't think you can find a better western erotic author or better, sexier cowboys."

~ *Night Owl Reviews*

"...The characters in this book are multi-dimensional and the sex scenes smoke they're so hot. Ms. James creates heroes and heroines with serious flaws and then provides redemption for everyone...If you love it when true love wins out over everything, this book's for you. I highly recommend it."

~ *Two Lips Reviews*

"This latest installment of the series has it all in an erotic romance...Ms. James makes you shiver in ecstatic, steamy delight on one page and then become misty-eyed with emotion on the next. She makes you hanker for a good old knock-down drag-out one moment and then soothes you with gentleness and kindness within minutes..."

~ *The Good, The Bad, and the Unread*

Raising Kane

Lorelei James

SAMHAIN
PUBLISHING

Samhain Publishing, Ltd.
577 Mulberry Street, Suite 1520
Macon, GA 31201
www.samhainpublishing.com

Raising Kane
Copyright © 2011 by Lorelei James
Print ISBN: 978-1-60928-095-6
Digital ISBN: 978-1-60928-063-5

Editing by Lindsey Faber
Cover by Scott Carpenter

First Samhain Publishing, Ltd. electronic publication: June 2010
First Samhain Publishing, Ltd. print publication: May 2011

Author's note

Although this is Rough Riders book 9, it takes place between the epilogue of book 7, *Shoulda Been a Cowboy*, and book 8, *All Jacked Up*...

Chapter One

When Ginger Paulson's horoscope hinted she'd take an unexpected trip, she hadn't anticipated tripping down a flight of stairs.

The wool scarf muffled her shriek as she became airborne. Everything happened in slow motion, yet lightning fast. She twisted her body, colliding with the ground in a bone-jarring thump. Her left shin smacked into the cement step. Heat bloomed as that section of her skin ruptured. Her right leg collapsed; her knee went one direction, her ankle the other. Burning pain shot through her as the cartilage in her right shoulder popped. Screaming in agony wasn't an option—the impact had knocked every bit of air from her lungs.

Can't breathe, can't breathe, oh God, I'm dying.

Dots swam in front of her eyes. First black, then white, then gray, then nothing.

No sight. No sound. No feeling.

Was she dead?

Immediately her pain receptors came back online, kicked into overdrive and she gasped in lungfuls of air.

Oh shit. Oh holy mother of God every inch of her body hurt.

Time blurred as Ginger lay at the bottom of the stairs in pain, stunned. She needed help.

Yeah, good luck with that one. You never ask for help.

This time, she had no choice.

As Ginger tried to roll to her right side, using her left hand to push herself upright, she lost her balance. The heel of her left palm skidded across the coarse pavement, grinding off her skin, clear down to the bone—or so it felt as a new stinging sensation assaulted her.

Goddammit. Her vision blurred, her ears rang, her body throbbed. She wanted to curl into a ball and weep.

Think. Crying won't solve the problem. Call for help.

Call. Right. If she could just reach her cell phone... Not an easy task, considering her right arm was useless. Despite the bloodied skin on her left palm and the pain pounding from every molecule of her body, she managed to snag the cell phone from her right jacket pocket.

Breathing hard, hurting, mortified and feeling a little loopy, Ginger used her thumb to dial 911.

"Nine-one-one. What's your emergency?"

"Help me. I've fallen and I can't get up."

Ginger managed to relay the basic information of her whereabouts without cackling hysterically about the "I've fallen" line until after she'd hung up. She laughed and laughed until her stomach muscles hurt.

Huh. Maybe she had hit her head harder than she'd thought.

Sundance, Wyoming wasn't exactly a metropolis. The wait for the ambulance wouldn't be long. The bitterly cold wind whipped snow crystals around her. Since she couldn't move, she laid flat on her back on the icy pavement, staring at the bleak winter sky.

The tears she'd been holding in finally poured out and froze to her cheeks.

Chapter Two

Kane "Buck" McKay had just pulled the plastic sheeting from his Hungry-Man Salisbury steak dinner when his cell phone rang.

"Sonuvabitch." Fingers smarting from the steam burn, he flipped his phone open with a curt "McKay."

"Buck?"

Kane's flash of temper mellowed and his lips formed a genuine grin. "Hayden. I'm surprised you're callin' me on a school night. What's up?"

The little boy babbled a mile a minute and Kane's smile dried.

"Whoa, whoa, whoa there. I can't understand a word you're sayin', buddy. Come on. Take a deep breath and start over."

Hayden spoke a little slower, but not much.

By the time Hayden finished, Kane had his coat and his boots on. "Okay, Hayden, calm down. You're gonna get your breathing outta whack if you don't take it easy. Slow and steady. That's good." He waited, listening to the wheezing silence on the line as he shoved his wallet in his back pocket, grabbed his keys and plunked his hat on his head. "You're at home with your grandpa?"

"Uh-huh."

"Lemme talk to him."

Urgently whispered words sounded in the background and then, "This is Dash Paulson."

"Dash? Kane McKay. Hayden called and said Ginger had some kind of accident?"

"I don't know why in the devil the boy called you."

There's gratitude for ya.

Pause. "But I'm glad he did. Evidently Ginger fell down the stairs at the office and that's all I know. She called about an hour ago from the hospital, told us not to worry and she'd keep us updated. We've heard nothing since. It's frustrating not able to go to her and see for myself what's up."

Dash Paulson was wheelchair-bound, which put him in a shitty situation because he was also housebound. "How about if I head to the hospital and see what's goin' on?"

"I'd appreciate it," Dash said.

"Sit tight. Lemme talk to Hayden again." Before Hayden could ask a million questions, Kane cut him off. "I'm goin' to check on your mama. It might be a bit before I know anything, so in the meantime I want you take your grandpa's mind off his worryin'. Play chess or work on that five-thousand-piece puzzle. Stay off the phone."

"Promise you'll call?"

"I promise, sport."

Kane jammed his hands in his gloves and patted his dog's head before he climbed in his truck. He tried to focus on something—anything—besides his mounting worry on the drive to Sundance. Not only was Ginger Paulson a single mother, she was also her father's caretaker, and she maintained a law practice.

Ginger. Just the mention of her name stirred something inside him. She'd captured his interest like no other woman he'd ever met. She redefined the term stacked—six feet of curves, curves and more curves. A red-haired, hazel-eyed beauty whose Amazonian size was only topped by her Amazonian intellect.

Too bad Ginger was way out of his league. And since she'd enrolled her son in the Little Buddies program, she was strictly off limits, which was a damn crying shame.

Out of loneliness and boredom, Kane had signed up as a volunteer for the Big Buddies/Little Buddies program, a program that paired young boys without a male influence with local male mentors. Once Kane had completed the training, he'd received his first Little Buddy. Problem was, the boy's mother was looking for a husband for herself, not a mentor for her son. When Kane rebuffed her advances and requested the boy be removed from his mentoring, she'd claimed to the program director that Kane had hit on her, resulting in Kane almost getting kicked out of the program in his very first month. That'd chapped his ass. Big time.

No one had expected him to stick with the program. So he'd worked damn hard to prove he had what it takes to be a good example to young boys. He'd had hits and misses.

Then he was paired with Hayden Paulson.

It'd been a rocky start. The boy was painfully shy, small for his age and freakishly smart—none of those descriptions had ever been applied to Kane McKay. After the first month, Kane wondered if he and Hayden would ever find common ground. But Kane saw something special in Hayden and forged a mentorship based on friendship.

Over the course of the last two years, he'd managed to coax Hayden out of his shell. Hayden was more outgoing, more confident in his own interests, plus he was eager to try new experiences. One of Kane's proudest moments came when the kid out-fished him on a camping trip. Spending time with the little boy with the big brain was the highlight of Kane's week.

The bonus? Mama hung around whenever Kane showed up on their doorstep. And sometimes he lingered, chatting her up, trying like hell to charm her, while Hayden impatiently tugged at him to get a move on.

But damn. Ginger Paulson was something else. That amazingly hot body, that amazingly expressive face, those amazingly tasty lips. The woman had turned him inside out and upside down since he'd given into temptation and taken the kiss she'd offered.

How much farther would it've gone if he hadn't done the right thing for once and backed off?

All the way.

Keep thinking about the hot mama and prove your indecent thoughts by showing up at the hospital with a hard-on.

Still...Ginger intrigued Kane on several levels. After she'd relocated from southern California to take over her dad's law practice, she'd involved herself in the community, but she didn't date. Ever. A fact he'd learned directly from her son. On occasion she whooped it up with Libby McKay and Dr. Monroe, but mostly she handled her family responsibilities and kept a low profile.

That's where he and Ginger had boatloads in common. Wild

Kane McKay, part of the infamous bad boy McKays, once the terror of four Wyoming counties with his boozing, brawling and babes, was no more. He'd foresworn the love 'em and leave 'em lifestyle after his cousin Colt had entered rehab. Since his twin brother Kade's marriage, a matrimony epidemic had consumed most of his hell-raisin' McKay cousins. Kane really had no one to party with anyway and surprisingly, he hadn't missed it at all.

His late nights were few and far between unless he counted the poker games he hosted for his remaining single McKay cousins. Kane didn't spend much time with Kade in their off-the-ranch hours. Same went for his cousin Colt. Both men were married, with families. Sometimes Kane longed for the life they'd led at the Boars Nest. Not the nonstop partying, or the orgies, but the camaraderie they'd shared. Everyone had grown up and moved on, it seemed.

Everyone but him.

Or so people thought.

Because he wasn't married with two-point-five kids, the consensus, even among his own family members, was he didn't want to grow up. But admitting his loneliness seemed fucking pathetic, so he hadn't done a damn thing to change those misperceptions.

The truck had warmed up by the time he'd reached Sundance. January was always miserable in the cattle business and in Wyoming in general. They'd positioned their calving season for early spring. Spring snowstorms were always a threat to the health of the cows and the calves, but he'd take wet and muddy over bone-chilling cold any day.

Kane parked in the nearly empty hospital parking lot. He entered through the front doors. After shaking the snow off his hat, he stood there like a dumbass, wondering what the hell to do next.

The blowsy blonde manning the information desk looked all of seventeen. But that didn't stop her from offering him a lewd once-over and licking her shellacked lips. "Well, hello, cowboy. You lost? Or is something broken and needin' some fixin'?"

"Neither. A...friend of mine was brought in a little while ago."

"Male or female friend?" the receptionist cooed.

"Female. Her family can't get here so they sent me to get

some information."

"Sorry, I can't give it out, no matter how cute you are. It was a wasted trip for you Mr...."

"McKay. Kane McKay."

"McKay?" Her raccoon eyes lit up. "Any relation to that hot, awesome bull rider Chase McKay? Is he your son?"

Son? Jesus. Chase was only ten years younger than him. Even on his worst day Kane knew he didn't look that damn old. "No, he's my cousin."

"Omigod I love to watch him ride. He's like...so incredible. Sheer poetry on the back of a bull." The girl actually stood and craned her neck, trying to look behind him. "Is Chase with you?"

"No." Wasn't the first time his cousin's groupies grilled him for the elusive Chase McKay's whereabouts. "Is there any way you can just—"

"Kane?"

He whirled around to see Libby, his cousin Quinn's wife, hustling toward him. Unease punched him in the gut. His gaze dropped to Adam, perched on Libby's hip. The kid didn't appear sick—he was his same stout-bodied, chubby-cheeked, blowing-spit-bubbles, happy-baby self. "What are you doin' here?"

"Joely—Doc Monroe—called me about Ginger." Adam squealed and Libby shushed him. "What are you doing here?"

"Ginger called Dash and Hayden and only gave them enough information to freak them out, so I showed up to figure out what's really goin' on."

"Typical Ginger behavior," Libby sniffed. "She's been moved from emergency into a private room. Come on."

Kane didn't bother to check with the chickie behind the desk to see if he was breaking any rules by following Libby.

Halfway down the hall, Libby stopped in front of a closed door. "She's already had her shoulder reset and they're putting a walking cast on her calf to immobilize the sprain."

"What the hell happened to her?"

"Doc Monroe can explain better than I can." Libby brushed her lips across Adam's dark head when he fussed again. "Ginger is lucky she didn't break her damn fool neck." She pushed open the door.

Kane followed her inside. And froze.

Ginger was sprawled on the hospital bed, damn near naked. The hospital gown left little to the imagination, exposing the deep "V" of her cleavage and stopping mid-thigh. Her right arm was tucked in a sling. Her left hand was heavily bandaged. He dragged his gaze up to Ginger's face. Her hair was an untamed cloud of red, spread across the white pillow behind her head. Her face was perfectly beautiful, nary a scratch, but it held the too-white shade of shock and pain.

Her eyes opened, narrowed. "What are you doing here, McKay?"

"Hello, to you too, Red," he drawled. "I'm here because a very scared little boy called me and asked me to check on you."

"Hayden called you?"

"Yeah, and I talked to your dad too." He jammed his hands in his pockets and ambled across the room. "They're worried, since you didn't let them know what'd happened, beyond that you fell down the stairs and ended up in the hospital."

Any semblance of Ginger's bravado fled.

"I can call Dash and let him know what's going on," Dr. Monroe said. "Including the bit where I'm keeping you overnight."

"But I can't stay in the hospital. I can't leave my son and my father alone. Not even for a night."

"Accidents happen, Ginger."

"They don't happen to me. I'm fine. Really."

He exchanged a look with Libby. They both knew Ginger was far from fine.

Dr. Monroe got right in Ginger's face. "How much pain are you in?"

Ginger swallowed and looked away.

"Answer me. Scale of one to ten."

"Five," Ginger admitted softly.

Kane sucked in a breath. Knowing how hardheaded Ginger was meant her pain was a least a seven, if not an eight.

The doc piggybacked a small, clear pack of solution onto the IV and popped the needle into the tubing. "Now listen up. You dislocated your shoulder. You have a severe sprain that I'm still not sure isn't a ligament tear. Knowing you, I was forced to put a cast on it to keep you from injuring it further until I can ascertain just how bad it is. You have a deep laceration on your shin, which was filled with metal flakes and salt, requiring an antibiotic to stave off an infection. You sustained multiple bruises from your fall. You claimed you didn't hit your head, but I can't take a chance you did and just don't remember.

"So given those injuries...you have to stay in the hospital, Ginger. Just one night. If you're improved tomorrow, I'll let you go home. But tonight, I'm not giving you a choice."

"Joely, please—"

"Right now I'm your doctor, not your friend. I'm doing what's best for my patient." Doc Monroe squeezed Ginger's left shoulder. "You need to heal and it's my job to ensure that happens. The best way to do that is to drug you up and let you sleep uninterrupted."

Kane knew Ginger and the doc were good friends, and it had to be hard as hell for the doc to do what was right, not what was easiest, not what Ginger wanted.

Ginger's teary eyes searched the doctor's face. "Who will take care of Hayden and my dad while I'm in here? You know I don't have anyone else."

Silence.

Libby said, "If you don't mind me bringing Adam, I can—"

"I'll do it," Kane interjected.

All three women looked at him as if he'd caught fire.

He bristled. "What? Hayden's camped out with me plenty of times. Takin' care of him will be a breeze. And Dash just needs me there in case Hayden needs something, right? I don't gotta bathe him or nothin'?"

"You might have to help him get into bed. If he rolls out of it for some reason during the night, you have to get him back in. Sometimes in the morning he needs assistance getting out of bed and into the chair..."

Kane stared at Ginger. "You do all that for your dad every day?"

"Yes, sometimes twice a day. So I just don't think this is your thing, Kane. No offense."

No offense? Bullshit. Before he could snap at her, Dr. Monroe jumped in.

"This would have to be for more than one night. If I release her tomorrow she'll need someone to help her out for at least five days. Would that be a problem for you?"

19

Five days, hanging with Hayden? Five days of playing fetch and carry for a scantily clad Ginger?

Sign. Him. Up.

"Nah. I can get Kade or my cousins to fill in for me for a few days. We're pretty slow right now."

"I'll talk to Quinn and Ben too," Libby said.

"Good. Then it's settled."

"Don't I have a say in this?" Ginger demanded.

Doc Monroe said, "Nope. Besides, I'll be more inclined to release you if I know you've lined up aftercare. You do want to go home tomorrow, right?"

Ginger huffed out an impatient "Yes."

The doc pointed at Kane. "Then there's your answer."

Kane focused on a wide-eyed, surly-mouthed Ginger and grinned. "Well, roomie, probably we should iron out the details before I head on back to your place and start fluffing your pillows."

"I don't need to tell you if anything happens tonight that you can't handle with either Hayden or Dash, call 911," Dr. Monroe said to him.

"No. I know my medical limitations."

"Good. I'll be back later to check on you, Ginger." As Dr. Monroe walked past Kane, she muttered, "The drugs will start to take effect in a few minutes. She'll be loopy, so say what you need to while she's still coherent."

Libby leaned over and rubbed Ginger's upper arm. "Take care. I'll swing by tomorrow."

Ginger reached for Adam's chubby leg, realizing at the last second she couldn't touch him due to her injuries. Frustration darkened her eyes as she watched Libby and Adam leave.

Finding themselves alone, they stared at each other in the sudden silence.

"You want to call your dad and Hayden and fill them in? Or do you want me to do it?"

Ginger bowed her head. "I can't even hold a phone, Kane. Just tell them I love them and I'm...sorry."

"Sorry for what?"

"All this."

She intended to apologize for an accident? Again, Kane forced himself not to chew her out for something that wasn't her fault. He turned his back on her and dialed. Dash answered and Kane explained the situation, sensing the older man's relief. Then Hayden came on the line. "Hey, buddy. Your mama is a little banged up but she's gonna be fine. Yes, I promise. I know you miss her, but she has to stay here overnight."

Ginger made a pitiful-sounding gasp and Kane spun to face her.

"She misses you too. Uh-huh. Tell you what, I'll be stayin' with you for a few days to help out. That sound all right?" Kane smiled. "Sure we can do that. I'm callin' the bottom bunk in your room, so get all them robot parts put away before I get there." He locked his gaze to Ginger's. "No, I'm sure your mama don't want me sleepin' in her bed."

She blushed and looked away.

Interesting.

"I'll cook something when I get there. No pizza. 'Cause I know you've got a milk allergy, that's why. See you soon." Kane snapped the phone shut and wandered to Ginger's bedside.

"Thank you. I'm sorry if I seemed ungrateful, I'm very grateful, it's just...I'm not used to needing help, let alone asking anyone for it."

"I know."

"And you're being so sweet and thoughtful, volunteering to take care of my son, my dad and me."

Really interesting that she put herself last.

"I can't help but worry that you're getting roped into something you didn't want and you're too much of a gentleman to say no." Tears seeped from the corners of her eyes.

Dammit. What was he supposed to do when she cried? Kane had little experience with women's tears, except the manipulative variety. And these were borne of pain and frustration.

He grabbed a Kleenex. "Come on, sugar, you're breakin' my heart here." He gently blotted her tear-dampened face. "You in a lot of pain?"

"Yes. It's like my whole body is throbbing. Not a good kind of throbbing."

He laughed softly. "I do believe the drugs are finally kickin' in."

"Maybe." Ginger blinked at him. It didn't help; her eyes had taken on a dreamy, unfocused look. "Can I ask you something?"

"I suspect you will ask me regardless if I say no."

"Why did you kiss me that night?"

Kane's heart skipped a beat. His gaze dropped to her lips. God, he still fantasized about that lush mouth. How aggressive he'd been with the kiss, how eagerly she'd welcomed it. How his wanting of her overrode his common sense, but he had zero regrets. Even now. Months later.

"Kane?"

He met her eyes again. "Why you askin' me this now?"

"Because we've never talked about it. We both pretended it never happened. Or was that kiss so easy for you to forget, McKay?"

He angled close enough that her breath teased his lips. "Not. Even. Fucking. Close. You have no idea how much I still..." *Crave you. Fantasize about you. Wish I would've taken what we both wanted.*

However, Kane said none of that. He backed off just like he had that night. "Never mind. This definitely ain't the time or the place to talk about this."

"No. Tell me. Please."

"I kissed you because you needed to be kissed."

Her lips formed a half pout. "That's all?"

Goddammit she was beautiful, even in pain, and Kane couldn't resist touching her. "No, that ain't all. But that's all I'm gonna admit to when you're drugged up and hurtin'."

Her lashes fluttered coquettishly. "See? Just like I thought."

"What did you think?" *Did you imagine I came this close to fucking you up against that wall until you screamed loud enough to wake your kid and your dad?*

Unlikely.

Ginger gifted him with a dreamy smile. "I think that you are a gentleman."

"You have no idea how badly I want to challenge that statement," he murmured, moving his thumb up to caress the arch of her cheekbone and the dark circle beneath her closed eye.

"Bring it, cowboy. Maybe I'm not as much the prim and proper mother that you see me as."

Right. Kane doubted she'd be on board with some of the kinkier things that did it for him. "Sugar, you're babbling."

"No. I'll remember every word of this conversation. I have perfect recall."

"I don't doubt that a bit, counselor."

She shivered.

He grabbed a spare blanket from the dresser and covered her completely. "Better?"

"Uh-huh. Thank you."

"Good. Get some rest. I'll be back to get you tomorrow." Kane made it to the door when her raspy voice stopped him.

"You're wrong."

"About what?"

"About the sleeping arrangements."

Had to be the drugs talking.

He didn't even turn around. He just kept walking.

Chapter Three

"Mom!"

Ginger smiled at Hayden when he skidded to a stop in front of her. "It's okay. You can hug me. Just don't squeeze too hard."

He buried his face in her neck and heaved a deep sigh.

She placed her forehead on the top of his damp head, breathing him in. The scent of her little boy, baby shampoo beneath the hint of sweat and the cold tang of the outdoors. "I missed you, baby."

"I'm not a baby."

"My mistake." She smooched his crown before he squirmed back. He never used to try and escape her hugs, but from the day he'd turned eight, he'd gotten stingy with maternal affection. She looked over at Kane, lounging in the doorway.

Good thing she wasn't hooked up to a heart rate monitor.

Holy buckets the man looked commanding, even leaning nonchalantly against the doorjamb. Commanding and an utterly striking example of masculine perfection. Scuffed black boots crossed at the ankle anchored the long line of his denim-clad legs. He wore a shaggy sheepskin coat and folded his arms over his broad chest. His ever-present black cowboy hat shadowed his face—a shame really, because Kane McKay had a beautiful face. Sharp angles defined his strong jawline. The neatly trimmed dark mustache and goatee framed those perfectly kissable lips. And his eyes. Lord have mercy on her soul. She could lose her train of thought in a heartbeat, gazing into those dark blue depths.

Don't you mean you could lose your panties in a heartbeat?

The man epitomized rugged cowboy, down to the inscrutable way he looked at her, so she wasn't quite sure what he was thinking.

Which was probably why she'd never made a move on him.

Well, that and it was against the rules of the Big Buddies/Little Buddies program for them to fraternize.

And man, she'd thought about fraternizing with him naked a whole lot. Ever since the night last year that she'd gone out and found trouble with his assorted McKay cousins' wives at the Twin Pines. Not only had she ended up drinking too much, she'd found herself in the middle of a bar fight, and coming home in the backseat of a cop car, courtesy of Deputy Cam McKay. She'd panicked to see Kane's truck parked in her driveway, fearing something had happened to Hayden, but Kane had calmed her down immediately... And then he revved her back up, with his sexy whispered, "How about if you let me take you to bed?"

"Mom?"

Feeling guilty about her impure thoughts, she said, "Aren't you supposed to be in school?" to Hayden and then shot a questioning glance at Kane.

Kane shrugged. "I wanted to swing by and tell Libby you were goin' home, so I just picked him up early." His gaze moved over her at a snail's pace and she shivered. "You ready?"

"I signed myself out. Got my cache of drugs. Just waiting on the wheelchair." She scowled. Seemed an unnecessary rule in her opinion.

Hayden's eyes grew big. "You have to be in a wheelchair?"

"No, sweetie. They'll wheel me out in one, that's all."

"Too bad. I thought maybe you and Gramps could have wheelchair races."

"He'd beat me for sure. He's pretty speedy."

Hayden crouched over the pink plaster. "Buck said you had a cast. Can I sign it?"

"First thing when we get home."

The nurse wheeled in the chair and Kane left to pull his pickup around. Hayden didn't say a word as the nurse helped Ginger into the chair. At least they'd removed the full bandage on her left hand so she wasn't a total invalid.

Face it. You are completely helpless for the next few days.

Once they reached the patient pickup area, Ginger debated on how she'd climb into Kane's monster truck. Hayden had no such qualms; he clambered into the back seat like a monkey. Good idea. Maybe she should just go for it. She attempted to stand and Kane was right there, gently shouldering aside the nurse.

"Thanks." He smiled at the nurse. "I got it from here." He put his mouth on Ginger's ear. Tingles ran from neck to her midsection, tightening everything in its wake. "Trust me?"

"I guess."

"On three I'm gonna lift you."

"Kane—"

His arm slipped behind the bend of her knee. He gently cradled the right side of her body to the hard strength of his. "One. Two. Three."

Then she was airborne, efficiently being stuffed in the front seat of Kane's truck. "You're lucky you didn't wind up in the hospital yourself, McKay, with my weight straining your back."

"Nah. I'm used to movin' around heifers."

She would've snapped at him if not for the twinkle in his eye and the smirk curling his lips. "You are a regular riot."

"So you can take a joke," he murmured. "I'd wondered. Besides, you smell way better than heifers and you didn't try to knock me on my ass. That's always a plus."

"There's always next time," she said sweetly.

"Lookin' forward to it." He fiddled with the seatbelt. "I'm thinkin' we'd better put this strap behind your head so it don't strain your shoulder and only use the lap belt." The intimate way Kane's fingers straightened the belt across her abdomen sent her heart galloping and a small gasp escaped.

Mr. Twinkling Blue Eyes was right in her face. "Shit, sorry, I thought I was bein' careful. Did I hurt you?"

"Umm. No."

He squinted at her. "Then what's wrong?"

I just discovered my whole body goes haywire from your slightest touch. "Ah. Nothing. I'm just anxious to get home."

He smiled. His damn smile was as sexy as his teasing eyes. "Once we get there, don't bail outta the truck on your own. I'm here to help you, and that includes carryin' you into the house if I have to, understand?"

"And if I don't?"

"Red, you might learn firsthand exactly how good I am with

ropes."

Gulp.

Kane grinned and spoke to Hayden. "All buckled in?"

"Yes sir."

"Good. Let's get your mama on home, hmm?"

Hayden filled the air with chatter, which Ginger mostly tuned out due to the reappearance of a vicious headache.

Once they'd reached her house, she couldn't wait to crash in her own bed and sleep. She depressed the seatbelt locking mechanism and turned toward the door.

"Ah ah ah. My threats ain't idle, sugar, so stay put."

Dammit.

The man lifted her out and wrapped his arm around her waist, holding her tightly to his side.

"I can manage."

"No, you can't," he argued with entirely too much cheer.

Glaring at him didn't cause his sexy smile to slip.

"You're gonna have to learn to lean on me." They took three steps. "There you go. See? That ain't so hard."

"Yes, it is." But Ginger wouldn't admit the hardest part was being pressed against Kane's muscular body and feeling the need to surrender to his raw magnetism.

Definitely loopy from the drugs.

Kane stopped on the top step. "You okay?"

"Sleepy. Sore. Starving. And crabby about being all three to be real honest."

"That's totally understandable. Let's get you inside."

In the kitchen, she sagged into a kitchen chair. "Give me a minute."

"No rush."

Ginger heard the soft squeak of her dad's wheels on the wood floor and looked up.

This aged version of her father caught her by surprise. During her childhood, this soft-spoken man had loomed larger than life. Tall, slender, with a shock of red hair. Now that red hair had turned white. His frame had shrunk, leaving his shoulders hunched, his arms and legs slightly shriveled. The arthritis confined him to a wheelchair, destroyed his body, but not his will, and his mind was as sharp as ever.

Ginger had always adored him. Even when her mother

used lies and manipulation to keep them apart. He'd given up his position as a federal prosecutor in California and retreated to Wyoming after the demise of his marriage to Ginger's mother. Although they both regretted the years they'd lost, she was grateful they'd worked to build a new relationship.

She attempted a smile. "Hey, Dad."

"Dearest daughter." His shrewd eyes took in every injury and assessed it before moving on to the next. "You all right?"

"I've been better."

"We'll talk about what happened after you've rested." He tapped his fingers on the arms of his chair. "Maybe it's none of my business, but who's going to help you get undressed?"

Ginger hadn't thought about that. She'd left the hospital wearing the camisole top she'd worn under her suit jacket and a borrowed pair of baggy scrubs-type pants. She'd only needed one shoe, so the nurse outfitted her with a pair of shower shoes, covering both her feet with socks and surgical booties to protect her from the cold.

"That young McKay has been quite a help, but I'm not comfortable with him...helping you get your clothes off, even though rumor around town is he's helped plenty of women out of their clothes. *Plenty* of women," he reiterated.

"Dad. That's not fair."

"I suppose you're right. But I'd feel better if you had a female around to help you do those types of things." He pinned her with a paternal look. "It's what you insisted on for me, remember? The male nurse who comes every other day to help me?"

"Fine. I'll call Libby. Or maybe Joely can swing by."

"Good." He rolled toward the living room.

"Your dad have that opinion of all McKays? Or just me?" Kane asked tersely from the hallway.

Ginger glanced up and saw a hard glint in Kane's eyes. "Since your family has been my dad's clients for thirty years, I'm betting it's just you."

"At least you didn't sugarcoat it," he drawled. "Come on, let's get you to bed."

"I thought you'd never ask."

"Careful, a man could take that the wrong way."

She stood too quickly and swayed, but Kane was right

there to catch her. He snarled and practically carried her to her bedroom, leaving her no time to protest.

You don't want to protest. You like his take-charge nature and all that big, strong, blustering manly goodness.

Ginger didn't dissect her reaction. She sighed when her back hit the mattress. How sweet was it that Kane set an extra folded fleece blanket next to her? Knowing she was always cold?

Hayden ducked around Kane and curled up beside her. "I could stay and keep you company."

Her heart swelled with love at her son's sweetness and concern.

But Kane shook his head. "Sorry. Maybe later. Your mama needs to rest." When Hayden's face fell, Kane amended, "Tell you what. I am gonna force her to eat so she can take her pain pills. You wanna make her a couple of slices of toast?"

"Sure." He raced off.

She sank into her pillows, too tired to argue with Kane about his use of the word force, too tired to keep her eyes open. "I don't need the pain meds right now."

"You will in about an hour. I'd hate for the pain to wake you up."

"True." The bed shifted as Kane sat next to her. Ginger didn't open her eyes.

"Look, I understand your dad's concerns about me, but if you need help changin' outta these clothes, I could probably keep it...umm, clinical."

"Probably?" she asked lightly.

Pause. Then soft laughter. "Ah, hell, who am I kiddin'? If I get even the barest glimpse of your nekkidness, my thoughts would be impure enough to warrant your daddy getting out the shotgun. So scratch that goddamn temptation."

Ginger's eyes flew open.

Kane stroked his closely trimmed mustache and stared at her breasts, spilling out the sides of the lace camisole. His avid gaze didn't return to her face for several long moments.

When Kane did look at her, the lust raging in his blue eyes caught her completely off guard. She blurted, "You've never—"

"Acted as if I've thought about takin' you to my bed and keepin' you there for a solid month?"

"Oh. Umm. No."

"I have, sugar. Have I ever. It's an impulse I've ignored because I'm supposed to provide 'moral character' for your son. So I feel guilty as hell when I see you and imagine all the immoral things I'd like to do to you."

"What types of things?" she breathed.

Kane traced the length of her bare arm with the tip of his index finger. "Things that'll make you stammer and blush." He smiled when goose flesh broke out across her skin from his touch. "And shiver like this."

"Why are you telling me this now?"

"Because we'll be in close quarters the next few days."

She blinked at him.

"So if you catch me starin' at you, understand you can trust me. I'd never act without an invitation from you."

Ginger stayed mum for a moment. "Is that why you kissed me and ran last year?"

"I already told you. I kissed you because you needed to be kissed. Besides, you were babbling and I wanted to shut you up."

"Maybe I'll have to babble more often," she murmured.

Hayden burst into the room and passed her a plate with two slices of peanut butter toast. "Here's your favorite," he said proudly.

"Thanks. Wow. Look at me, a lady of leisure, with two handsome men waiting on me."

A frown creased Hayden's brow behind the bridge of his glasses.

She chewed the toast, although it was hard to swallow. She choked out, "Could I get a glass of water, please?"

"Sure, Mom."

Ginger jammed another chunk of toast in her mouth to prevent asking Kane what was going on between them.

Kane leaned closer. "Using food to sidestep talkin' about the issue? Really, Red? Is that a legal tactic?"

She kept chewing, feigning total cluelessness.

"We will finish this discussion when you ain't stuffing your face. I'm damn tired of livin' in avoidance."

Hayden skipped back in, but he was strangely subdued as he doodled on her cast.

She rooted in the plastic hospital bag for the pain meds.

Kane handed her the glass of water and kept staring at her mouth after she popped the pills. "What?"

"You've got toast in your teeth."

Great. She swished water in her mouth and curled on her side before shooing them out of her room.

The drugs didn't immediately kick in, which allowed her thoughts to spin back to the night Kane had kissed her a few short months ago.

Ginger rarely went out, so it was ironic that the two times she'd let loose in the last year, Mr. Responsible, aka Kane McKay, had been a witness to it. She'd been at the Rusty Spur with Joely Monroe, celebrating their single sisterhood by knocking back a round or five of a delicious little drink called a screaming orgasm. Ginger wasn't much of a drinker, but the running joke about them having to buy their orgasms made them order a whole bunch. Usually at top volume and then they dissolved into hysterical laughter. Her pleasant buzz dimmed after their designated drivers, brothers Chet and Remy West, drove her home first and she saw Kane's pickup parked in her driveway. Again. Which just served as a reminder that she couldn't forget her responsibilities, even for one night. She always had to be available.

She raced inside, fearing the worst, since Hayden and Kane were supposed to be on an overnight camping trip—the only reason she'd agreed to a girls' night out in the first place. Fortunately, Hayden had only forgotten his inhaler. Once he'd gotten home and used it, he hadn't wanted to leave again so Kane had waited around to talk to her. Which was sweet and thoughtful and made her feel like complete shit.

She'd double-checked on her son amidst Kane's reassurances the boy was fine. In that moment Ginger was grateful that Kane was attuned to Hayden's unpredictable physical ailments and she appreciated Kane didn't think less of Hayden for them.

Ginger had slumped against the wall across from Hayden's room, feeling guilty. Feeling relieved. Feeling overwhelmed.

Kane moved close enough to her she felt the heat radiating from his body. "Ginger? You okay?"

"No. I feel like a horrible mother. Not being here when Hayden needed me."

"He didn't want to worry you because he really was fine. If I thought it'd been something serious, I would've called you. You know that, right?"

She nodded.

"If you're worried *I'll* think you're a horrible mother? Think again."

"Why's that?"

He laughed softly. "Sugar, I ain't one to cast stones. There's nothin' wrong with goin' out and havin' a good time once in a while. Especially since I know you're rarely whoopin' it up at the Golden Boot. Which is a damn cryin' shame."

"Why do you say that?"

"Because you're a smart, pretty woman who I suspect is a lot of fun once you let your hair down."

In such close proximity and in dim light, Kane's eyes glowed dark indigo. Such compelling eyes fringed by ridiculously long black eyelashes.

"You're lookin' at me like you're considering cuttin' loose."

Can I cut loose with you?

Bracing his hands on either side of her head, Kane studied her curiously. "Did you mean to say that out loud?"

Oh crap. She shook her head.

"Didn't think so." Kane's moist lips teased her ear and followed her jawline. A delicious slow, warm shudder worked through her entire body. He brushed his mouth across hers. Once. Then he eased back slightly to gauge her reaction.

Unconsciously, Ginger licked her lips.

A half growl rumbled from his chest and Kane captured her mouth and he kissed her.

Man, had he ever kissed her. A tongue-plundering, lip-gliding, hot, wet and conquering kiss. She figured she'd have a real screaming orgasm if she kept kissing Kane McKay, so she kept her lips locked on his. Lord, his kisses alone made her dizzy with desire. Drunk on his wicked sensuality.

The kiss ebbed and flowed, relaxed and intensified, and seemed to go on forever, but not nearly long enough.

Who knows how much farther it would've gone if Hayden hadn't called out for her.

Kane retreated immediately. Ginger began to apologize, but Kane very gently put his finger over her kiss-swollen lips. "No need. I'll let myself out."

After she'd soothed her son, she half hoped Kane had changed his mind. But he'd been gone and they'd never spoken of the kiss again.

Kane glanced out the window at the setting sun. As much as he didn't want to leave, he had a couple of things to tend before dark. He grabbed his coat and stopped in front of Dash. "I'll be back in a bit."

Dash waved him off. "No rush. I imagine she'll sleep for a while yet."

"Where are you going?" Hayden asked, looking up from the chess game.

"Home to do some chores. Got to make sure Shep has food."

"I wish you could bring Shep here."

"Me too. But I've stashed him in the barn where it's warm and dry." Kane missed his dog, but he knew he couldn't keep Shep in Ginger's house, despite Hayden's continuous claims he wasn't allergic to dogs, just cats.

"Can I come along?"

Kane looked at Dash, then back at Hayden. "Tell you what, if you stay here and keep an eye on your mama, I'll take you tomorrow and you can help me check cattle, okay?"

"Okay." Hayden returned his focus to the chessboard.

The cold air bit into him and he wasn't surprised to see the temperature had dropped to a single digit. He huddled in his coat and cranked the heat in his truck. Icy fingers of snow slithered across the road. Somehow he managed to block out the conversation with Ginger because chances we're high she either wouldn't remember it, or she'd ignore it.

At his place he parked under the carport. He checked the house first, finding it eerily quiet inside. He didn't bother to take off his boots as he wandered to his bedroom. He'd purchased the trailer after his cousin Cam bought the Boars Nest from him and Colt. By that time Colt had already built his new house, Kade was married to Skylar and Kane was used to living alone.

As a bachelor, Kane had no desire to design room layouts or choose kitchen cabinetry and countertops or pick plumbing fixtures. He'd wanted a ready-made house and this mobile home bought at an oil company auction fit him perfectly. Not too big, not too small and easily moved onto McKay land.

Kane poked his head into the extra bedroom and debated on grabbing his laptop, but knowing Hayden's tendency to monopolize his time, he doubted he'd have a chance to work on updating cattle records.

He'd taken a six-pack of Bud Light from the fridge when he saw his brother Kade's rig park out front. It was about the time Kade headed home to his wife and kids in Moorcroft.

The instant he stepped outside, a purple fur-lined hood bobbed as the pink streak raced toward him. "Uncle Buck!"

Kane grinned at his oldest niece. The girl was a spitfire, all sweet girlie goodness one second, wild and ornery as a mustang the next.

She threw herself at him.

"Eliza, did you sweet-talk your daddy into lettin' you help him today?"

"Sweet-talk." Kade snorted. "She browbeat me. Up at the crack of nothin' waitin' by the damn door for me this mornin' and she wouldn't take no for an answer."

"A stubborn McKay child. Imagine that." Kane whispered, "That's my girl. What's up?"

"Me'n Grammy baked cookies today! With rainbow sprinkles and we bringed you some, 'cause Grammy said it's a shame you don't got a woman to bake sweets for you."

Kane exchanged a look with his brother. Then he smooched Eliza's forehead. "I don't need a woman when I have you. Come on. You can help me feed Shep. He's probably mighty lonesome out in the barn."

"Why's he in the barn? Was he bad?"

He laughed. "No, I'm helpin' out Hayden's mama for a few days and Shep can't come with me."

"But why not?"

"Because he can't sleep in Ginger's house and they don't have a barn. He'll be better off here."

Her enormous blue eyes pooled with tears. "Oh no. Poor Shep's all alone?"

Ah hell, he'd done it now. His softhearted, hardheaded niece constantly dragged home injured critters—birds, frogs, turtles, feral cats. "He'll be fine, Eliza."

"I wanna see for myself," she harrumphed, exactly like her mother, and marched to the barn.

Kade sighed. "Thanks a lot. She ain't gonna leave here without Shep. That girl, I swear I'm gonna have a zoo instead of a ranch."

"A llama, a goat, two sheep, chickens, cats, dogs and horses... Yep, as soon as Eliza Belle convinces you to buy an ostrich you can rename the place McKay's Menagerie."

"Fuck off."

Kane laughed. "You love it. Although the inside of your house is as much of a zoo as the outside."

"True. I swear all three girls talk at the same time, from the moment I pick them up until we tuck them in bed."

Between Eliza and fraternal twins Peyton and Shannie, Kade and Sky definitely had their hands full. "You ain't really complainin'."

"That's also true."

"If Eliza wants to babysit Shep for a couple of days, I'd appreciate it. That way I won't worry about him."

Eliza and Shep loped out of the barn. Kane bent down and ruffled the dog's ears. "What do you say, Shep? Wanna stay with Miz Eliza for a couple days?"

Shep wagged his tail.

"Yay!"

Kane looked at Kade. "Got time for a beer before you head back?"

"Just one."

Once they were inside, Eliza made herself at home. She shed her coat, the Hello Kitty snow boots Kane had bought her for Christmas, and opened the kitchen cupboard where Kane kept the dog food. She chattered away while Shep chowed down.

Kane handed his brother a beer.

Kade twisted the cap off the beer, took a long pull and looked at Kane suspiciously. "So, what's really goin' on with you and Ginger Paulson?"

"Nothin'." Kane flicked the metal beer cap into the garbage can. "She fell down her office stairs. Ended up with her arm in a sling, her lower leg in a cast and she's got no one else to help her out, so I volunteered."

"Why?"

Because I am crazy about her. "Just bein' a good neighbor."

Kade waggled the beer bottle at him. "Bullshit. I know you, bro. Need I remind you what happened with Brandi?"

"Christ. No. It ain't the same. Not at all." Brandi, the mother who'd been so desperate to hook him, had shown up at his trailer late one night. She'd removed her trench coat to reveal her naked body beneath it. Things had gone downhill when he'd learned she'd left her six-year-old son home alone so she could strip for him. He hadn't exactly been nice to her, requesting reassignment, and she'd caused problems for him.

"You've no interest in Ginger at all?"

Lie. Lie through your damn teeth, fool.

But Kane couldn't snow his brother. "There's interest. And sparks. But I don't wanna do anything to jeopardize my relationship with Hayden." He swigged his beer. "Ginger is a temptation that I've resisted." *So far.*

"And yet, you willingly put yourself in close quarters with her?"

"Yeah, I ain't exactly the brightest crayon in the box, am I?"

Mouth tight, jaw set, Kade stared at him.

"Jesus. What?"

"Is that part of it? You think she's smarter than you?"

"*Think?*" Kane repeated. "I know it. I barely graduated from high school, remember?"

"So? I don't think she gives a shit what grade you got in world history."

Kane raised his beer bottle. "That would've been a D-plus."

Kade laughed.

"Hey, I was extremely proud of the plus. Anyway, in addition to her kid, her daddy lives with her, so ain't nothin' happening. Like I said. I'm just helpin' out."

"How is Dash? You don't have to like...help him to the bathroom and stuff?"

Kane shrugged, not entirely comfortable discussing the man's private issues. He'd helped Dash last night, but the ornery coot hadn't been any happier for Kane's help than Ginger had been. Like father like daughter. "Not so far. Do you know why Dash moved to Sundance from sunny California?"

"Afraid to ask him?"

"Yes sir. And I know Ginger did some legal work for Sky, which means Sky told you."

"And you want me to tell you?" Kade asked.

"Yep. If you can't trust me, who can you trust, bro?"

Kade snorted. "Fine. Ginger and Sky got to swappin' stories, bein's they're both from California. Evidently Dash's divorce from Ginger's mother was nasty. The mother hired some high-falutin' divorce attorney and she demanded all their physical property as well as excessive alimony. So Dash handed over all the real estate and gave up half of his future earnings to her for a period of fourteen years, until Ginger turned eighteen." Kade swallowed a drink of beer. "Then he turned around and quit his judgeship, and signed on as Dirk Whitmore's partner in Wyoming. The ex-wife was beyond pissed about the loss of income and refused to share custody of Ginger. So Dash was allowed to see Ginger for two weeks in the summertime—in California. That was it."

Kane whistled. "Harsh."

"Yeah. Makes me grateful we never had to go through any of that shit."

"Daddy. You're not s'posed to swear."

"Princess, if you don't tell your mama you caught me swearin', I won't tell her I caught you with her lipstick."

Eliza immediately said, "Deal." She yawned and crawled on her daddy's lap. "I wanna go home. I miss Mama and my sissies."

"We're goin'. Get your winter stuff back on and me'n Uncle Buck will load Shep and his food."

Seemed strange that the only ones who called him Buck were his nieces, his cousins' boys, who he considered his nephews, and the kids in the Little Buddies program. The great experiment with changing his name to something completely different from his twin brother's had lasted until the night he'd picked up a brunette in a bar outside of Gillette. Her continual cries of "Fuck me, Buck" and "Buck me, Buck" and "Suck me, Buck" were enough to make him ditch the name altogether—not that it'd really caught on.

While they were outside, Kane said, "Can you handle everything Monday and Tuesday?"

"I guess. Gonna be a long weekend for you, huh?"

"Yep."

"Before I forget, Colt said something about you pickin' up the generators and takin' 'em in to Brown's Repair before we hit calving."

"Why doesn't Colt do it? It ain't like I don't have plenty of my own shit to take care of around here and I'm helpin' out Brandt and the boys."

Kade frowned. "I don't know. He just told me to tell you."

"*Tell* me," Kane sneered. "More like command me. Asshole."

"Whoa. I'm just the messenger." Kade's eyes narrowed. "I don't know what the hell has been goin' on between you and Colt the last month, but I'm pretty sick of bein' the go between—"

"And I'm sick and tired of his—"

"Hey! Look." Eliza stood on the seat and passed him a Ziploc bag of cookies through the sliding beer window—after she'd given one to Shep. "You can share with Hayden if you want."

"Huh-uh, short stuff. I don't share."

"Mama says it ain't nice not to share. Isn't nice," she corrected herself.

"How many bags of cookies you got stashed in your jacket so you don't have to share them with your sisters?"

She smiled coyly and blew him a kiss. "Bye, Uncle Buck."

Kane shook his head, charmed by his niece's sweet slyness.

Chapter Four

Ginger woke to a spike of pain in her shoulder. Both her legs ached. Her hand smarted. Her mouth was dry.

Last night she'd only stayed conscious long enough to use the bathroom, eat more toast and swallow more painkillers.

And dream. Good Lord had the dreams been spectacular. All starring one hunky, built cowboy, who'd shed his gentlemanly persona right along with every stitch of his western clothes. He'd bound her. Gagged her. Tied her up. Tied her down. Spread her out. Bent her over. Displayed her body solely for his pleasure. He'd demanded sexual obedience. He showed his bedroom prowess, demonstrating kinky things she'd only read about. So it was disorienting to wake up alone and realize she'd been hallucinating about the sexy gentleman rancher.

No wonder she started out the day cranky.

Since personal grooming had fallen by the wayside for the last two days, cleaning herself up was her first priority. She desperately needed a change of clothes. A change of scenery. Ginger felt like a prisoner in her own body, in her own room, in her own home.

Enough feeling sorry for yourself. Your father deals with this every damn day.

After three false starts, Ginger draped fresh clothes around her neck and hobbled to her master bathroom before Kane bulled his way in and took over. Much as his take-charge nature appealed to her, the last thing she needed was her good-smelling sexy helper to get a whiff of her very rank self.

Carefully unhooking the sling, she kept her right arm immobile as she slowly removed her clothes. It was mortifying to be coated in sweat by the time she'd stripped to just her skin.

When she got a glimpse in the mirror of the injuries to her body, she literally gasped.

She looked hideous. Bruises dotted her ribcage. A few were scattered across her upper thigh. An ugly welt protruded on her left shin below the deep gash. Luckily, her coat had protected her arms from cement burns, although her left palm had borne the brunt of her graceless skid across the frozen pavement.

The snappish voice—*stop sniveling, it could've been worse*—dried the moisture forming in her eyes.

A shower wasn't a possibility due to her cast, but she had to wash her hair. Had to. Thankfully she'd invested in a removable handheld showerhead and she wouldn't have to wedge her aching body between the toilet and the tub to reach the main spigot.

She filled the sink with hot water and loaded her washcloth with suds from her favorite Sky Blue soap—a creamy mix of sweet lavender and mint. It was harder than she'd anticipated, scrubbing herself with her left hand. By the time she finished, she felt a million times better, but she was exhausted from the effort. And she still had to wash her hair.

Ask for help.

No. She'd done fine on her own, maybe slower than she preferred, but she could do this.

Ginger set extra towels on the floor to cushion the cast and her shin. She cranked on the water, placing the shampoo bottle within reach before bending over the edge of the tub. Her fingers circled the hose for the sprayer and she jerked it close.

Ready. Set. Clean.

Getting her head wet? Easy. Washing her scalp and her long hair one-handed? That sucked. Bad. Trying to rinse out the shampoo, when she couldn't feel with her other hand if suds still matted her hair? Beyond frustrating.

In attempting to rinse her nape, water poured into her ears. She hated that echoey, squishing sound in her head. As she adjusted the angle of the spray nozzle, soapy water trickled down her spine, following the crack of her ass to flow between her thighs. When she repositioned the rotating showerhead again, this time to rinse the front of her hairline, she nailed herself right square in the face with the water. For some reason, she screamed, flinging the sprayer aside like it'd been shooting acid rain at her.

Stupid, stupid, Ginger. What is wrong with you? It's just water.

Gritting her teeth, she opened her eyes to see where she'd tossed the sprayer. Thick rivulets of soap slithered down her forehead and puddled in the corners of her eyes.

She couldn't see, she couldn't hear, she couldn't move. The soap started to burn. "Shit! Shit! Shit!"

The door banged open. "Ginger? Jesus, what are you—"

Was that Kane? She shrieked, "Get out! Get out of here right now!" Her eyeballs stung. Her naked body burned with utter humiliation. God. Of all the positions to be stuck in, on her knees, her fat white ass flapping in the wind.

"Why don't I—"

"Get the fuck out? Good plan."

The door slammed shut.

She blindly reached for the hose for the hand sprayer. Unable to see a damn thing, she leaned over too far, smacking her shoulder into the bottom of the tub. "Fuck!"

"That's it, goddammit, hold still." Kane moved in behind her, straddling her upper torso, squeezing his knees on either side of her ribcage. He reached for the hose and placed the nozzle on the back of her head. "Close your eyes and tilt your head down," he said tersely.

If Ginger was surprised by how quickly she acquiesced, she was even more surprised by Kane's thoroughness. His gentleness.

He rinsed her hair. Her face. Her eyes.

"I can take it from here," she said curtly.

"Like hell. I'm gonna help you to your feet whether you like it or not." He wrapped his arms around her midsection.

She sucked in a breath when the muscular backs of his forearms brushed the underswell of her breasts. Her nipples constricted. Her whole body quivered.

"Steady. I know you're cold. Let's get you upright first. Then we'll see about getting you dried off and warmed up." He lifted her with almost no effort. Instead of letting her go, he held her tightly against his body.

She whimpered.

"Am I hurtin' you?"

"No. I'm just...mortally embarrassed."

"Listen to me. I am here to help you. With everything. Including this kinda stuff. So all you need to do, Ginger, is let me help you. Can you do that?"

"No."

He laughed. "Tough shit."

She nearly smiled through her chattering teeth.

"No more of this 'you don't need my help' attitude. From now on, I'm gonna stick to your goddamn side like glue, understand?"

"Uh-huh."

"Good." He released her. "Now brace your hand on the sink and I'll dry you off."

With brisk, but calm efficiency, Kane toweled off every section of her wet body. She had to admit that he didn't let his gaze linger on her naked body parts. Until he had to help her get dressed. He muttered something about going straight to hell.

Kane slipped the straps of her favorite lime green bra up her arms and pulled the cups to cover her breasts. After he snapped the front clasp of the separate sections together, his fingertips swept the deep "V" of her cleavage, lingering on the upper curves.

Her nipples hardened at his touch, despite the echo of her father's warning about Kane's deftness with female undergarments. *He's helped plenty of women out of their clothes.*

He lifted a brow at her shirt choice. "A button-up, long-sleeved western shirt?"

"I thought it'd be easier to put on."

"Not easier to snap with one hand. Let's start with your bum arm." Once he had the shirt snapped, he slipped the sling over her head. "Careful."

Ginger fought the urge to tell him to hurry, because hello? She was naked from the waist down. The glint in Kane's eye warned that if she complained, he'd take even longer dressing her.

When he dropped to his knees, she couldn't tear her eyes away from his dark head so close to her pussy. If he moved his face, just a couple of inches, he could put his mouth right where she most wanted it. Would he comment about her being a natural redhead?

But Kane didn't say a word. He didn't slowly, sensuously ease the soft cotton yoga pants up her legs. One fast tug and the waistband hugged her hips.

Not only did Ginger feel ashamed of her less-than-perfect body, she was embarrassed by her conflicting emotions—on one hand wanting Kane to notice her, on the other hand wanting to cringe away from his scrutiny.

Kane stood and hung up the towels.

How much of a freak did it make her that she felt more vulnerable dressed than she had stark naked? Keeping her head bowed, she whispered, "Thank you."

Then Kane was right there, tipping her face up to meet his gaze. "Hey now, what's with the waterworks? I just got you dried off."

"I'm sorry I'm such a pain in the ass."

He studied her. "Why do you have such a hard time askin' for help?"

"Because I've never needed it before."

"Well, you need it now."

"Thanks for pointing that out."

"I'm gonna be pointing it out over and over until it's through that thick skull of yours, so suck it up. Get used to takin' my help, Ginger, because I'm just as goddamn stubborn as you are. And I ain't gonna wait for you to ask me for it."

Hayden knocked and rushed in without waiting for the obligatory "come in", oblivious to the fact she and Kane had been within kissing distance.

"Mom? You okay?"

"Yeah, baby, I'm fine."

Hayden squinted at her hair. "Except you look like a mad porcupine."

Her hair snarled like a Brillo pad if she forgot to put conditioner in, which she had. Combing it without the benefit of conditioner? Near impossible, especially since she'd be forced to use her left hand. The thought of hobbling around her house with her hair looking like an electrocuted porcupine made her want to cry.

"Hayden, buddy, why don't you give your mama a minute?"

"I didn't mean to—"

"She knows. Go on."

If Ginger couldn't even look at herself in the mirror she couldn't imagine what Kane saw when he looked at her.

Silence, thick as steam, floated around them.

Kane curled his hands around her face. "You don't look like a mad porcupine. Maybe just a rabid squirrel."

She laughed and sobbed simultaneously.

His too-kind eyes searched hers. "Find me a brush and I'll comb out your hair."

"You'd do that?"

His hands fell to his sides. "Why? Don't you trust me?" he said with an edge to his voice.

Way to insult the man when he's gone above and beyond. Ginger backtracked. "It's not that."

"Then what? Because it doesn't take a damn doctorate to untangle hair, Ginger."

What did that have to do with anything? Kane wasn't feeling intimidated by her...was he?

That was beyond ridiculous. The man was...a super hero—according to her son. And from what she'd seen so far? She'd have to agree.

"Red?" he prompted brusquely.

Keep it light. "I was just wondering if it'd be presumptuous to ask you for a pedicure too."

"Definitely." He flashed her that knee-weakening grin.

In her bedroom, she perched on the edge of her bed. Kane followed a beat later, wielding a brush and a comb. He closed the door behind him and propped a knee on the mattress. "If I pull too hard, let me know."

Ginger let her eyes drift shut, allowing herself to enjoy the feel of Kane's hands on her head, straightening and smoothing the coarse strands, one section at a time.

"I see them wheels turnin', counselor. You're wondering how many heads of women's hair I've combed before yours, aren't you?"

Was she that transparent? "Maybe."

"No women, but I have untangled wild child Eliza's hair a time or two."

Grateful for the subject change, she asked, "Do you spend much time with Kade and Skylar's girls?"

"As much as I can. Eliza more than the twins, since she's

older." He chuckled. "Last year? She was complaining to her parents about them goin' away for 'alone' time and demanded alone time too."

"What did they do?"

"Sent her to my house for the weekend. We ate junk food and watched girlie movies and played High Ho! Cherry-O and Go Fish. However, I drew the line at playin' Barbies or painting her nails," he said dryly. "So your pedicure chances are slim to none."

Ginger laughed.

"And while I was workin' on the tractor? Little sneak ran off to play with Shep in the shelterbelt. She came back an hour later with her hair in knots. I figured Kade and Sky would throw a fit if I chopped off Little Miss's long locks, which woulda been a damn sight easier than combin' through it. Took me two solid hours to untangle that rat's nest."

He couldn't fool her. Warm amusement for his niece's antics lurked beneath the words. It appeared the man was great with all kids, not just hers.

"So yesterday when I went to check on Shep, Kade and Miz Eliza showed up. She got teary eyed that my dog was 'all alone' and convinced her daddy to take him home for the weekend." He sighed. "Poor Shep will probably have pink ribbons attached to his collar when I pick him up."

Ginger had forgotten Kane had a dog. And he hadn't asked to bring him along, knowing Hayden's allergies. "I'm sorry you had to make other arrangements for Shep, Kane."

The brush stopped.

"What?"

"I like hearin' the sexy way you say my name."

A blush spread across her cheeks. Her heart pounded. "Oh. Really?"

"There's no need to apologize since I volunteered to be here and Shep would've been fine sleepin' in the barn."

Silence stretched. Not uncomfortable. The gentle, yet thorough way his hands stroked her hair was as relaxing as it was arousing. Unconsciously, Ginger rubbed her thighs together. How amazing would those stroking motions feel all over? Her breasts? Her belly? Her pussy? A sound of pure pleasure escaped before she could stop it.

"You like this," he murmured in her ear.

"Yes."

"Me too." Then he didn't say another word, but he seemed to take even more care, even more time.

The soft sound of the bristles gliding through her hair slowed.

"As much as I like seein' this red mass down around your pretty face, I'm gonna pull it into a ponytail." Once her hair was slicked back, he said, "You wanna check my handiwork to see if it's up to your standards?"

"I trust you."

"You shouldn't trust me. 'Cause I've been havin' all sorts of naughty thoughts about you."

"Since when?"

"Truthfully? Since always." His silky voice drifted across her ear. "But it's gotten much more intense in the last hour since I busted in on you in the bathroom."

A dizzy, disconnected feeling buzzed through her system and she found it difficult to breathe. "And yet you were a perfect gentleman."

His deep-throated laugh vibrated through her body.

"Oh, maybe I looked like that on the outside. But on the inside? I would've liked nothin' better than to lock that damn bathroom door behind me and put my hands and my mouth all over your perfectly lush curves. All over. Every inch. Over and over. Until I knew that body as well as my own."

Ginger looked sideways at the bulge in the crotch of his jeans and then met his dark gaze. "You're attracted to me after the very unsexy way I mooned you?"

"Are you serious? Lord woman. With you bent over like that?" He rubbed his fingers across his goatee, staring at her hungrily from beneath lowered lashes. "'Bout the sexiest damn thing I've ever seen. Took every ounce of restraint for me not to drop my jeans and just drive into you. No sweet-talkin', no foreplay. Just down-and-dirty, hard-and-fast sex."

A wave of lust swamped her.

"But I ain't the type to take advantage."

Talk about a cold dash of reality. "Meaning what? Since I'm a captive audience, my attractiveness has markedly increased for you solely because we're in such close proximity?"

"You wanna explain that in English, counselor?"

She huffed out a breath. "Fine. You find me appealing because I'm the only woman who's here."

Kane bent down so they were nose to nose. "Not. Even. Fucking. Close."

The door opened and Hayden raced in.

She and Kane broke apart, but not as fast as she imagined they would.

Without preamble Hayden blurted, "I didn't mean to hurt your feelings—"

"I know. Look." She flattened her palm over her scalp. "No more porcupine." She brought him down beside her on the bed and brushed the hair from his brow. "Now I'm ready to get out of this bedroom for a while. I'm starved. What did you guys eat last night?"

"Spaghetti. And we had chicken noodle soup today."

"Sounds yummy."

"Let me help you up," Kane said.

"I'm fine."

He moved in front of her and growled, "That was not a request, Red. Give me your damn hand."

Using Kane for support instead of the wall did have advantages. Muscles, muscles and more muscles. Plus, he smelled good. She let him maneuver her to the kitchen.

Her dad watched their progress, silently, but his shrewd gaze flicked back and forth between her and Kane.

No reason to feel guilty. She was an adult woman. It was her house. And besides, nothing had happened between them except hot looks and teasing banter.

"Glad to see you up and about, daughter."

"I'm glad to be up and about." She glanced at the kitchen, expecting a disaster area, but it was clean except for the pot on the stove.

"Would you like some soup?" Kane asked her.

"Sure." She'd never seen the domestic side of the rancher, and she watched him shamelessly as he ladled soup into the bowl. He set it in front of her and she looked up at him with astonishment. "Homemade chicken noodle soup?"

"Yes, ma'am. My mama's recipe. She made sure both Kade and I knew our way around the kitchen before she kicked us out."

"You are too good to be true," Ginger muttered. She dipped the spoon into the broth and slurped. Delicious. She ate like she'd never seen food. Kane refilled her bowl without asking or without commenting on her ravenous appetite.

"So can I watch *Transformers* tonight?" Hayden asked.

"I figured you'd probably watched it last night."

"Huh-uh. Last night we played games."

"You all played chess?"

Hayden sighed. "Mom. Three people can't play chess. Besides Buck doesn't like chess."

Ginger sent Kane an inquiring look.

Kane shrugged. "Intellectual games ain't really my thing. I'd rather play cards. Plus, chess is something you play with your gramps. When I was your age, I played checkers with my grandpa. It was our thing."

"What about your brother? Didn't he feel left out?" Hayden asked.

"Nah. Gramps played cribbage with him. And trust me, we were awful protective of 'our' game with grandpa. I'd never horn in where I didn't belong."

Again, Ginger was bowled over by Kane's sweet side.

Are you? Are you really? Haven't you watched him with your son and marveled at his patience and thoughtfulness? Haven't you seen him treat you the same way?

"Ginger?"

She blinked at Kane. "Sorry. Were you speaking to me?"

"Just wonderin' if you want more soup?"

"No. Thank you."

"I've gotta head to my place and check a couple things. I told Hayden he could come along...if that's all right with you?"

Ginger appreciated Kane didn't presume anything with her son. "Fine with me. I'll hang out and keep Dad company."

"I don't need a babysitter, Ginger," her father said crossly.

"Maybe you don't, Dash, but she does," Kane answered. "I don't trust Red not to get into trouble while we're gone, so keep an eye on her to see if she needs any help, 'cause God knows the stubborn woman won't ask for it."

"Hey!"

Her father sent her a sly look. "Redheads are always

trouble."

After Hayden and Kane left, Ginger nestled into the couch and snagged the remote. "Anything good on TV?"

"There's a documentary on Catherine the Great on The History Channel."

"No offense, Dad, but that'd put me to sleep."

He shook his finger at her. "No offense, but you *are* supposed to be resting."

"I'm tired of resting. I'm restless. It's driving me nuts."

He pulled himself out of his wheelchair to sit on the opposite end of the couch. "Dr. Monroe called me and gave me the official medical breakdown of your injuries, but that doesn't tell me how it happened."

Ginger explained and wasn't surprised by her father's drawn-out sigh.

"You're lucky."

"I know."

"Not only do I love and adore you, Gigi, I count on you. So does Hayden. I couldn't handle it if something happened to you."

Gigi. He only used his pet name when he was really upset. "Maybe I'll call West Construction and have them check the downspouts to see why we have an icy spot on the steps. Be just our luck if someone sued us."

He harrumphed. "Did you make any progress on the Jensen case?"

Now they were back to the status quo. "Not really. I can't find a precedent. I know I'm overlooking something simple."

He offered a few suggestions she hadn't considered. And for the millionth time, she was grateful there wasn't a blessed thing wrong with his mind.

Shoptalk faded. Ginger stretched out on the couch, allowing her dad to settle her foot and cast on his lap. He confiscated the remote and picked the most boring TV show ever. She dozed off.

Insistent taps on her shoulder awakened her. She blinked sleepily at her impatient son as she swung her feet to the floor. "You're back. Did you have fun?"

"Yep. Buck let me bring some of his cookies. Want one?"

"Absolutely." Kane sauntered closer. With his feline grace

and King of the Jungle swagger, when he walked into a room he owned it. Why did Ginger have the urge to offer him her neck in submission? Or show him her tail?

Kane smiled, as if he could read her thoughts, and flashed his teeth before he sat next to her on the couch.

"Normally I don't share my sweets, especially when they're from my niece."

Ginger bit into the cookie and the rich, buttery taste burst into her mouth. "Eliza made these?"

"With a little help from Grandma."

Hayden inserted himself between them and looked at Kane. "Did you have grandmas to bake cookies with?"

"Nope. So I guess you and I are in the same boat, sport. Havin' to beg cookies from whoever we can."

"Not to rain on your cookie parade, but how many have you had? I don't want Kane to have to deal with you getting sick."

"I've had four...maybe five."

"No more today, okay?"

Hayden sighed. But he didn't complain. The poor kid had been dealing with food allergy issues his whole life.

"Your mama's right. I don't need to eat any more cookies either. I'll just put them away for tomorrow."

Kane's comment mollified her son. "So guess what else? Buck's going to teach me how to play poker and Texas Hold 'Em. Cool, huh?"

"Very. I assume there won't be betting?"

"Mom," Hayden said with exasperation.

"No ma'am. No betting," Kane said. "This is strictly for fun."

"Then count me out," Dash said.

Three sets of eyes zoomed to the family patriarch.

"After I teach Hayden, I'd be up for a game or two with real stakes," Kane offered.

"Poker or blackjack?" Dash asked.

"How about a little of both? With a side of Texas Hold 'Em just to make it interesting?"

Dash smirked. "I'll get my wallet."

After Dash disappeared into his bedroom, Kane lowered his voice. "Level with me. Is your grandpa any good at cards?"

Hayden shrugged. "He's always talking about playing cribbage for a quarter a point at the senior center."

"Does he win?"

"All the time. You should see the jars of quarters in his room."

Kane groaned. "I do believe I've been had."

Ginger grinned.

For the next hour, they convened around the kitchen table. Kane was extremely patient in teaching Hayden the basics. He didn't criticize his choices nor did he offer him false praise. He explained.

The most entertaining aspect was watching her father and Kane measuring each other, gauging their opponent's skill level, trying to figure out each other's tells.

Ginger called a halt to the card competition so they could eat supper.

Again Kane wouldn't let her do anything. He made her sit as he heated up the soup. Between the four of them they finished the pot. Hayden flopped on the living room rug with his Lego set. He could amuse himself for hours. Ginger counted herself lucky her son was such an easygoing kid.

They'd conned Ginger into playing banker for the McKay versus Paulson card tournament. Both Kane and her father bought in with twenty-five bucks worth of poker chips.

Despite the throbbing in her shoulder, Ginger gritted her teeth, determined not to take a pain pill. She propped her cast on an extra chair and sipped a glass of water.

Watching Kane deal kept her focus on his hands. Long fingers, thick in width, but surprisingly nimble with big, rough-skinned knuckles. Little spots of black hair dotted the backs, above his wrists. She imagined those masculine hands caressing her body. The deftness of his fingers moving inside her. The coarseness of his calluses dancing across her skin. The sheer size of his palms on her breasts or spanning her hips.

"Ginger?"

Startled out of her mental skin flick starring one high-handed cowboy, Ginger looked over at her father. "Sorry. What?"

"Do you want a beer?"

Her dad was drinking beer? Didn't he prefer wine? "Probably better not mix alcohol with my medication."

Kane passed Dash the deck of cards. "Your deal. Your

choice."

"Blackjack."

"Figures."

The rheumatoid arthritis had done a serious number on her father's body; the most obvious place was his hands. Some days he had difficulty eating, or holding a pen, or poking buttons on the remote. She didn't baby him and offer to help him—unless he specifically asked. Respecting his privacy meant she had to watch him wrestle with simple tasks such as brushing his teeth and cleaning the lenses on his glasses. Seeing his gnarled fingers struggling to shuffle the deck of cards caused an ache inside her. But he hid his frustration well.

Her father's slowness didn't bother Kane in the slightest. He sipped his beer, toyed with his chips. Not once did he offer to shuffle and deal for Dash. Not once did he urge the man to hurry up. Not once did he sigh or stare.

Kane's consideration brought a lump to Ginger's throat. This man was so much...more than she'd ever imagined. Sexy. Thoughtful. Sweet.

"Read 'em and weep, boy," her father taunted.

"Yee-haw, here's a chance to win some money back from the card sharp. I'll double down and split," Kane said.

Dash had an ace showing. He flipped over a Queen of Hearts on·one of Kane's cards.

"That one's good. Hit this one."

He turned over a nine of clubs on the other.

"Good. Now let's see what you've got."

Her father turned over his hidden card. A Six of Spades. "Seventeen. Dealer stays on seventeen. Let's see them."

Kane had split a pair of tens, winding up winning with both twenty and nineteen. He grinned and scooped the chips to his side of the table.

The give and take of the game went on for another hour. Ginger almost felt invisible, listening to her dad and Kane talk about their gambling experiences. The highs and lows. The Vegas trips. The rhythm of the male voices soothed her and she drifted off.

She jerked awake with a gasp and found herself the center of three different scowls. "What? I was just resting my eyes."

"Right. You've been out for a good ten minutes."

"No way."

"Mom. You were snoring."

She blushed.

Kane stood. "It's time for you to call it a night, Red."

"But—"

"You're supposed to be restin', remember? And somehow I don't think fallin' asleep at the table is what Doc Monroe had in mind."

Hayden hopped off his grandpa's lap, slipped his arms around her neck. "Night, Mommy."

"Night." She whispered, "No goodnight kiss?"

He kissed her cheek.

"Don't stay up too late and no drinking beer."

His nose wrinkled. "I don't like beer."

"No whiskey either."

He smiled that sweet little boy grin that turned her insides as gooey as a marshmallow. "I promise."

"Good." She swung her cast around and stood.

Kane lifted a challenging brow. "I'll help you and make sure you don't fall on your face before you get to bed."

The automatic response to deny his help was strong, but she let it go. "That'd be great."

"Play a couple of practice hands for me and keep an eye on your grandpa so he ain't stackin' the deck against me."

Dash rolled his eyes.

Ginger kissed his cheek. "Night, Dad."

Kane's body heat nearly scorched her back as he escorted Ginger to her room. The bed she'd cursed hours earlier looked like an oasis. "I'm so tired."

"I know you are. C'mere." Kane gently wrapped her in his arms. "It ain't so bad, havin' my help, is it?"

"Yes."

He whispered, "Liar."

"Okay. You're right. It's not all bad." She sighed and relaxed into him.

Kane didn't seem to mind holding her. "Since I'm the only one who didn't get a goodnight kiss, I'll take a rain check."

"Maybe you could come and get it later."

His eyebrows lifted. "You invitin' me into your room,

counselor?"

"Is that so surprising?"

"I'm not sure if that's the best idea I've ever heard or the worst."

Ooh. Rejection. "Forget it. Kissing me goodnight is not part of your caretaking duties."

"Now, don't go and get all pissy on me. We both know there'd be more between us than just one kiss."

"That's what I want. Don't you?"

"Like you wouldn't fuckin' believe." He sighed. "Look. I've kept my hands off you because of Hayden. That's it. You and me bein' together, especially now, would confuse him. He's a great kid. I won't hurt him, Ginger. Not for anything in the world."

Right then, her heart stumbled. She knew she should've probably left it at that.

But she couldn't.

Ginger wanted to explore this sexual sizzle, a one-two punch of lust she'd never experienced with any other man. "I won't hurt him either, but I'm more than just a mother. Didn't you tell me you required an invitation? Well, here it is. And..." Dammit. She sounded needy. Horny. Stupid. She turned her head away.

Kane placed a finger under her chin, forcing her to look at him. "And...what?"

"I want you like crazy, Kane."

"Since when?"

"Truthfully? Since always."

"You find me appealin' because I'm the only man around here that you ain't related to?"

Smartass man, tossing her words back at her. She drilled him in the chest with her index finger. "Not. Even. Fucking. Close."

Kane blinked at her, slowly, sexily, gifting her with the captivating grin that transformed his face from merely handsome to devastatingly gorgeous. "I'm likin' this sneaky, wild streak, Red."

"I'm trying it out; it's brand new."

"Lucky me," he murmured. "I'll accept your invite. But you oughta know I have a condition if you wanna fuck around with me."

"Which is?"

Kane loomed over her. His eyes darkened. His entire posture changed. "I'm in charge of what goes on between us behind closed bedroom doors. Period. Leave the lawyer out of it because there ain't gonna be any negotiating for a more even split of who's in control. You need to be fully aware of what I am."

"What are you?"

The bad-boy smile he gave her rivaled the devil's. "In bed? About as far from gentlemanly as you can imagine. Think you can handle that?"

Hell yes, she was on board with handing over all sexual responsibility to him. But the lawyer in her had to poke him. "No humiliation and pain games. Because if that's what you're into, I'm afraid I'll have to decline."

"Good pain is subjective as well as erotic. But when I've got you nekkid and at my mercy, the last thing I'm gonna be thinkin' about is humiliation. I'll be too focused on seein' how many times I can make you come."

A man with his purported sexual experience could afford to brag about his inventiveness. She swayed a little.

"You're fallin' asleep on your feet. Let's get you in bed."

Once she was settled, Kane brushed his warm lips from her temple to her ear. "Keep your door unlocked tonight. Try to get some rest." He shut off the lamp and left her in the darkness.

How was she supposed to sleep now?

Chapter Five

Kane felt like a horny teen as he snuck down the hallway toward Ginger's room. He almost turned around and climbed back into the bottom bunk.

Almost.

He slipped inside her bedroom, pressing his back against the door as he shut and locked it behind him.

Mmm. Mmm. Mmm. Would you look at that?

Ginger had fallen asleep on her back with her left arm gracefully curved above her head. The arc of her hip mimicked the angle of her arm, creating the impression of a 1940s pinup queen.

Jesus. He wanted her. Yet, he knew having her just once would be like a fucking gateway drug. He'd become addicted. He'd want more from her than sex. He'd want everything.

As he debated on the best way to wake her, her eyelids lifted and she peered at him drowsily. Her shy smile proved to be his undoing. He took the kiss he craved, bringing his mouth down on hers hard.

Right away her lips parted, her tongue eagerly sought his and the kiss caught fire.

Kane groaned, lost in the rush, lost in the give and take of the kiss. Pulse-pounding passion tinged with sweetness. No roving hands. No body parts grinding together. Only their mouths touched. Wet lips. Swirling tongues. Nips of teeth. Gliding, sliding, falling headfirst into the kiss, well past the point of no return, he never wanted to stop kissing her. Somehow, Kane eased back from the pleasure of her mouth.

Ginger stared at him, wide-eyed, tracing her kiss-swollen lips with the tips of her fingers.

"What?" he said thickly.

"I'd wondered if I'd embellished that kiss from a few months back, but I hadn't. You sure know how to make my head spin, Kane McKay." She reached up, letting her fingertips trail over the lower half of his face. "I love the way your mustache and goatee feel when you're kissing me."

"Imagine how it'll feel other places." He threw back the covers. "If I unhook your sling are you gonna be able to keep your bum arm still?"

She cocked her head. "Depends. What do you plan on doing to me?"

Kane grinned. "Oh, I've got a couple of real good ideas, Red, but sharin' them at this point would spoil the surprise. I'd rather demonstrate than explain."

"Then no guarantees I can hold still."

"Then the sling stays on."

"Fine." Ginger gave him a head-to-toe perusal. "You wear flannel pants and a wife beater as pajamas?"

"Normally I don't wear pajamas at all."

Her hazel eyes enlarged when he climbed onto the bed, straddling her pelvis, with a knee on either side of her hips. He whipped off his tank top.

She sighed gustily. "You should never ever wear a shirt. In fact, it should be illegal for you to cover that magnificent chest."

Kane reveled in the way her hungry gaze roamed over every ounce of his exposed flesh. "That so, counselor?"

"Yes sir. Do you work out to maintain this fantastic physique?"

"If feedin' cattle and doin' stuff around the ranch is considered workin' out, then yes. Sometimes I meet up with Colt at the community center and we lift weights." Not recently, since his cousin had been a serious dick lately.

You really wanna think about Colt when you're finally in Ginger's bed?

No.

"I cannot wait to put my hands all over you, cowboy."

"Same goes. My turn first." Kane rested on his haunches and reached for the snaps on her shirt. "Keep your eyes on mine as I undress you."

She opened her mouth to argue, then thought better of it.

Tempting, to yank the sides of her shirt apart and be done with it. Especially since he'd forced himself not to gawk at her beautifully tempting body parts earlier. Now faced with the luxury of memorizing every abundant inch, he wasn't about to rush.

He popped the first pearl-snap button. Then the next. Then the next until a long strip of her luminescent skin, from her neck to her belly, peeked out from beneath the lapels. Carefully, Kane peeled back the left half of her shirt, tucking the right side beneath her sling. He traced the delicate line of her clavicle to the hollow of her throat. With every teasing stroke, the pulse along the side of her neck jumped.

Not as calm and cool as she appeared.

Kane let the backs of his fingers drift, paying particular attention to the patterns of freckles. He murmured, "I love the way these spread across your skin. Looks like mud spatters on alabaster."

Her body went rigid.

Kane met her gaze, surprised to see a hint of anger. "What did I say?"

"Don't spout poetry about my stupid freckles. They don't resemble 'cinnamon sprinkled on cream' or 'nature's polka dots on a flesh canvas'. They're ugly. They're weird. They're blotchy. There's too damn many of them. They've been the bane of my existence since the day I realized the more time I spend in the sun, the more freckles show up. And that really sucks when you live in sunny California."

He closed the distance until they were nose to nose. "If I wanna spout poetry about your beauty marks, then I'll damn well do it. So suck it up." He bent his head and his tongue zigzagged random patterns across the brown dots, switching it up to nuzzle her neck, nibble her earlobes, nip the strong line of her jaw. He teased, tormenting until she moaned his name.

"Something you need?" he asked, trilling his lips down the pointed tip of her chin.

"You. More of this."

"I could get used to hearin' that sexy squeak when I taste you right here." He opened his mouth along the side of her neck and sucked.

"Maybe I have other noises, you know, when you lavish attention with that talented mouth...elsewhere."

"Such impatience. You hintin' about some place in particular?"

"You could do a freckle check by my nipples," she suggested.

Kane chuckled against her skin, then sucked another spot in the middle of her breastbone.

"Hey, no hickeys."

"Tough. I wanna leave my mark on you. So when you're alone in your bed? And you look down? You'll see it and remember me puttin' my mouth all over you."

"Like I'm ever going to forget this."

"I hope not." He kissed a path down the center of her body, right through her deep cleavage. When he reached the front clasp on her bra, he took it between his teeth and bit down, expecting it to snap open.

Nothing happened.

Damn. It'd been a few years since he'd tried this trick of removing a woman's bra with just his mouth.

He tried it again.

The plastic didn't budge.

Maybe he'd lost his touch.

Maybe that's a good thing.

Kane glanced at Ginger to see that luscious mouth forming a smirk.

"Problems, cowboy?"

"Seems I'm a bit rusty."

"And yet, I'm not exactly sorry to hear that," she demurred.

"Time to get serious about this clothes removal business."

He rose on his knees and cracked his knuckles.

Ginger laughed.

The husky sound of her amusement zinged straight to his crotch.

One deft twist of his fingers and the bra cups separated, revealing the pearly flesh, but the green lace edge kept her nipples hidden. He curled his right hand over her rib cage and traced the heavy underswell of her breast, leisurely sliding the fabric aside with his thumb.

Her chest rose and fell with anticipation. Her teeth dug into her lower lip.

The second that pale peach tip became visible, Kane's

mouth was on it.

Ginger arched up hard and moaned.

He suckled and teased. Using his mouth, his lips, dragging his goatee across the taut peak.

"I...oh. I like that."

He could spend a solid day learning how she liked to be touched on her tits. What made her squirm. What made her come.

"Sweet Jesus, I feel like I'm going to..."

He kept sucking until the restless rubbing of her thighs beneath him increased. He switched sides, devoting the same ruthless attention to this nipple, while his fingers manipulated the one still warm and wet from his mouth.

Breathy moans built, urging him on. Her pelvis shot up and she gasped, "Oh. My. God."

Kane swore he felt the pulse of her orgasm in his mouth as he vigorously sucked her to the peak of her climax.

At some point Ginger had latched onto his head, digging her fingernails into his scalp. That bite of pain was a serious fucking turn on.

Her body quivered beneath him and she sighed the contentment of a satisfied woman.

He intended to hear that sound many more times; he was nowhere near done with her. Not tonight. Not ever. If he had to use sex to win her over, then he'd goddamn well do it.

Kane released her nipple. His mouth wandered down her body. Kissing her sternum. The defined line of her upper belly, pausing at the indent of her navel. Upon reaching the waistband of her yoga pants, he gazed at her across the length of her torso. "Lift up."

Ginger canted her hips.

He tugged her pants off. Before he focused his attention on that sweet slice of heaven between her thighs, he repositioned her cast. "Lie back."

Beautiful. Bright red curls covered her mound. Kane was just so damn eager he skipped the buildup. No teasing touches. No teasing remarks on the sexy freckles scattered across her curvy, muscular thighs.

Keeping his grip on the inside of her legs, Kane pressed a kiss to the top of her pubic bone. Then he dragged his tongue through the cleft to the source of that deliciously spicy scent.

Warm. Sticky. Sweet.

Kane closed his eyes and devoured her pussy. He lapped at the cream gathered at the opening to her body, alternating long sensual strokes with short jabs. Wiggling his tongue deep, retreating to wrap his lips around her clit. But Kane only sucked that nub one time and returned his oral worship to the mouth of her sex. Licking her. Exploring every hidden fold of her soft, wet cunt. Swallowing her honey like ambrosia.

Her whimpers increased. Her legs shook.

And still he didn't relent or change his pace.

"Kane. Please. I'm about to crawl out of my skin. My shoulder is throbbing and I didn't take pain meds because I wanted to be fully conscious for when you came to me tonight."

"Such a convincin' argument, counselor. I'll let you play the injury card this time." He blew across her engorged pussy and she whimpered. "But next time? Fair warning. I ain't gonna stop kissin' my fill of your sweet spot until *I've* had enough. Not even if you beg."

He lifted up, so their eyes met over the plane of her body. "Watch me." He lowered his head, rubbing his cheeks, his jawline and his lips into those tight red curls, coating his facial hair with her juices. "I love the way you smell almost as much as I love the way you taste." He slid his thumbs up through the wetness and pulled back the supple skin hiding that pleasure pearl.

Her belly rippled with anticipation.

Kane nimbly flicked his tongue across the nub, not too hard, or too fast, just a consistent pressure.

"Yes. Yes. Don't stop."

When her pelvis arched, his lips enclosed her clit and he sucked, matching the rhythm of her pounding pulse.

Sexy whimpers surrounded him as she came, hard, fast, wet, and then she was done.

After gifting her pussy with one last soft-lipped kiss, Kane pushed up, placing his hands by her head.

Ginger's generous mouth curved into a lopsided smile. She reached her arm above her head, stretching like a contented feline. "Wow."

"How's the throbbing shoulder?"

Another satisfied sigh escaped. "Completely forgot all about it."

Kane pressed his mouth to hers, sharing her taste. He wanted to kick off his pants. Feel the tight clasp of her cunt around his cock as he sank into her over and over. But Ginger wasn't up for sex, especially not the raw, urgent fucking he had in mind. After several easy, lingering smooches, he forced himself to retreat. "You need a more comfortable shirt to sleep in."

She blinked at him with complete confusion. "But. You haven't... We could... I want to, I mean..."

"As much as I love hearin' how flustered my kisses make you, Red, the truth is, you're injured. I probably already took advantage of you." He grabbed her pants and motioned for her to raise her hips.

Her eyes narrowed, but she let him shimmy the yoga pants up her legs. "Your mouth sucking on my tits until I came and then that same hot mouth sucking on my pussy until I came? I fail to see how that's *you* taking advantage of me, when you didn't come at all."

Whoa. Kane hadn't expected such coarse, common words from the woman with the gigantic vocabulary.

"Shocking, isn't it? How I prefer dirty-talking to sweet-talking?"

"Maybe some."

"I can see how hard you are. I could give you a hand job? Shoot. I'm probably not very good with my left hand."

"Neither am I."

She laughed softly. "How about if I whisper dirty nothings in your ear while you jack off?"

His dick actually jumped at that sexy visual. "Another time. What shirt you wanna wear?"

"There's a black tank top on the hamper."

He snagged it and sat on the edge of the bed. "Up you go." He unhooked the sling. The shirt came off first, then the bra. Before he covered her with the tank top, he drew a circle around each of her nipples, watching as they puckered into stiff points. He couldn't resist granting each one an openmouthed kiss.

"You are a tit guy, aren't you?"

"Yes ma'am."

"I've never gotten off just from a man sucking on my tits. I've been close a couple of times, but they've always stopped too soon. Too eager to get to the good stuff, I guess."

"These babies are the good stuff." Kane cupped the globes in his hands and rubbed his goatee across the tips. "I've got plans for these beauties."

"Like?" Ginger prompted.

Kane locked his gaze go hers. "Like watchin' them bounce as you're ridin' me. Holdin' onto them as you fuck me reverse cowgirl. Slidin' my dick in here until I'm ready to explode—" he dragged his index finger through the center of her cleavage, "—and then comin' all over your chest, seein' how those freckles look covered in my seed."

She swallowed hard.

"Shockin', ain't it?" he teased. "How I prefer down and dirty sex to sweet, sweet love making?"

"Not shocking at all, Kane. Just hot as hell. I can't wait to prove to you that I like it as down and dirty as you do."

"Always full of surprises, counselor. But tonight, you're done in."

Ginger ran her fingers up the length of his fully erect cock and circled her hand around it. "Am I?"

Kane placed his hand over hers, squeezed once and removed her hand from his dick. "Yes."

"What are you going to do now?"

"Sneak into the bathroom and whack off. Probably twice."

She smiled cheekily.

And Kane did just that. Thinking of Ginger the entire time.

Chapter Six

Ginger managed to brush her teeth, wash her face and change into a fresh pair of yoga pants all by herself. It took forever, but she had to do it. If for no other reason than to prove to Kane that she was on the mend and she was up for anything tonight.

She'd shuffled to the kitchen to start a pot of coffee when she heard Kane come up behind her.

"Just what do you think you're doin'?"

His raspy morning voice sent tingles zipping across her nerve receptors. She turned her head and his mouth was right there. Sweet, minty breath drifted from between his parted lips.

"Ah hell, Red, how am I supposed to resist kissin' you when you look as fresh and pretty as a damn daisy?" He pressed his lips to hers, bestowing the type of gentle, warm kiss lovers shared after a passion-filled night.

She'd barely caught her balance from his sweetness when he scrambled her brain cells with a no-hold-barred-I-want-you-now zealous kiss of intent.

"Why you tremblin'?"

"Just thinking about last night."

Kane pushed a piece of her hair behind her ear. "No regrets?"

"Only that I didn't get a chance to touch you at all."

"There's always tonight, if you're feelin' up to it."

Ginger's eyes searched his. "You aren't bothered by the fact that all I did was lay there and wasn't an active participant?"

"Not in the least." He nipped her mouth with firm-lipped sugar bites. "Although, I am hard as a fuckin' brick thinkin' about your mouth on my cock. That's the image I jacked off to last night. You, on your knees, lookin' up at me, your soft hair teasin' my thighs as my dick is buried in your hot mouth."

Heat moistened her pussy. "What are you doing right now?"

"Not draggin' you to your bedroom, as much as I'd like to." He backed off to mutter, "Maybe we better talk about something else. Park that sexy ass on the chair and I'll make us some coffee."

"Bossy much?" Ginger shuffled to the kitchen table.

"You don't know the half of it."

"But I'll bet you're dying to show me."

"Yes, ma'am."

This man could get her all kinds of fired up just with molten looks and sexy words.

Kane rested his backside against the counter as the coffee brewed. "So what do you guys do on Sundays?"

"Depends. Sometimes Hayden has a friend over. Sometimes you two do Little Buddies stuff. Sometimes we spend a couple of hours playing Xbox."

"Is it true you only let Hayden play the Xbox once a week?"

She nodded. "Probably sounds crazy. But it'd be easy as a single parent to let him fill up the hours with TV or video games while I'm working. I don't want to socially stunt him by keeping him away from video games entirely, but there are better things he can do with his time. So far he hasn't fought me on the one day a week rule."

He cocked his head. "Do you follow that same rule, counselor? Or are you addicted to the Internet and your cell phone?"

"I spend plenty of time on the phone and the computer during working hours. It's a respite when I'm done for the day. I have a BlackBerry, but I don't know how to do half the shit on it. Sometimes I take pictures. What about you? You texting like crazy and always checking your email?"

"Not hardly. I have a BlackBerry, but we don't get cell reception everywhere on the ranch, so it's dead more'n half the time. I do text. I'm online once a day, usually to check stock prices, do a little research. I use my laptop for updating the databases about our herd. The dams and sires, calf live birth weights, milk weight gain ratios, that sort of stuff."

Living in an ag community, she was aware that ranchers, especially the younger generation, used computer technology for everything. "Do Kade and your father do that much computer work too?"

"Kade could do it if he wants to. I always send him backup files of my work in case something happens to me or to the computer, but Kade has way more on his plate after workin' hours than I do. It makes sense the responsibility falls to me."

Ginger didn't respond.

Kane brought her a cup of coffee and sat across from her. "I see the wheels a'turnin', counselor." He blew across his cup. "You shocked I'm mildly technologically savvy?"

Her gaze hooked his. "Not at all. It just makes me wonder how many more responsibilities fall to you because you don't have a wife and three kids waiting on you after you drop off the last bale of hay."

"You worried I'm doin' more than my fair share?" he asked, his tone slightly amused.

"I guess I am. I'm not sure how the McKay Ranches Inc. or McKay Cattle Company works. Your family ranching businesses are the only clients Dad has kept on since his retirement and he's slowly easing me into it. But it does seem unfair if you're bearing a bigger workload."

"Sometimes I forget you're a lawyer, and you look at things differently than normal folks."

She gazed at him coolly. "So I'm abnormal? Was that an insult, McKay?"

"Whoa. You iced over my coffee with that cold glare, sugar."

"Not funny."

"Look. The division of duties ain't the same on the ranch as it is in a traditional nine-to-five workplace. We do what needs done. Sometimes there's a helluva lot that needs done. During calving season. During haying and branding. Like when Skylar was pregnant with the twins? I sure as hell wasn't gonna make Kade stick around and check the herd in the middle of the night. Especially when he lives a lot farther away than Dad or me. Besides, he wouldn't have been worth a shit anyway, worryin' about his wife."

"Calving is a busy time?"

"Exhausting. I don't get more'n a couple hours sleep for at least three weeks. In the last few years, Kade handled the daytime chores. Dad switches back and forth between helpin' both of us. If Dad gets too tired, then Ma pitches in. I'm usually out at the bunkhouse with my cousins during that time, since we've staggered the calving season. So, see? It all works out." He got up and grabbed the coffee pot, refilled both their cups. "For instance, Kade is takin' care of things while I'm here with you."

"I'll remember to thank him," Ginger murmured. "And you. Thank you, Kane. I know you probably had more important things to do than babysit me."

"I'm here because I want to be. You know that, right?"

"I'm a little more convinced now than I was when you first showed up at the hospital."

At his smoky gaze, and his gravelly "Is that so?" heat curled in her belly.

"While you're restin' today, do you mind if I take Hayden into town for the high school basketball game? We don't have to stay for all four quarters, but he's been lookin' forward to it. Thought we could pick up something for supper and bring it home."

"I don't see why not. It'll be good for him to get out."

Kane was quiet as he fiddled with his coffee mug.

"I see the wheels a'turnin', cowboy. What's on your mind?"

"This might sound weird, but would Dash want to come to the game? There's this scrimmage thing at halftime, and Hayden's been practicing his sprint drills. We'd intended to ask you as a surprise, but bein's you're laid up... I think it's important that Hayden has family there."

Kane continually shocked her with his attention to detail and the genuine affection he held for her son. "Sometimes Dad—"

"Is perfectly capable of making up his own mind," Dash supplied as he rolled up to the table.

"Morning, Dad."

"Ginger. How are you feeling?"

Admitting she felt fantastic might encourage him to ask why she felt so fantastic. She couldn't admit two orgasms courtesy of Kane McKay were just what she needed. She shrugged. "Okay. How about you?"

"I'm feeling a little stir crazy, if you want to know the truth.

Since tomorrow is a holiday, the bus won't be picking me up to take me to the senior's center."

"I forgot there was no school tomorrow," Ginger said.

Dash addressed Kane. "Were you serious about letting me tag along today?"

"Yep."

"I appreciate it. I wouldn't want to miss the opportunity to cheer on my grandson."

"Good. Is the mechanical handicapped platform in the van easy to run?" Kane brought Dash a cup of coffee.

"Far as I know. Ginger doesn't have a problem with it."

Interesting that Kane hadn't asked *her* if the equipment was hard to handle.

"We'll have to get an earlier start. But don't let on you know about Hayden's surprise," Kane warned.

"I was an attorney for fifty years, boy. I know how to keep a secret."

"You've got a damn fine poker face too," he muttered.

Dash gave him a sly grin. "A necessity, being a judge and living in a small community."

"Well, I want a chance to earn back my twenty-five bucks."

Ginger looked at Kane. "You lost to my dad?"

"Yep. That'll teach me to go all in." Kane drained his coffee. "What do you guys want for breakfast? Eggs? Toast? Cereal?"

"Cereal is fine with me," Dash said.

Ginger rolled her eyes. Another thing her father and her son had in common: love of sugar-laden cereals. "I'll have eggs."

"Hang on. I've gotta wake up my egg cracker." Kane strode off.

She felt her father staring at her. "What?"

"I can't place it. You seem different today. More relaxed or something."

Ginger slipped on her poker face. "I must be on the mend."

"You slept all right?"

Why was he pushing her on this? Normally he couldn't give a rip about her sleep patterns.

Shit. He knew. Her dad knew that Kane had snuck into her room last night.

Stay calm.

For fuck's sake. She was a thirty-seven-year-old woman.

This was her house. If she wanted to invite a man into her bed, it was none of her dad's business. She'd buck up, and just...

Lie her ass off.

"Yeah. That pain pill really knocked me out."

Her dad harrumphed.

Hayden trudged into the kitchen. His sleep-tousled blond hair stuck up every direction and his glasses were on crooked. He snuggled into her, wrapping his arms around her neck. Wouldn't be too much longer before he wouldn't want morning snuggles and hugs. She kissed the top of his head. "Morning."

"Hayden, it might be better if you didn't squish your mama, and sat next to her instead of on her."

Hayden shook his head and burrowed deeper into her neck.

Kane frowned but didn't say a word.

Her son used to be clingy, but not so much in the past two years, so she was perplexed by his suddenly shy behavior.

Kane set out two bowls, spoons, a carton of soymilk and a box of Frosted Cheerios.

Her father helped himself to breakfast. The only sounds were the hum of the heater and the crunching cereal.

"I hear there's a basketball game today. Grandpa is going."

"I wanted *you* to come to the basketball game, Mommy."

"I know, baby. And I'm sorry that I'll be stuck here while you're having a good time with Grandpa and Kane."

"His name is Buck," Hayden said snottily.

"Actually, my name is Kane. Buck was a nickname I tried out for a while, hopin' it'd distinguish me from my twin brother and my McKay cousins, whose names, for some reason, all seem to start with the letter C or K."

"I wasn't talking to you," Hayden retorted.

Shocked, Ginger leaned back and looked at her son sternly. "Hayden Michael Paulson. What is wrong with you? That was just plain rude. Apologize to Kane right now."

Silence. Surly, stubborn silence.

Ginger waited about another fifteen seconds. Then she instructed, "Back to your room. You can come out only when you're ready to be civilized and apologize to Kane."

"But Mom—"

"No buts. Go on."

He climbed off her lap and ran to his room, slamming the

door behind him.

She closed her eyes. Kids and drama went hand in hand. Chances were high Hayden's snit would only last a few minutes. But she'd learned early on if she let him exhibit bratty behavior, he'd use it whenever possible to get his way.

"Ginger?" Kane said.

Please. Don't offer me parenting advice right now. "What?"

"Would you like a reheat?"

"Yes. Thank you."

He'd filled her cup and cleared her father's bowl.

Sure enough, less than five minutes later, the bedroom door opened and Hayden appeared. He started to climb onto her lap, but she shook her head and pointed to Kane.

Hayden stood behind his grandfather's wheelchair, his fingers curled around the handgrips. "Umm. I'm sorry for being rude to you, Buck."

"Thanks for the apology, sport."

"So you're not mad?"

"Nope. Takes courage to admit you were wrong."

Hayden slid into the chair next to her. "What am I supposed to call you? I've always called you Buck, but everyone else calls you Kane."

"My nieces Eliza, Peyton, Shannie and Liesl call me Buck. So do Kyler, Gib, Thane, Anton, Parker, Braxton, Spencer, Westin... Shoot, I know I'm forgetting a couple that can talk now."

"You consider all your McKay cousins' offspring your nieces and nephews?" Ginger asked.

"Pretty much. Me'n Kade were with them all the time growin' up. And we're ranching together, so the kids think of me the same as their other McKay uncles." He winked. "I've gotta admit to havin' a real soft spot for Kade's girls."

"Anton and Ky are cool," Hayden offered. "They're always talking about all their cousins." He dumped cereal in his bowl and poured soymilk over it.

"Seems my cousins' wives are in a race to see who can have the most kids in the shortest amount of time."

"Who's winning?"

"Colby and Channing were, but with Cam and Domini adopting Liesl and the twins a few months back...they're tied.

Four and four."

Ginger looked at Kane. "Lots of twins in the McKay family tree."

He nodded. "Mostly fraternal. Kade and I are the only identical twins in our McKay generation, but it seems genetics—and adoption—is makin' up for it in this next generation."

Kane's phone buzzed and he plucked it out of his front shirt pocket. "Mornin' Ma." Pause. "No." Another pause. "Because it ain't a story Ginger wants spread all over town." He held the phone away from his ear as his mother railed on him.

Ginger detected humor in his tone, not anger as he said, "Sorry. No, I *am* sincerely sorry, Ma. Yes ma'am." Then he hung up.

He gave Hayden a conspiratorial wink. "See? My mama still makes me apologize too."

"Wow. What did you do?"

"Forgot to tell her I'm helpin' out over here."

"Oh." Hayden tucked into his cereal, hiding behind the box.

"What time do we have to leave for the basketball game?" Dash asked Kane.

"'Bout two hours."

"I'll be ready. I have a few things to finish up in my room." Dash left the table and his door closed behind him.

"As soon as you're done with breakfast, you need to hop in the shower, Hayden."

"Aw, Mom. I'm probably just gonna get sweaty at the game. I'll shower when I get home."

"No dice."

"Why do you make me shower every day? It's a waste of water," Hayden grumbled. He shoved the cereal box aside and challenged Kane. "Do you shower once a day?"

"Nope."

A triumphant expression crossed Hayden's face. "See?"

Kane mock-whispered, "Sometimes I shower twice a day."

"No fair." Hayden picked up his bowl and drank the last of the soymilk as he walked to the sink.

Before he made it to his room, Ginger yelled, "A shower means getting your hair wet and scrubbing it with shampoo."

"Aw man" echoed back to her and she and Kane smiled at each other.

"You busted him on a technicality, Mom, nice goin'."

"Were you determined to do your part to save the environment when you were a boy by not showering? Because this is a foreign concept to me."

"Once Kade and I had a contest to see who could go the longest." He grinned. "We tied at three weeks until Ma couldn't stand the smell of us and hosed us both down in the front yard."

"I knew an iron-fisted disciplinarian lurked beneath Kimi's sweeter-than-honey demeanor."

"She puts the 'mean' in demeanor. She's small, but she's mighty."

Then playful Kane vanished and he stared at her with the inscrutable gaze that caused her nerve endings to twitch.

"What are you thinking about?"

He practically growled, "How badly I want to throw you over my shoulder and drag you to bed."

The rush of lust unfurled her flirty side. "What would you do with me, once you had me where you wanted me?"

"Fuck you. After I fucked you on the bed, I'd fuck you against the wall. Then I'd bend you over the chair and fuck you from behind as we're watching ourselves in your mirror. Then I'd fuck you in the shower."

Ginger's heart galloped. For a man of few words, he used them well. She could almost feel the soft mattress against her spine and his muscular body covering hers from chest to feet. She could almost feel the hot, hard thickness of his cock filling her as he braced his hands by her head. He'd look into her eyes, alternating his sexy penetrating stare with bone-melting kisses. Wordlessly urging her to new sexual heights as he rammed his flesh into hers, until they both exploded with satisfaction.

"Ah sugar, you're playin' with fire, eyeballin' me like that."

"Same goes," she shot back.

"It's gonna be a long goddamn day," he muttered and exited the kitchen.

Kane's mother, being the snoopy sort, showed up just as they were getting ready to leave. "Ma. What're you doin' here?"

Kimi McKay had to stand on tiptoe to kiss her son's cheek. "Just being neighborly. I brought over a casserole and a few of the cookies Eliza and I made."

Hayden peeked in the bag. "Cool. Sprinkles."

"You like sprinkles?" Kimi asked.

He nodded.

"Maybe sometime your mama will let you come over and bake cookies with me. Been years since I had a little boy in my kitchen helpin' me out."

"That'd be fun. Me'n Buck had a cooking class with Domini."

"I heard. What did you learn?"

Hayden scowled. "That I can still taste broccoli even if it's hidden in food."

Kimi laughed. "No broccoli in the casserole, I promise. Now you guys better get goin'. I'll stick around. Keep Ginger company. You know, in case she needs something."

Kane froze. Dammit. How could he force his mother to leave without it seeming like he was trying to get rid of her?

He couldn't. Kimi West McKay knew that. She'd counted on Kane being polite in mixed company because that's how she'd raised him.

A well-played move by the blonde tornado.

His mother lovingly patted his arm—and then heaved him out the door. "Have fun, boys!"

Dash wore a funny smirk as he rolled down the wheelchair ramp. "I see Kimi still rules the roost."

"Yep. Always has. I suspect she always will."

"Makes sense."

He bristled. "What makes sense?"

"Why you aren't put off by strong women."

That comment came completely out of left field. And it made him bristle even more. Like Dash thought that he didn't have the smarts to know when to stand up for himself?

Hayden said, "I know what we need to do first."

Kane was grateful for a chance to focus on something besides what Ginger's dad thought of him—which apparently wasn't much.

After the van door opened and the mechanical platform was on the ground, Dash could roll himself onto it. Then Kane just hit a switch to load man and chair inside the van. Impressive, how slick the whole set up worked. Must've cost a pretty penny, but it was worth it since it kept Dash from being totally housebound.

At the community center, they unloaded in the handicapped zone. Kane hadn't realized how tight the fit was between parking places for a mechanized wheelchair platform. Despite Dash's insistence he could maneuver himself into the gymnasium, Kane wheeled Dash inside, Hayden loping alongside them. When people called out to Dash, Kane wondered if Dash's insistence about handling himself was a smokescreen: maybe Dash was embarrassed to be seen with him.

"Hey, look! There's the signup sheet for the halftime race," Hayden said.

"Let's get you on the list." Kane spoke to Dash. "You wanna wait here until we're done so we can find seats?"

"I have to stay in the handicapped section on the main floor. You two go on, I'll be fine on my own."

"But Grandpa, I wanna sit with you."

Dash looked at Kane briefly, then back at his grandson. "We can sit in the same vicinity, but the handicapped section is small. If you sit by me, that means someone in a wheelchair won't have a seat." Dash set his twisted hand on Hayden's shoulder. "Go sign up. Hayden raced to the table. Dash glanced at someone behind Kane and muttered, "Crap."

"Why, Dash Paulson. Long time no see."

Kane recognized his cousin Keely's voice and turned around.

She squealed, "Kane! I hoped you'd be here." She hugged him effusively and punched him in the stomach.

"Hey, what was that for?"

"For not inviting me to the last McKay poker game. You macho guys were just pissed because I handed you your collective asses last time."

"I seem to recall you bein' out of town." His eyes narrowed on his only female McKay cousin. Circles darkened the pale skin beneath her tired eyes. Her sunny smile seemed a tad forced. "Whatcha been doin'?"

"Workin', workin', and more workin'." She sighed. "I was coming to this basketball game to support my lamebrain brother Colt, but he backed out at the last minute."

Kane said, "That's too bad," without any disappointment.

Keely ignored his sarcastic reply and invaded Dash's personal space. "So Mr. Paulson...happy as I am to see you out and about, you wanna tell me why you've been ditching our physical therapy sessions?"

Dash scowled at Keely. "They're pointless. I'm never getting out of this chair."

"Probably not. But you don't want to lose what strength and agility you have now, do you?"

"No."

"Does Ginger know you're skipping class?"

Another grimace. "No. I also know you can't tell her because of patient confidentiality, so you'd best be keeping this to yourself, missy."

"Mr. Paulson, we both know there are ways around those pesky rules. So if you don't show..."

"I'll show," he grumbled.

"Excellent." Keely rubbed her hands together with utter glee. "Fair warning. Wednesday is gonna suck. I'm putting you through the wringer. See you then." She gave him a finger wave and a haughty grin before she whirled on her boot heel and vanished into the crowd.

Dash pointed at Kane. "Not a word to my daughter about this business."

"You have my word. But I agree with Keely. And I've seen firsthand how much her therapy has benefited my cousin Cam. Think about that."

Kane wandered off in search of Hayden. They found two seats in the lower bleacher section. Kane kept Hayden's junk food intake to a grape snow cone and a box of red licorice. With the kid's food allergies, he was careful to stick to the tried and true. The guilt would eat him alive if Hayden got sick on his watch.

At halftime, Kane headed down to the main floor and crouched beside Dash as Hayden participated in the footrace.

Hayden finished third. Kane snapped a couple of pictures of the ceremony and the green ribbon with his cell phone and sent it to Ginger.

Near the end of the third quarter, he saw the back of

Dash's wheelchair as he exited the gym. He and Hayden followed.

Dash was parked outside the restroom, wearing a scowl.

"Is everything all right?"

Two spots of color dotted the man's sallow cheeks. "I need to use the facilities but this handicapped bathroom isn't conducive to my needs."

Kane scratched his head. "How about if you repeat that in plain English?"

"This particular bathroom is impossible for me to use."

"Do you need help?"

The muscle in Dash's jaw tightened. "No. That's not the issue."

Like hell that wasn't the issue. Like father like daughter. Neither one wanted to accept his help. Rather than snap, or embarrass the man, or point out the obvious, Kane said, "Fine. Let's get you back home."

"I thought you'd prefer to stay until the end of the game."

"In the future, maybe it'd be better if you asked my plans instead of assuming they'll conflict with yours."

Dash had no response.

Kane buttoned his sheepskin coat and slipped on his gloves. "Everyone ready to go?"

"Wait a sec. I gotta say goodbye to someone." Hayden raced off and ducked beneath the bleachers.

The silence between him and Dash was decidedly chilly and didn't owe a damn thing to the frigid temperatures outside.

"McKay, I apologize. I can be a bit of a curmudgeon sometimes."

At least the members of the Paulson family didn't have a problem admitting when they were wrong.

"I understand. We're cool. Know what's funny? My mama used that same word to describe my grandpa. Course, me'n Kade thought it meant mean."

Dash smiled. "Thanks for bringing me here today."

"You're welcome."

Hayden bounded back, grinning from ear to ear. "This is so great. I wish we could do guy stuff like this with all of us every weekend."

Kane looked at Dash, who rather pointedly focused his gaze on his hands in his lap and didn't respond.

"Me too, sport," Kane said. "Me too."

Chapter Seven

"Kimi, don't feel obligated to stay if you have other things to do," Ginger said, after twenty minutes of general small talk.

"I'm happy to stick around. And to be honest? You'd be doin' me a favor by lettin' me stay."

Ginger eyed the petite blonde. How this small woman birthed twins boggled her mind. "How would you getting stuck with me be a favor?"

Kimi cracked open a can of diet soda and poured the fizzy liquid over a glass of ice. "First off, it's Sunday. Which means football, which I don't care a lick about. But my husband and his brother Carson are huge fans. They turn the TV so damn loud I can't stand to be in the same room with them." She winked. "I'm pretty sure that's what they're countin' on."

"You're left to your own devices every Sunday?"

"It ain't so bad. About half the time I head over to my sister Caro's place, since Carson is parked in my den. But today, Caro has all her grandkids over. Now don't get me wrong, I adore my grandnephews and grandnieces. There are just so darn many of them. Cryin', fightin', screamin', kids and dogs runnin' in and out of the house. Plus diapers, and at least one of them always vomits. Caro's in her element, but she's used to bein' surrounded by kids, as she had half a dozen."

Kimi set the soda on a coaster next to Ginger, and then poured herself a soda on ice too.

"Of course, my granddaughters are perfect angels. Here. See for yourself." From a saddle-shaped purse, Kimi whipped out a four-by-six photo album and handed it over. "Since Sky works so much during the week, her and Kade's weekends are devoted to their girls, and I can't fault them for that. Even when

I don't get to see my girlies as much as I'd like."

"Do you ever hang out with Kane on Sundays?"

"Rarely."

"Why's that?"

Kimi shrugged. "Used to be he'd still be enjoying female companionship from his Saturday night adventures in whatever bar he'd been trolling in the night before."

"Used to be?"

"Not for lack of women vying for his attention. My boys are good lookin' men. Lord, they've been rating a second and third glance from women of all ages since they turned fourteen. Kane took advantage of that female attention, way more than Kade ever did. But in the last few years, it's like Kane had a complete personality makeover."

Getting the goods on Kane McKay straight from his mother's mouth? Too good an opportunity to pass up. "How's he changed?"

"His cousin Dag died. Colt went into rehab. Cord got married. Kade got married. Then they sold the Boars Nest to Cam. It was like everybody grew up and moved on. Everyone but him. And don't get me started on that ridiculous name change.

"I've thought a lot about it and the bottom line is this—I don't think Kane wanted to give up his party-boy ways. It's made him a little bitter, so he keeps to himself. It bugs the crap out of me that he's alone so much." Kimi sighed. "Then again, near as I can figure, he's not bouncing on every woman with a pulse in the tri-county area. Good Lord. That man had lousy taste in women."

Cheeks burning, Ginger sipped her soda, keeping her mouth shut.

But Kimi was perceptive and recognized Ginger's intentional silence. "If you've got something to say about Kane, by all means, spit it out."

Her internal debate lasted all of fifteen seconds. "No offense, Kimi. I hate to say you're wrong about your son...but you're wrong. Kane keeps to himself because he's just plain tired. Sounds to me like he's picked up a considerable amount of slack since Kade became a family man." Ginger lifted a finger when Kimi started to argue. "He wasn't whining or complaining when we talked about it, just explaining.

"Kane spends time with Hayden at least once a week. Maybe he isn't hanging out with his married McKay cousins, but he plays poker with his single McKay cousins every other week. Maybe the difference is Kane doesn't feel compelled to live up to his former wild reputation. And near as I can tell? He isn't bitter. But I suspect he is lonely."

Kimi flat-out gaped at her. Then she got up and walked into the kitchen. She stared out the window, keeping her back to Ginger.

Way to insult Kane's mother first thing. Sometimes you have the tact of your mother.

Ginger waited for Kimi to either leave in a huff or lash out at her, figured she deserved either or both reactions.

Finally she came back and sat next to Ginger on the couch. Ginger's stomach churned seeing tear tracks on Kimi's face.

"Sorry if I stepped over the line."

"You didn't." Kimi laughed. "Okay, you did. It's just...you think you know your child. Straight down to the bone. Then someone shows you how arrogant that is. I should never assume anything. It makes me mad when other people do it, and I've done the same damn thing with my own child. So I don't know which is worse, how impressed I am by your insight into my son, or how embarrassed I am because of my lack of it."

Somewhat relieved, Ginger sagged into the couch. "I entrust Kane with the most important thing in my life—my son—so I probably see him in another light than you do."

A shrewd look entered Kimi's eyes. "How do you see my son?"

I'd like to see the gorgeous, thoughtful, kind, sweet, funny man naked a whole lot more, especially with his innate ability to make my earlobes sweat when he puts those callused hands on me.

"Not only is Kane multi-faceted, Kimi, he's great at multi-tasking. I don't know what I would've done if he hadn't volunteered to stay here and take care of us after my accident." Ginger tilted her head back and stared at the ceiling.

"Speaking of caretakers, are you Dash's primary caretaker?"

"Yes. And no. We built this one-level house to accommodate his wheelchair. Everything is handicapped-accessible. I hired a male nurse to deal with Dad's personal hygiene stuff because the stubborn man refuses to let me help him.'"

"Men need their pride," Kimi said softly. "My father hated being seen as weak. But Cal's dad, God rest his soul, accepted he'd never be the man he was and kept a great sense of humor about his 'failings' until the day he died."

"At this point...my Dad is between those two mindsets. Luckily he's still a social guy, so he's off to the senior center or community center three times a week. Although he's retired, he comes into the office and helps me."

"Cal said Dash intends to pass all the McKay legal work on to you."

"There's a lot more to it than I imagined."

"Big ranch. Big secrets. I hope you're up for it."

That was a strange thing for Kimi to say.

The silence didn't last long and Ginger appreciated Kimi kept the conversation rolling.

"I'm not surprised Dash kept his health issues a secret while he was dealing with Linda's illness." Kimi clucked her tongue. "Linda was such a sweet woman."

"That's what I hear. I didn't know her at all."

"Is that because you were close with your mother? I don't believe I've ever heard her mentioned."

Ginger tensed up at the mere mention of her mother. "As you probably know from local gossip, my parents' divorce was less than amicable. My relationship with my mother wasn't that great growing up, but it worsened after I left for college."

"Why? You'd think she'd be proud to have such a successful, smart, driven woman for a daughter."

"Wrong. She hated I'd followed in my dad's footsteps. Then Hayden's birth knocked her for a loop, because frankly, she wasn't ready to be a grandma. Plus, it embarrassed her I'd become an unmarried single mother and refused to disclose the name of Hayden's sperm donor. She cut all ties with me when we moved to Wyoming."

"Where does she live?"

"No clue. Last I heard it was...Australia? Or New Zealand."

Kimi's eyes widened. "She doesn't have any contact with Hayden?"

"She's never seen him, besides in pictures. It's a pretty screwed up situation."

"Sounds like it. But then I've learned that there's no such thing as the perfect family."

Her cell phone buzzed. She opened the picture message from Kane, showing Hayden receiving his third place ribbon. How much did it suck she couldn't be there?

"Honey? What's wrong?"

She passed the phone to Kimi. "Mother's guilt. Kane sent me a picture of Hayden and his award."

"How thoughtful."

"I know. He's always doing stuff like that. But it makes me feel so guilty."

"Part of bein' a mom."

"Do you ever still feel guilty?"

Kimi pinned her with an arch look. "Yes. Especially when it's pointed out to me that I don't know my own son as well as I thought I did."

Ginger blushed. "I didn't mean—"

"I know you didn't. I'm glad you talked to me. I really liked seein' Kane through your eyes, Ginger. And I hope..." She waved dismissively. "Forget it."

"No, Kimi, tell me. You hope what?"

"I hope Kane knows how proud I am of him, not only for helpin' you out, but for the time he spends with Hayden. I've never thought of him as overly responsible besides when it comes to his duties at the ranch."

"Maybe you should tell him. It'd be good for him to hear it from you."

"Maybe I will."

Ginger's head pounded, a byproduct of thinking about her mother.

Kimi stood. "Come on. Let's get you a pain pill and tuck you in. I fear my son'd have my hide for talkin' your ear off when you're supposed to be restin'."

"I can't believe how tired I am."

"Which is a sign you need to get some shut-eye."

Kimi stayed by Ginger's side until she drifted off, offering comfort and silent support. Her last coherent thought was *Like mother, like son.*

"Hey, Red." A soft kiss teased her forehead.

"Am I still dreaming?"

"Are we nekkid in this dream?"

"Yes. Completely. Rolling around on satin sheets and you're kissing me in that panty-drenching way of yours."

Kane chuckled. "Maybe we'll have to act out the good parts of the dream later. But it's time for you to get up."

Ginger opened her eyes, sighing dreamily that Kane's handsome face was so close to hers.

"What was that sigh for?"

"Because you're just so damn pretty, Kane McKay."

His neck flushed. "How many of them damn drugs did you take?"

"Funny." She ran the tips of her fingers down the section of skin where the blush met his goatee. "You could have any woman in town. You have had most of them, to hear your mother talk. So what are you doing with me?"

Hurt flashed in his eyes. She could've bitten her tongue for her careless comment.

"My ma was here tellin' stories about me, was she? Fillin' you in on all the women I bedded and discarded? Did she tell you that the reason Kade and Sky ended up together was because he pretended to be me after I was an asshole to her on our first and only date?"

"No. She didn't mention that one."

Kane stood abruptly. Angrily. "Don't matter. We've been back awhile. Are you hungry?"

Ginger reached for his hand. "Don't run off in a fit of pique."

"Say what?"

"Don't leave because you're mad. Kimi didn't name off your conquests, Kane. She just said you used to be quite the wild one and you've mellowed. Now instead of worrying about you being too rowdy, she worries about you being alone too much."

He frowned. "Ma said that?"

"Yes."

"I'm alone by choice."

There was more to his statement, but she didn't push. Instead, she brought his hand to her mouth and placed a soft kiss in the palm. "So does that 'alone by choice' comment include tonight?"

"Is that an invite, counselor?"

"Yes. But I feel the need to point out it is an open-ended invitation."

Kane's eyes turned dark with liquid heat. He cupped her chin in his hand, sweeping his thumb across the inside of her lower lip. "Know one thing about me that ain't mellowed? That I'm in charge even when *you're* touchin' me."

His bold statement caused her belly to jump. She stared at him, wondering how far he'd take things.

"You look nervous, Red."

"I've never met a man like you."

"Simple? Or highly experienced?"

"Neither."

He huffed, "Then what?" a little impatiently.

"You distract me to the point that's all I can think about...being with you."

Kane's lethally sexy grin appeared. "I can live with being a distraction, sugar. In fact, I intend to bump up my attentions and see if I can't become your obsession."

Hours later, Ginger reflected on Kane's words when he waltzed into her bedroom and she realized he could become an obsession.

Hayden had hit the sack earlier than usual. Her father had retreated to his room directly after Hayden.

And now Kane had come to her.

A thrill of anticipation electrified her, starting at her toes, ending at her scalp.

She'd purposely dimmed the lights to enhance the mood. Hoping the ambient glow would mask her physical flaws and her nervousness.

Instantly he flipped on all the switches, growling a warning, "No hidin' from me. Ever. I like to watch."

"Watch what?"

"You." Kane gestured to the edge of the bed. "Sit there."

"Am I supposed to get undressed?"

"Did I tell you to get undressed?"

"No."

"There's your answer. This time you're undressing me." Kane stood in front of her, legs braced apart, arms crossed. A master directing his slave. "Pants first."

His high-handed behavior wasn't what she'd expected. No kissing, no seduction. Using her good hand, she tugged one side of the elastic band, then the other, until the flannel pooled at his bare feet. He kicked his pajama pants aside.

Ginger's gaze didn't waver from her first up-close look at his cock. Oh wow. Circumcised? Check. Long? Check. Thick? Check. She wanted to rub the smooth and shiny purple head across her lips.

He grabbed the edges of his tank top and yanked it off.

Confused, Ginger met his eyes. "I thought I was supposed to undress you?"

"You were. Until I saw the way you were lickin' your lips. I'm dyin' to feel your mouth on my cock." Kane wrapped one hand around her jaw. The other hand circled his dick and he brought it in line with her lips. "Use your mouth only, and only on the tip."

He painted her lips with the polished skin of the head. Once the slit was close enough to taste, her tongue darted out to catch the drop of fluid beading in the center. She moaned at her first taste of him.

"You keep makin' sounds like that and this'll be over too damn quick."

"You want me to make those sounds when this bad boy is completely buried my mouth?"

"Eventually. For now, focus on the head."

She circled her lips around the crown and sucked, alternating with flicks of her tongue. Working the sweet spot beneath the thick rim brought forth Kane's masculine groans of approval, but it wasn't enough. She wanted to feel the rigid length gliding over her tongue. She wanted to feel his girth stretching her mouth wide. She wanted to feel his pubic hair ticking her nose as she took him deep. She wanted total submersion in this intimacy.

So yeah, maybe she resented his dictate of control.

Without warning, Kane tilted her head and pushed past her lips, over her teeth, across her tongue, bumping her soft palate, until his cock was fully seated in her mouth and halfway down her throat.

Ginger fought the gag reflex, focusing on her breathing. Trying not to feel smug she'd gotten exactly what she'd wanted.

Brusquely, Kane said, "Look at me."

The only things she could move were her eyes. She gazed up at him. God. He was something. So overpoweringly male.

"You were testy about me parceling out a taste of my cock an inch at a time, weren't you, sugar?"

Her affirmative growl traveled up his shaft.

He trembled.

Ginger smiled, hard as it was with her lips stretched around the base of his cock.

"You are stubborn about getting your way," he murmured. His thumb traced the hollowed section of her cheek. "Truth is, that makes me fuckin' hot." He let his fingers drift up her face to circle the shell of her ear before coming back to rest on her jaw. "But I'm gonna enjoy teachin' you obedience."

His big, rough-skinned hands landed on her head. "Hold on."

Her left hand gripped his muscular quad.

Kane pulled his cock out, letting the rim of the cockhead rest on her lower lip. Then he thrust back in fully. He did that three more times a slow withdrawal, a fast plunge to the root.

Saliva built in her mouth, coating his shaft, making the glide easier. Ginger kept her eyes closed, reveling in the silken push and pull of his hard flesh across her soft tissues.

"That's it," he rasped. "Get me wet."

She let her teeth graze the underside of his cock as he eased out. Then she playfully flicked her tongue into the slit.

"No teasing." He shoved deep. "Now suck harder. That's it. Lemme feel those throat muscles workin'."

Kane picked up the pace.

Ginger loosened her jaw, loving his loss of control with every grunting thrust into the wet recess of her mouth. Her panties were soaked. Her sex throbbed with want, jealous her mouth was being so thoroughly filled.

The strokes increased. Kane's breathing turned even more ragged. "I'm close. Jesus. Fuck." Two more deep thrusts and he stilled. His cock twitched on the back of her tongue and he groaned, "Swallow. Now. All of it. Christ." His hips continued to bump against her face.

Her cheeks were compressed tightly to the rigid shaft. Her throat muscles contracted around the head as his seed flowed down the back of her throat. A pleasant buzz reverberated in her head.

First time she'd experienced that euphoric feeling from giving a blowjob. Usually her orgasms gave her that floating, melting sensation.

Seriously fucking hot, seriously fucking heady, this obedience stuff.

"Hey. Red. Look at me."

She blinked at him.

Satisfaction and pure possession were etched on his face. And his mouth. That sinful, talented, knowing mouth, curled into a naughty smile. "You liked that."

Ginger couldn't even nod with the fierce grip he had on her head.

Kane's cock remained in her throat. "Beautiful, sexy Ginger. Prim and proper mama no more. Christ, woman, you blew my fuckin' mind."

She kept her eyes riveted to the fire blazing in the blue depths. She finally understood his need for control—because his sexual hunger could be overpowering. All encompassing. Addictive.

"But you can let go of my dick now. In fact, sugar, you're teeth are startin' to hurt a little."

What? She was keeping his cock in place? Not him? That was new. She relaxed her jaw.

Kane's greedy gaze was locked on his semi-hard cock slipping from between her lips. "Soon as you catch your breath, we're goin' again."

She nuzzled his hip, breathing his musky scent deep into her lungs. Her fingernails were still embedded in his thigh with enough force she'd marked him.

He seemed content to stroke her hair, brushing back the tendrils sticking to her sweat dampened face.

Several insistent knocks on the door brought them both out their sexual trance.

"Mommy?"

Ginger's head snapped up.

Kane said, "Shit," and quickly—and rather comically—

dragged on his pajama bottoms and pulled on his tank top, inside out.

Good thing she had her clothes on and she looked sleep tousled, not sex-ravaged. Kane unlocked the door, ending up behind it as it opened.

Hayden rushed in and started to fling himself at her, but Kane deftly stopped him mid-leap.

"Gently, sport. Your mama still ain't up to tackle hugs."

If it surprised Hayden that Kane was in her room, he didn't show it. He burrowed into her.

"Sweetie? What's wrong?"

"I had a bad dream. And you died and Grandpa changed into a tornado, with robot arms and he chased me in his wheelchair. He was gonna cut off my head!"

"Sounds scary. But I'm thinking no more *Transformers* before bed," she murmured, looking up at Kane.

Kane mouthed, "Sorry."

"Can I sleep with you?"

Hayden rarely asked to crawl in bed with her so she knew he was shaken up. She kissed the top of his head. "Of course. Do you need a drink or anything first?"

"No. Just need you, Mommy."

Her heart tumbled. "I'm here. Not going anywhere, okay?"

"Okay." He released a heavy sigh. "I'm tired."

"Maybe Kane can tuck us both in."

"No problem."

Ginger rolled back onto the mattress. Hayden snuggled beside her, heeding Kane's warning not to jiggle her sling. They wiggled until comfortable positions were attained.

Kane tugged the blankets over them. "Do you want pillows to prop up your cast?"

She shook her head.

He clicked off the lights. "I'll leave the door open in case you need anything."

"Thanks."

Usually Hayden was a restless sleeper but it didn't take long before his breathing leveled. He mumbled, "Love you, Mommy."

"Love you too, baby."

She thought she'd be too keyed up from the sexual shenanigans with Kane to fall asleep right away. But right after closing her eyes, she drifted off.

Chapter Eight

By the time Ginger hobbled into the kitchen the next morning, Kane had already showered, shoveled the steps and the wheelchair ramp and brewed a pot of coffee.

Yeah, he was a little anxious.

She didn't wait for him to bring her a cup; she walked right past him poured her own. "You've been a busy bee this morning," she said, gazing out the window.

"I'm used to getting up early. Did Hayden settle down all right last night?"

"Surprisingly, yes. He's still completely sacked out."

"I checked on you guys about three and you were both sound asleep."

Ginger turned around. "Why'd you check on us?"

"Habit. I've been checkin' in on you at some point every night since I got here."

She stared at him. Hard. "So? Do I drool? Snore? Babble in my sleep?"

"You're not usually this cranky before you've had your first shot of caffeine. Something botherin' you?"

"Just...never mind. Drop it, okay?"

Kane stopped in front of her. "No. Talk to me."

"You're doing everything. I'm doing nothing. I'm tired of being helpless. I need a real shower so badly I can smell myself. I look horrible. I hate the way the pain pills knock me out. I hate that if I don't take them I hurt."

"Anything else?"

Ginger lifted her head. "Like my total helplessness, my total dependence on you isn't enough reason for me to be cranky?"

She scowled at him. "Why in the hell are you so damn chipper this morning?"

"Do you want a *blow by blow* account of what's put a big ol' grin on my face?"

"Smartass." She hid her smile behind her coffee cup. "I didn't expect you'd be happy. I thought you'd be upset we were interrupted."

"I didn't expect anything less than you givin' Hayden your full attention when he needed it."

"Really?"

"Uh-huh. I thought maybe you were peckish because I hadn't kissed you good mornin' yet. Come to think of it, I didn't kiss you goodnight, either."

"Slacking on your caretaking duties, McKay."

"Do you want me to kiss you?"

Her gaze darted to Dash's room.

"I checked on him too. He's still snoring away." Kane set her coffee cup on the counter and held her face in his hands. "Good mornin', beautiful." He kissed her with as much tenderness he could muster, needing her acceptance. Her surrender.

Ginger tried to crank the heat up, but he wouldn't allow it. He gently bit down on her lower lip and briefly held it hostage between his teeth. "Ah. Ah. Ah. My pace. And I'm wantin' slow, wet and sweet kisses from you right now, counselor."

"Kane. I want more than kisses."

His cock, already stirring with interest, went fully erect. "Same goes, but I ain't gonna start something we can't finish. Neither your daddy nor your son needs to see me bending you facedown across the counter as I fuck you like a madman."

The pulse in her throat jumped.

With deliberate slowness, Kane bent down, breathing on the spot before he placed his lips on it. "I love the way you taste right here."

Ginger shivered, releasing a husky moan.

"I want you under me, on top of me, in front of me, every which way I've ever thought about takin' you and then some. But let's be realistic, Red. It's probably not gonna happen tonight."

Silence.

"Having second thoughts about getting mixed up with a single mother who's rarely alone?"

"Nope. I'm thinkin' we're gonna hafta get creative to carve out our own alone time." He kissed a path to her ear. "Tomorrow's a school day, and the bus picks Hayden up out front, right?"

"Yes. No. Umm. Maybe."

"Which is it?"

"Shit, I don't know. Yes, tomorrow is a school day. And God, I cannot think straight when you whisper in my ear, Kane McKay. You could recite the constitutional amendments and I'd get turned on."

Kane smiled against her temple. "And the senior bus picks your dad up...early?"

"Uh-huh."

"So let's plan on spending tomorrow—the whole day—alone together, in bed."

She leaned back to look at him. "That'd be perfect. But I have to work. I've already missed—"

"Too bad. Doc Monroe said you needed a minimum of five days recovery time. Tomorrow is the fifth day. Doctor's orders are doctor's orders, sugar. And it's my job to make sure they're followed to the letter."

After a brief pause, Ginger giggled.

Giggled.

The brilliant, sexy, headstrong bombshell with too many responsibilities and too little personal time...actually giggled like a girl.

That's when Kane knew he was done for.

He smashed his mouth to hers, kissing her with the passion that he could finally unleash tomorrow.

She matched his every tongue tangling, lip gliding, teeth nipping move, adding a few of her own, until he was dizzy with lust. Why did he have the strangest urge to break out into song like some cheesy romantic comedy hero?

Hero. Right. He was far from being a hero, but it looked as if he was about to get the girl of his dreams—for one day, anyway.

Kane eased back from the reckless kiss, pressing his forehead to hers.

"Is it tomorrow yet?" she murmured.

He chuckled, pleased as punch that she was just as anxious. "No. But as soon as everybody's up, I'm gonna need to go outside and work off this extra energy. Got a wood pile that needs split or something?"

"Was your use of the word 'wood' intentional?"

"Smartass."

"You need help chopping your wood?" She snickered.

"No. I've got plenty of experience, even if it's been one-handed experience recently."

Ginger nuzzled his neck. "Care to elaborate on that 'recently' time frame?"

"Sure. Not since the night you goaded me into kissin' you."

She froze.

"Surprised?"

"Completely."

Kane whispered, "Your turn."

"I haven't had any wood in my shed since I moved here."

Simultaneously, they tilted their heads back and stared at one another. Then simultaneously, they grinned.

"Red, we are so gonna combust as soon as I see them bus taillights turnin' onto the highway tomorrow mornin'."

"I can't wait."

At 5 a.m. Kane rolled out of bed and shoveled. Again.

At 6 a.m. Kane showered. Shaved. Trimmed his mustache and goatee. Did a little manscaping.

At 6:30 a.m. the coffee finished brewing.

At 6:35 a.m. he heard Ginger's door open. She woke Hayden. Then her father. Then she entered the kitchen.

Okay. He'd half hoped she'd slink in wearing the silky green robe he'd seen hanging on the back of her bedroom door. But no. She wore black yoga pants that hugged her every mouth-watering curve and an old T-shirt that barely skimmed her navel.

Hello gorgeous.

But she wouldn't look at him. She poured herself a cup of coffee. Knocked it back and poured another.

"Ginger? You okay?"

She whirled on him and growled, "No. Don't touch me. Don't talk to me. Don't even look at me."

Shit. Had she changed her mind? "Why not?"

"Because if you do, I will jump you and ride you like a pony, right fucking here, right fucking now, on my dirty kitchen linoleum."

Whoa. Guess she hadn't changed her mind.

Heh heh.

Grinning, Kane held up his hands in mock surrender. "I'll just umm...watch The Weather Channel or something."

"You do that."

If Hayden or Dash noticed her edginess, they didn't mention it. She packed Hayden's lunch. He bundled the boy up and sent him out to wait for the school bus.

One down; one to go.

Dash seemed to be dragging his wheels. Even after the senior bus pulled into the driveway and honked. He slowly put on his coat. Buttoned it. Double-checking each button.

At one point Kane swore he caught a knowing, ornery smirk on the man's face.

Dash wrapped his scarf around his neck, then rewrapped it. He settled his Elmer Fudd hat with the earflaps on his head. Tugged on his gloves with his teeth. Took them off and tried it again.

Finally.

But the man bundled up and ready for a trip to Siberia, simply waited at the door.

"Do they usually come in and get you?" Kane asked.

"No."

Pause.

"Need me to help you out to the van, Dash?"

"A little eager to get rid of me this morning, McKay?"

Dammit. "Nope. I thought you might be worried the ramp is icy. I shoveled it, so you don't have to worry about careening out of control."

The horn honked again.

Dash stayed put.

Now Kane was really starting to sweat. What if the bus left? He could drive Dash into town in the van, although that'd eat up some time, but that'd still leave him and Ginger...

94

"Later," Dash said and Kane scrambled to hold the door open while Dash rolled out.

8:37 a.m. Dash was on the bus's loading platform and the driver opened the door to load Dash's wheelchair into the bus.

8:40 a.m. the bus started backing down the driveway.

8:41 a.m. the senior bus disappeared down the highway.

8:42 a.m. Kane locked the front door.

At 8:42 and sixteen seconds Kane stood at the foot of Ginger's bed.

The sexy vixen had draped the green robe across her body. "They're gone?" she asked.

"They're gone."

"For sure?"

"For positive."

"Then strip."

Kane raised an eyebrow. "Excuse me?"

"No control games. I want you naked."

"Control ain't a game for me, Red. No master-slave scenarios. No collars. No fake punishments for disobedience. No crops or whips or spankins...unless you ask. Or maybe, even if you don't." Kane yanked his T-shirt off. Unbuckled his belt and unzipped. And stopped.

If the glazed look in her eyes was an indication, she'd quit listening to him when he'd started shedding clothes.

He whistled to get her attention.

Ginger's gaze zoomed back to him. "Umm. What were you saying?"

"This isn't a game. I'm in control when that bedroom door shuts. You cede all power to me. Period."

"Why?"

"Well, one—because I like it and bein' in control is my true nature. And two—because I know you're the take-charge type. You're always worryin' about everyone else in your family, makin' sure your career and every aspect of your life are kept under control. Which is fine. Perfect actually. Because it'll be so much more freeing when you hand that tightly held control over to me when we're in the bedroom." Kane shucked his Wranglers and his socks, keeping her focus trained on him. "No one has to know but us. I'm willin' to compromise on a lot of things, but this ain't one of them. So tell me now if you're on board with this."

"If I'm not?"

"I'll put my clothes back on and we'll chalk it up to differing philosophies."

She blinked at him. He recognized the wheels in her head were spinning frantically, trying to justify this action with all that lawyer speak that made her so damn appealing.

"Say yes. Let me take care of you, Ginger. I'll give you everything that you never knew you needed in bed." And out, but she wasn't ready to hear that part yet.

"Yes," she whispered.

Kane wrapped his fist in the silken material of the green robe and yanked, revealing her...fully clothed body.

Her porcelain-colored skin flushed a deep crimson. "I wanted to be a temptress, to wear my skimpiest lace panties and matching bra, but I couldn't get undressed by myself. So, sorry I'm in the same old crappy stuff I've worn for the last—"

"Stop." He crawled across the bed, his painfully hard dick bounced against his belly. "Lose the pants." Off they went. "Sit up."

She pushed upright with her good arm and studied him from beneath lowered lashes. "Take the sling off too. I'll be careful. I just need to touch you with both hands, Kane."

He unhooked the sling and maneuvered her shirt off. She wore the lime-green bra. He twisted the front clasp, slid it free from her arms and it met the rest of her clothes on the floor.

Once he tore his greedy gaze away from her drool-worthy tits, he sealed his lips to hers. As Kane kissed her, he slowly rolled her onto her back.

By the time they came up for air, Kane teetered on the edge of just plowing into her and getting this first time out of the way so he could take it slower the second go round.

Fuck that. Ginger deserved better. Hell, he deserved better.

He pushed onto his haunches; his gaze started at the sassy dent in her chin and winged to the pale peach tips of her hardened nipples and ended at the triangle of red curls. Kane bent his head and lapped her slit from the mouth of her sex to her clit.

Damn. She was already wet. Really wet. Completely ready.

"Kane—"

"I know." With *now, now, now* pounding in his head, he slid her left foot up until it was flat on the mattress. Then he did the same with the cast. He braced his left hand above her shoulder and directed his cock to the warm, wet place between her thighs.

Then Kane snapped his hips. With one fast stroke he was fully seated inside her. He levered his body over hers, so they were belly to belly, chest to chest, eye to eye. "You okay?"

Ginger's left hand touched his face. "Don't stop, don't think, just fuck me."

Growling, Kane pulled out and slammed back in. "Good thing you said that, because I couldn't hold back right now if I tried."

He withdrew. Shoved in to the root again. Each stroke gained momentum. Faster and faster until he was fucking her without pause.

She squirmed, delicately arching her neck, canting her hips, urging him to go deeper. Her free hand gripped his ass and her breath whooshed out with his every forceful thrust.

"God, that feels so good," she moaned.

"Too goddamn good." Yeah, it'd been a long time since he'd had sex, but he never remembered it being this good. Maybe the buildup of sexual tension heightened his senses.

"I'm already close. Shift your hips a little to the... Oh yes, right there."

On every upstroke he pressed into her pubic bone, grinding against her clit. Shortening each thrust so he kept nearly constant pressure where she needed it most.

Her cunt muscles clamped down on his cock, keeping it in place and she came with a husky, drawn-out wail.

Steady. Steady. Steady.

Kane clenched his jaw and rode out her orgasm, memorizing the play of emotions crossing her exquisite face. The look of pain morphed into an expression of bliss and she released a wholly feminine, wholly satisfied sigh.

The sigh set him off. He jackhammered his cock into her without restraint, watching her tits shake, watching her smile grow as his control unraveled.

His balls constricted. He shouted as pulses of hot seed shot out of his dick into the slippery, wet heat of her pussy. At each ripple of pleasure zipping down his spine, he couldn't stop his pelvis from thrusting, trying to prolong the almost violent electric bursts as long as possible.

As soon as he stopped moving, Ginger's mouth was on his. Unrelenting and hungry. Kane remained in the pushup position as long as he dared, letting her control the kiss, but his arms needed a break. The last thing he wanted was to crush her dislocated shoulder.

Ginger made a soft protest when he broke the kiss.

"I know, darlin', but give me a second, okay?" He shifted back, dislodging his cock. Wetness trickled down her leg and it occurred to him why it'd felt so goddamn good: they'd forgotten a condom.

Fuck.

She realized the oversight the same time he did.

"Shit, Ginger, I'm so sorry. I was just so damn crazed to be with you that I forgot." He rested on his haunches, dropping his palms to his thighs. "I've always used a condom. Always. And it's been a while for me, so I'm clean. I know that doesn't probably ease your mind as far as—"

"Kane." She sat up and placed her hand in the center of his chest. "It's okay. We should've thought of birth control—both of us—but I was just as eager as you were. Besides, I'm on the pill."

"You are? But...why?" The spike of jealousy surprised him. "If you're not seein' anyone regular?"

"I had one unintended pregnancy. I've been on the pill since Hayden was a baby."

"Ah. Well, that's good, I guess."

"And the few times I've let myself act like a woman, and not a mother, I've insisted on condoms." Her hand inched down and she swept her thumb across his nipple. "I loved the feel of you in me, no barriers. Just you bare."

"Me too." Goose bumps prickled his skin from her lazy stroking motion on his chest.

"So we can skip the condoms entirely, if you want."

Kane's hand slid into her hair. He tilted her head back while bringing her closer. "Oh, I want, all right."

Silence passed between them as they looked at each other. Lust built quickly, reflected in equal measure.

He softly brushed his lips across hers. "Again. Right now."

Ginger's gaze dropped to his cock. "Here I thought I'd get to use my hand to help you rise to the occasion."

"I ain't stoppin' you."

She reached between them and fondled his balls. Then she wrapped her fingers around his girth and stroked, keeping her eyes glued to his. "See? I'm not very good with my left hand."

"That's the thing, darlin', you don't have to be good. Just puttin' your hand on me does all sorts of good." He loosened his hold on her hair. "Need help climbin' up on my lap?"

"What do you mean?"

Kane adjusted his legs beneath hers. "Hold onto my shoulder." As soon as Ginger had some semblance of balance, he lifted her so her legs were half-wrapped around his waist as they faced each other.

"Oh. I like this," she murmured.

He aligned his cock and slid into her in a single slow glide.

"I really like that."

"This way I can have my hands free to touch you."

"Not to mention I can kiss all those spots that've been tempting me." Ginger used her teeth to follow the muscles corded in his neck. She methodically tasted the section of skin under his strong jaw. She slid her lips to his ear. "While this control thing is a turn on? I want equal time to explore your body."

"Ah. Okay, Jesus."

"Move in me, Kane. Put your hands on me. God, I love the way your rough hands feel on me."

Kane grabbed her ass cheeks and rocked into her. In this position he couldn't pull his cock out, but there was something very intimate about staying connected while hands and mouths explored. While pulses raced and sweat beaded on skin.

And Ginger took her own sweet time in her exploration. She kissed, nibbled and licked the slope of his shoulder, his jaw, all the while making very satisfied, very approving noises. He loved the way her tits pressed into his chest. The stiff nipples rubbing the hair on his sweat-slickened skin when she shifted to touch him at another angle. He loved the feel of her quickened breath puffing out every time he lifted his hips and drove into her a little deeper.

He loved everything about this. About her.

Part of him wanted to stay locked with this highly sensual woman for the next hour, just existing in the physical reaction. Another part wanted that drive to orgasm.

When Ginger reconnected their mouths the urgency re-ignited.

His hands cupped her buttocks, lifting her completely off his cock so he could plunge in fully.

She ripped her mouth free, arching her neck. "It's right there."

"Bear down on me, oh fuck yeah, just like that." Kane buried his lips in her throat and sucked hard.

"Omigod. Yes. Yes!" Ginger's body tightened, inside, outside.

Kane came with a roar as her climax milked his with every rhythmic pulse. He was pretty sure he stopped breathing for a second or so. He was pretty sure the damn world stopped spinning. He was also pretty sure one day in bed with her wouldn't nearly be enough.

Soft kisses tracked his hairline.

His eyes fluttered open.

Ginger smiled at him.

"Jesus. That was fucking amazing."

"Or amazing fucking," she teased, kissing his nose.

"That too," he murmured. He sensed her restlessness and need to move. "Hang on. Lemme help you." He lifted her, turning so she balanced on her good arm before lowering her to the mattress.

She immediately closed her eyes and rested her bum arm on her bare belly.

Kane crawled beside her and swept the damp hair from her rosy cheek. "You okay? Need anything?"

"Some recovery time before round three."

"Funny, Red, that's supposed to be my line."

"I could use a drink of water."

"Be right back." Kane slipped on his boxer shorts and wandered to the kitchen. He checked the time, checked his phone and washed his hands and face in the sink. He half expected to find her asleep when returned to her bedroom.

But Ginger was wide-awake. Looking sexy as hell propped

up on the pile of pillows on her bed.

"Here." He handed her the glass of water and she drained it. "More?"

"No. But we worked up a powerful thirst, didn't we?"

"More like a powerful hunger for me."

Both her auburn eyebrows lifted. "There's going to be a third round, isn't there?"

"Uh-huh." Kane kissed the top of her foot. "And a fourth." He kissed above and below the bandage covering the gash on her shin. And the cute dimple above her knee. Then the bruises on her upper thigh. "And possibly a fifth." Finally he kissed the sexy curve of her hip. "Just not right now."

She shivered.

"You cold?"

"Always."

"Maybe I can warm you up." He carefully pulled her into his arms.

She wiggled until she could press her cheek into his chest. Her cast clunked into his shin as she attempted to twine their legs together. "Sorry."

"It's okay." His fingers trailed lazily up and down her spine.

After a bit, Ginger sighed. "Want to know something that's embarrassing to admit? It's been so long since I've been with a man, I was worried I wouldn't remember how."

Amused, he said, "Remember how to have sex?"

"No. Remember how to be a woman."

His heart lurched. He wanted to reassure her she was all woman, but he didn't interrupt, as he suspected this was something she'd never admitted to herself, let alone to anyone else.

"I've been asexual for so long, mother, professional woman, daughter, that I let the part of me that loves sex, that loves to be bold and fun in bed, the part that loves the feel of a man's hands on me, his arms around me...God. Just to be held like this. Do you know how long it's been? It's like I slammed the door on that part of myself and never even peeked inside."

"So, do you regret me kickin' that door wide open?"

She laughed. "No. Never. Especially now that I know what I was missing behind that door with you. Do you think it's weird I had the overwhelming urge to tell you the truth?"

"A lawyer speaking the truth? What is the world comin' to?"

Ginger laughed again.

"When did that door on your sexual being close?"

"Right after Hayden was born. I tried to recoup some of what I'd lost. But then I realized I never had it in the first place."

"Was it Hayden's father who did such a number on you?"

Her body went rigid. "I never talk about it. About him. Whatever."

Kane ignored her clipped tone. "Then sugar, I think it's long past time you did."

Chapter Nine

Ginger had wondered if this would ever come up.

So far she'd avoided the subject with her son.

But she knew there'd be no avoiding it with this man.

But strangely, she trusted him. She wanted to tell him.

"Ginger?"

"Sorry. Just wrestling with where to even start."

"How about at the beginning?"

She toyed with his chest hair, purposely not looking at him. "After I graduated from law school I landed a job with a big law firm in Los Angeles that specialized in contractual law in the entertainment industry. It was a highly sought-after job and I was damn lucky to have gotten it."

"Good perks?"

"Amazing perks. Anyway, after my intern period passed, I was assigned permanently to the contractual dissolution team."

"What's that?"

"We were hired to find loopholes to break existing contracts."

His fingers never stopped moving on her back. "Is that big business?"

"Very big business. I worked directly under the senior partner, Chas Daly. I admired him because he was brilliant and charismatic. He treated me like a rising star. He introduced me that way. 'Here's Ginger, our newest rising star.' It was heady stuff."

"I imagine."

"With the late nights, case overload and me being a rookie who needed supervision, Chas and I spent a lot of time together. One thing led to another, and within a year of my assignment we were engaged in this torrid affair."

At that comment Kane's fingers stilled.

"Chas was married, which I knew. He fed me those clichéd bullshit lines about he and his wife drifting apart, she didn't fulfill his sexual needs. The man had a voracious sexual appetite. In hindsight it was probably due to Viagra. I eagerly bought his lies, becoming the adventurous lover his wife wasn't. Even if we only hooked up in his office. I knew if I stayed the course, Chas would eventually leave her for me. Obviously that didn't happen."

"What did happen?"

"I found out three pieces of information that absolutely devastated me. One—his wife's father had started the law firm and he was inexplicably tied to it and to her. Two—he was older than I'd thought."

"How much older?"

"Thirty years. I was twenty-seven. He was fifty-seven." Shame burned her cheeks. "But it was LA. Everyone looks at least a decade younger. I figured he was in his late forties, because that's how old his wife looked."

"What was the third thing?"

"I wasn't the only woman he was having an affair with. The guy was a real womanizer with a string of conquests a mile long. Most of them bimbos. Anyway, after I found all this out, his wife, Lucinda, caught wind of our affair. I wasn't his run-of-the-mill stripper floozy. So I was summarily canned, without notice. And before you say something like 'why didn't I sue?' I'll remind you this law firm was the premier law firm in breaking contracts. I was seriously fucked.

"Three weeks after I lost my job, I moved out of my high-priced condo because I couldn't afford the rent without the high paycheck, I discovered I was pregnant. More than three and a half months, according to the doctor. It was a shocking development, to say the least."

"Did you contact Chas and let him know?"

"No. I muddled through the pregnancy on my own. From the day he was born, Hayden had health issues. Although we didn't have health insurance, my son received the very best care."

"And while you were struggling, you didn't consider askin'

Chas to support his child? To take responsibility for his actions?"

Ginger recognized Kane's anger. She lifted her head and looked at him. "Yes, I did. Several times. There were days when I suspected I'd doomed my baby by holding onto my pride. But when I held that sweet baby in my arms, I sure as hell wouldn't share custody of Hayden with Chas. Ever. It sucked. I had no one to talk to about any of it since I'd ostracized myself from my law colleagues."

"Why?"

"I didn't want anyone to know about my pregnancy. The sad fact was I'd been too busy building a career to maintain female friendships. My mother was embarrassed I'd become unwed, underemployed, single mother. My dad...well, my dad was great. For the first time in my life he supported me. Emotionally and financially. When we had a bad month...he was there to help out. He wasn't ashamed of me and he adored Hayden from the start." She swallowed hard.

Kane didn't speak.

"Maybe I'm just stubborn or stupid, but whenever I went to pick up the phone to call Chas, something stopped me. I knew myself well enough that if I hadn't set a firm date to let Chas know he had a son, I'd keep stalling. So I promised myself I'd tell Chas after Hayden's second birthday."

She closed her eyes. "I never got the chance. Chas had a massive heart attack out on a fishing boat off the Catalina coast and died when Hayden was twenty-two months old."

"Oh sugar."

"A few months later I found out through a mutual work friend that Chas's wife and his daughter from his first marriage were in a huge lawsuit over his estate. That's when I knew it was some kind of karma that'd kept me from contacting him. Chas wasn't meant to be in Hayden's life in any capacity. And I decided not to subject Hayden to any of Chas's bullshit family stuff. I finally realized there were more important things than money or prestige."

Kane tucked a stray hair behind her ear. "Did you love him?"

"Who? Chas?" She chewed her lip, considering her answer. Not for Kane's sake but for hers. "I thought I did. But when he sacrificed my career without even blinking? I hated him. I hated him for taking away everything I'd worked for. I hated him for a long time. Which is so bizarre because he gave me the most important thing in my life. He actually gave me the ability to love, because until I had Hayden, I didn't even know what love was."

Kane brought her face to his and kissed her. So sweetly tears pricked the back of her eyelids and seeped out the corners of her eyes. Then he kissed her tears away.

"Hayden doesn't know any of this, Kane. The only person I've ever told is my dad."

"Has Hayden ever asked about his father?"

"Has he asked you? While you two were doing Little Buddies stuff?"

"Nope. That's actually one of the topics we're supposed to steer clear of."

"Smart. I steer clear of it too." She dropped her head back onto his chest.

He toyed with her hair for a time before he spoke again. "Did you practice law after you had Hayden?"

"Sort of. I moved to San Diego and worked as a file clerk in the county prosecutor's office. I hated that job and decided to hang out my shingle for a solo law practice."

"That go better for you?"

"For the first month? I didn't have a single client walk through my door. Then one day, this seventeen-year-old punk with attitude swaggered in. She'd signed a modeling contract and paid the agency owner five grand for a portfolio. When she arrived at her first photographic 'shoot' she discovered the guy wasn't a modeling agent—he was making porn. She demanded her money back and the contract voided."

"The guy refused?"

"Of course. Most young girls would've walked away and chalked it up to a stupid mistake. Or they would've taken his offer of 'earning' the fee back by appearing in an adult film or two. That type of scam happens all the time in LA. But Ava, my client, refused to back down. I didn't find out until later that money wasn't an issue for her."

"Why wasn't it?"

"Her parents were loaded. They didn't approve of her chasing her dream to become an actress, so she'd hired this guy on the sly without their knowledge or approval. But it was her mess and she was determined to clean it up without Mommy and Daddy riding to her rescue.

"With my background in contract law, I sent the sleazeball a letter outlining my plans to file a lawsuit, regarding his blatant breaking of California sexual predator laws since Ava was a minor—which he knew when she signed the contract. Within two days we had the money and a voided contract." She smiled. "Despite our age difference, Ava and I became great friends. We still are. She was so impressed with the results, she sent me more clients. I vetted all her professional contracts up until I moved to Wyoming and she hit the big leagues."

"Big leagues?" he asked, puzzled.

"After her first TV series was a runaway smash, she transitioned into movies."

"Who we talkin' about here, Red?"

"Ava Dumond. Her stage name is Ava Cooper."

"No shit? The teeny blonde with the big—"

"Watch it," she warned.

"The big...role on that vampire show? *That* Ava Cooper?"

"One in the same."

"Whoa. I'd wondered if you knew any of them Hollywood stars, bein's you're from LA. Turns out you do."

"She's the only one I keep in contact with. I worry about her. She's highly driven, with boatloads of talent, and she'd avoided drugs and alcohol and all those self-destructive clichés. Now if she could just stay out of the tabloids. She's got lousy taste in men and a tendency to end up in compromising positions, which always seem to end up on tape."

"I can't imagine havin' that kinda lifestyle."

Ginger really loved this, being wrapped in Kane's arms. She honestly couldn't remember the last time she'd lolled around naked in bed with a hot man, just talking.

That's because this is a first.

Wouldn't Kane be shocked to know that?

So tell him.

No. She'd come across...pathetic, probably.

"You must be awful good at keepin' secrets."

"Comes with the territory of my job. Now that I've told you my biggest secret, let's hear some of yours."

"Nothin' to tell. I'm just a simple Wyoming rancher."

Was his tone a little testy? "You've never been married?"

"Nope."

"Ever come close?"

"Nope."

"Ever been in love?"

"Dozens of times."

Ginger went completely still.

"Lasted until I ditched the condom, sometimes even a day or two after that. Never longer than a month."

"Oh." That was a harsh insight.

"You sure you wanna hear my past secrets and lies, sugar? 'Cause they sure ain't pretty."

"Like mine were?" she shot back.

Kane laughed. "We're both a little touchy, ain't we?" He began that soothing stroking motion on her back again. "You showed me yours, I'll show you mine. I guess the easiest way to say this is that I lost my virginity at age fourteen. Got my first taste of sex and never looked back. When I wasn't workin' on the ranch or raisin' hell with my McKay cousins, I was sweet-talkin every woman in my path hopin' to get into her pants. And truth be told, it didn't take much for them to fall into my bed. Or into my truck. Or wherever.

"For the longest time it seemed like I had the perfect life. Workin' the land that's been in my family for a couple generations. Livin' in a house with my brother and my cousin. We had damn wild times. Lots of women, lots of booze, no regrets. We enjoyed the hell out of our bad-boy, love 'em and leave 'em reputations."

"The women you were with didn't mind?"

"Hell no. They wanted braggin' rights for bangin' a McKay. Or two. The more adventurous chickies? We'd invite them to get really wild. Threesomes, foursomes, you name it, we did it."

She thought back to his mother Kimi's comment that Kane had horrible taste in women. "So those were the women you...loved?"

"Loved 'em when I was with them. Afterward? Sometimes I couldn't even remember the woman's name. How's that for true love?"

Ginger wondered if Kane was trying to shock her.

"Disgusted yet?" he said with an edge.

"No. Just curious."

"About?"

"What happened that made you change. Was it intentional? And if not, do you regret being forced to accept the change? From what I've seen of you, you're not that same guy hustling to get laid all the time."

Kane kissed the top of her head. "Thanks."

"For what?"

"Not runnin' out of here screamin' about my raunchy past. Then again, you ain't exactly up to runnin', are you?"

Ginger poked him in the rib.

"Part of the change was intentional. For a year before Colt went into rehab, I knew he was outta control, bad kind of outta control. I couldn't do nothin' about him blowin' off his ranch responsibilities, but I figured if I went everywhere with him during prime bar cruisin' hours, I could at least keep an eye on him. Bastard got damn wily at ditchin' me. Then our cousin Dag died and I totally fucked up things between Kade and Skylar.

"Within a two-month period my life changed dramatically. Kade left for almost a year to head up a grazing experiment on a new stretch of land we'd bought. Colt quit drinkin' and whorin'."

"Did you quit too?"

"Yes ma'am. The changes in their lives forced me to change. Might make me sound like a simpleton, but I wouldn't have done it on my own. Guess I've always been more of a follower than a leader when it comes to that kind of stuff."

Ginger couldn't tell whether or not it bothered him. She ran her fingers down his arm.

"Here's something I've never told anyone. The biggest turning point in my life was the night I watched a guy beat the shit out of my brother because he thought Kade was me."

A beat of silence passed.

"Bein' a self-centered prick, I never realized how many times that'd happened to my brother. He'd been forced to deal with my messes our whole lives because we were born with the same face. Probably sounds stupid, but right after that? I grew a mustache and a beard, shaved most my hair off and tried to set us apart. Not for my sake, for his."

"Is that also when you changed your name?"

He groaned. "Jesus. What was my mother thinkin'? Naming identical twins Kane and Kade? And it don't help matters that Uncle Carson's boys all start with 'C'. It was like they purposely set out to confuse everyone. Anyway, the name Buck didn't stick. Pissed my mama off good, too, that I tried to change it. Kade, Colt and Keely thought callin' me Buck was hysterical. But only the kids call me that now. Mostly because of that movie *Uncle Buck.*"

"Good Lord, those kids can't possibly confuse you with John Candy?"

"Now that was downright sweet. When Colt built his own house and Cam offered to buy the Boars Nest, it was another decision I went along with. I bought a trailer and got me a dog, which I'm pretty sure in the world of bachelors, is equal to single women havin' cats."

She laughed.

"Then Kade startin' havin' kids, and it seemed all my McKay cousins paired off."

"Were you jealous?"

"Some. To combat the extra time on my hands since I wasn't out carousing, I took on more responsibilities at the ranch. Helped my other McKay cousins expand. And I joined up with the Little Buddies program, which is one of the best things I ever did."

"I agree." Ginger wanted to tell him how much his presence influenced her son. How she appreciated Kane not trying to make Hayden into a mini-me, how he'd played on Hayden's strengths, not exploiting Hayden's weaknesses.

They remained twined together, lost in thought.

Kane's mouth connected with her ear. "If you could do anything right now, what would it be?"

"Take a shower."

"Done. Sit up. Hold tight."

"But—" she said to his nicely muscled back.

Kane reappeared holding a garbage bag and a roll of packing tape.

"You're serious."

"Completely. I can make your cast leak proof. But that ain't what worries me."

"What worries you?"

He pointed to her shoulder. "You usin' your arm."

"I'll be careful when I'm washing my hair."

"Guess maybe you don't understand, but you won't be takin' this shower alone."

Her hormones, which had been lazing like a sated cat, leapt to attention.

"You wanna take a shower, and I wanna play some water games with you. Sounds like a perfect way for us both to get what we want." Kane slipped the garbage bag around her cast. He did some twisty thing with the tape, wrapping and rewrapping the plastic. More taping. Then he looked up at her. "Let's test 'er out and see if she's water tight."

"Okay."

"But first..." Kane tugged on the ponytail holder, releasing her hair. It fluffed around her head like an angry red cloud. She was about to apologize for her appearance, when he murmured, "Better."

Ginger wiggled until she sat on the side of the bed, cast on the floor and her bum arm dangling by her side. "I look ridiculous."

"No, you look hot as hell," Kane corrected.

"Silver-tongued cowboy."

He moved in front of her. She leaned forward and placed a kiss on the bulge tenting his boxers out.

He sucked in a breath. "Come on, let's get you wet."

"I'm already wet when you look at me like that, Kane."

Although his grin was quick and playful, his eyes smoldered. "You've got a bit of a silver tongue yourself, counselor."

In the bathroom, Kane dropped his boxers and climbed into the shower. Once he had the water settings where he wanted them, he held her steady as she stepped into the tub.

As soon as the curtain closed, Kane's mouth devoured hers. The need ignited between them. Ginger was surprised steam didn't rise off her body wherever his greedy hand roved.

Water pounded on her back as Kane kissed her, and kissed her, bringing the kiss to a level of passion where she thought of nothing but his lips, his tongue, his mouth. The synchronized beating of their hearts.

She whimpered when he tore his mouth free and buried his face in her neck.

"God. Ginger. I—" His labored breathing flowed across her wet skin, causing her to shiver. His entire body was rigid—not just his hard cock digging into her abdomen.

Finally, after holding her as if he couldn't bear to let her go, he lifted his head and kissed her softly on the lips. "Sorry. Just needed a second to get control."

"I don't mind. In fact—" she walked her fingers up his chest, "—your 'my way or the highway' attitude really does it for me."

"Yeah?"

"Oh yeah."

He gifted her with his devastating grin. "I'll give that idea a full test drive later. For now...how about if you let me wash your hair?"

"Please."

Kane turned her. "Be easiest if you brace your hand on the wall." He placed her palm above the soap dish. "Now tilt your head back and close your eyes."

Warm water cascaded down her scalp, soaking her hair completely. Droplets hit the plastic covering her cast, making dull *splat splat splat* sounds. Then Kane's big, strong hands were gently massaging her scalp, surrounding them with the sweet scent of her lavender shampoo. Soapsuds flowed down her back, over her buttocks and the outside of her legs.

He rinsed. He even repeated.

"I need conditioner—"

"I know sugar. I've got it right here." He smoothed it through her hair from roots to the tips. "Turn around." He pressed her back against the wall. "Now where else do you need scrubbed while we're lettin' the conditioner set?"

Ask him.

Don't be an idiot.

Kane leaned closer. "What's wrong?"

A blush crept up her neck. "I need to shave. And if I attempted it with my left hand, I'll just cut myself."

His lips quirked. "Can't have that."

She knew he was waiting for her to ask him. "Even though it might be kind of weird...would you mind shaving my legs and my underarms?"

"There. Askin' me for help wasn't so bad, was it?"

"Yes."

He smooched her wrinkled nose. "Suck it up. Lift your left arm above your head."

Kane circled her wrist with one hand and soaped her armpit with the other. His concentration was absolute as he passed the blade across her skin. Once. Twice. Three times. He held the razor under the shower spray. Then he cupped her right elbow and held her arm out chicken wing style. More soap, three quick passes with the razor and her underarms were smooth again.

"Legs next?"

"Uh-huh." But the suds his hands created were mesmerizing.

He noticed her focus was on his hands on her tits. "I figured I'd give you the whole body treatment. You know. Makin' sure you were clean everywhere."

"You just want to soap up my tits."

"Like you wouldn't believe." He started on her neck and quickly moved across her clavicle and shoulders. Then he coated his hands with more suds and swept them over her breasts. Under her breasts. Cupping and squeezing. Rasping his thumbs across the beaded tips of her nipples. Over and over.

Ginger watched him. The absolute lust in his eyes as his slippery hands mapped every inch and curve of her breasts.

"You have the greatest tits I've ever seen. Just so damn perfect. Responsive." He pinched the left nipple a little harder than she was used to and looked at her to gauge her reaction.

The initial sharp sting mellowed into a delicious heat. "Oh."

"You like that?"

"I'm not sure. It surprised me."

"You ever worn nipple clamps?"

She shook her head.

While he talked, he continued lathering every inch of her breasts. "I'd like to get them hard with my mouth and put clamps on. The kind with the chain between them. Then I'd fuck you. Slowly. Every so often I'd yank on the chain. When you were ready to come, I'd remove the clamp and suck hard until all the blood returned. Suck until you came again. Then I'd do the same thing to the other side."

A rush of moisture trickled from between her thighs. Moisture that owed nothing to water from the shower. "Kane—"

Kane's dark eyes searched hers. "There's so much I wanna do to you, Red. I wanna make you forget every man's touch but mine." He kissed her again, with the brutal intensity that stole her sanity.

Then just as quickly, he backed away. He snagged the handheld shower and rinsed her; his gaze tracked the rivulets of soap.

Her stomach cartwheeled when he dropped to his knees and the stubble of his closely shorn head brushed her belly.

"Hold still. I've never shaved a woman's legs before and I don't wanna cut you."

Right. He was down there to shave her legs. Not to bury his face in her pussy.

Ginger's whole body became a mass of goose bumps as his hands stroked her legs. She even forgot her embarrassment about being hairy. The plastic wrap around her cast rattled as he maneuvered the razor above it.

"There. Done." He rinsed her legs. As he stood to replace the handheld showerhead in the base on the wall, he looked at it, then her. "Do you ever get yourself off with this?"

Dammit. She was a thirty-seven-year-old woman. She wasn't supposed to blush.

Kane crowded her. "Do you?"

"Yes."

"Do you use the pulsing option full blast on your clit?"

"Yes. If I'm getting myself off, I want it to happen as fast as possible."

"No buildup?" he asked silkily. "No teasin', enjoying the feel of the warm water flowing over your cunt, makin' it wetter? Softer?"

Her pulse raced. Was there a question in there?

"Are you wet right now, Ginger? After havin' my hands all over you? After me tellin' you all the raunchy things I wanna do to you? After havin' my mouth—" he placed his lips on her ear, "—this close to that sweet, sweet pussy?"

His deep, husky voice zinged in an electric current as if

she'd stepped on a high wire. "Yes."

"I don't believe you."

Her eyes flew open when Kane was on his knees again. He uttered a harsh, "Spread your legs." The instant she gave him enough room, his mouth was on her.

"Oh God." His thumbs traced the shape of her sex from the top of her pubic bone through the slick folds to her opening. His tongue darted inside. Again and again. Kane lapped and licked and sucked. Biting. Growling. He fucked his tongue into her channel so deep she felt the press of his teeth into her tender tissues.

Ginger's legs shook. Her skin was on fire.

Kane retreated, rubbing his beard across her upper thighs, the rise of her pubic bone, the curve of her hip.

She glanced down at him.

He licked his lips and smiled naughtily. "Guess I was wrong. You are wet. Wet and soft and tasty. I'm gonna need another bite or two to tide me over until I fuck you." Then he bent his head again and ravaged her with his mouth.

But this time he also used his hands. This time he slid his thumb into her pussy as the fingers of his other hand held open the flesh above her clit so he could suck on it unimpeded. His thumb slipped in and out of her cunt, and he added another finger. Two, three, four times those digits plunged deep while he teasingly nibbled on her clit.

She wanted to beg him to hurry, but Ginger suspected it'd spur him to slow down even more. So she bit her lip, closed her eyes and let herself go, giving her pleasure over to him.

Kane sensed her surrender. He stopped tonguing her long enough to say, "Good girl." His thumb slipped back into her pussy, and his index finger, wet with her juices, began to stroke the bud of her anus. Lightly. Then persistently.

Her orgasm hovered close enough to taste.

He made a feral, snarling noise that vibrated against her sensitive tissues. His mouth suctioned to her clit and he sucked strongly as his finger slipped into her ass.

That bite of pain gave away to indescribable pleasure as he thrust the two digits in and out, pressing his thumb and finger together on the thin wall separating the two passages.

Ginger screamed as the climax overtook her. Every part of

her body, her clitoris throbbed against Kane's flickering tongue. Her internal muscles clamped down on his fingers, trying to bring them deeper into her body with each clenching pulse. Her nipples tightened, as if suckled by phantom mouths. The orgasm drew the breath from her lungs.

And still Kane didn't let up.

She should've pushed his head away, needing a break from the consuming sensitivity. But he remained in place. Sucking her. Fucking her pussy and her ass with his fingers. Rebuilding that ball of sexual energy until her skin prickled and another orgasm slammed into her.

"Oh. My. God. Yes. Yes!" She thrashed, against him, against the wall, unable to hold still. A slight tinge of pain reminded her of her bum arm. Her hand landed on Kane's head as she pressed his face into her needy cunt.

The blood quit pounding in her head, her ears, her nipples. Between her legs. The haze of pleasure cleared, but didn't fade completely.

Ginger glanced down at his dark crown. He'd pressed his forehead into her lower belly. His breathing stuttered across her wet skin.

Kane looked up at her, fire in his eyes. Without a word he removed his fingers lodged within her body. He stood. He placed a soft kiss on the section of her skin where neck met shoulder. Holding her by the waist, he turned her around to face the short wall. "Bend over."

Any relaxation she'd attained vanished when Kane layered his muscled body to hers. He put his knee between her legs and widened her stance, canting her hips to his liking.

Kane's chest felt like an electric blanket pressing on her back. He trailed firm-lipped kisses up her nape. The head of his cock nudged her pussy. Then he rocked his hips and filled her with a single stroke.

His impatience was arousing. Ginger gasped with his every forceful thrust. All the way out, all the way back in. Hard. Fast. Without pause.

He'd curled his hands around her hips. Even in his lust filled state, he showed his concern for her injury. Which was sweet.

But that was the only sweet thing about Kane McKay right now. Sounds of flesh slapping flesh, his guttural noises, the splash of water around their ankles, spun Ginger into distorted reality. That familiar sensation bloomed in her core. No. She couldn't. She'd just had the two best orgasms of her life—back to back. There was no way she could come again.

Was there?

The pressure of Kane's fingers on her hips increased and he switched to short, shallow jabs.

When Ginger felt his cock go harder yet inside her, she bore down and he flew apart. Ramming into her without care or concern.

His hips kept moving as he muttered. After he slowed and stilled, he slumped across her back, breathing hard, still lodged inside her.

Although he couldn't see it, she permitted a smug smile.

Kane pushed her hair aside to sink his teeth into the back of her neck.

She held very, very still. She'd sworn she'd seen or read something about the neck biting in the aftermath of mating as a mark to ward off other males.

He murmured, "We still need to rinse your hair."

"I'm sure the water has gone cold by now."

Kane took a step back and returned with the showerhead. "Tilt your head back. I see your hair flowing down your back and your ass at that sexy angle. Christ, Red. You make such a goddamn pretty picture, it almost makes me hard again."

His hot words washed over her, warming her as thoroughly as the lukewarm water that flowed through her hair. She pushed upright and turned to see Kane scrubbing his head with one hand and his body with the other. He grinned. "See? I'm pretty low maintenance."

"And yet you look damn fine all the time."

He placed a dot of soap on her nose.

Kane made her stay in the shower until he'd toweled off. He dried her off, removed the plastic from the cast and even combed her hair.

One thing he didn't do? Help her get dressed. He informed her he intended to have her at least once more before the school bus pulled up. Getting dressed was pointless.

When Ginger yawned, he tucked her in bed and told her to rest up while he fixed lunch.

Sex. More sex. Snuggling. A shower complete with multiple orgasms? Now food served by the virile cowboy who'd also served up the delicious orgasms?

In her estimation, days didn't get much better than this.

Chapter Ten

After five days of looking after Ginger and Hayden, Kane was at loose ends.

During Ginger's nap, after their mind-blowing shower, he'd rounded up Hayden and Dash's dirty clothes. He'd washed four loads of laundry. He'd fixed lunch and organized leftovers for supper. He'd loaded the dishwasher.

And he hadn't minded a bit. In fact, he would've done more if he could. Might make him a pussy, or at least as domesticated as a house cat, but he liked taking care of her.

By the time he'd sat down to read the paper, Ginger had woken up. Upon seeing her sleep-tousled hair, her drowsy smile and all that naked freckled skin, he'd wanted her again.

And he'd had her again. A bit less frenzied than the first three times, but the sexual heat erupting between them was astounding. He'd suspected Ginger would be an earthy, lusty lover once she'd become comfortable with his sexual demands and she definitely hadn't disappointed.

He had been disappointed this morning when he'd driven Ginger to work, wishing they could have a few more days together. But Ginger distanced herself from him the instant she'd donned that severe black business suit. She'd insisted on walking up the stairs to her office unaided. She'd dismissed his concerns that she wasn't up to a full day of work. Even with her receptionist, Rissa, at her disposal, Kane knew Ginger wouldn't ask for help until it was too late. Then she'd politely rejected his offer to take her to Doc Monroe's for her follow up visit and showed him the door.

It sucked. Kane was flat out crazy about the woman. And he hadn't a clue what he could do about it except show a little patience.

Luckily time was one thing he had plenty of.

Nine Days Later...

Another quiet Friday night. Kane sipped a cup of coffee liberally laced with Jameson whiskey and stared at some nameless comedy on the boob tube. He was fried. They'd spent all day rounding up strays. Most had been eager to rejoin the herd after the small blizzard had separated them the day before. A few older sows had gone to their favorite birthing spots, which worried him. They weren't set to start calving for another month.

The driving wind and blowing snow had taken it out of him. After spending the day with Kade crisscrossing the land on four-wheelers, he'd been damn tempted to burrow under the covers until morning.

Shep growled in his sleep and Kane automatically patted the dog's head. Shep had refused to venture into the frigid weather. Kane looked at the Border collie, concerned by his lethargy in recent weeks. Kade mentioned Shep hadn't been his usual sparky self with the girls over the long weekend. And this morning, the dog that lived to chase stray cows hadn't moved from the sofa when Kane called him. Shep wasn't a pup, but he'd never seen the dog so sluggish. He ruffled Shep's ears. "Must be the weather, eh?"

He'd begun to drift off when his cell phone rang. Never fucking failed. He'd left messages with his cousins about canceling their poker game, but one of them was probably calling to harass him. He answered without looking at the caller ID. "If you're gonna whine about poker night. Save it. I'm draggin' ass tonight and don't feel like losin' a pile of money. Catch me tomorrow."

A chuckle. "That's definitely a unique way to answer the phone."

Shit. Not his one of his cousins. "Sorry, Dash. Been a long damn day and I was half-asleep. What's up?"

"Two things. Hayden couldn't remember what time the workshop started tomorrow and I can't find the flyer with the information."

"It starts at ten. Does he still need me to pick him up?"

"Probably, since it's not like I can hop into my Mercedes and get him there."

"Speaking of... That is one sweet ride." Far as Kane knew, the SL500 Mercedes Ginger drove used to belong to Dash. "How fast will it go?"

"I had it up to one forty the last time I cut loose."

Kane whistled. "Nice. As much as I love to bullshit about cars I can't afford, what was the other reason you called?"

A heavy sigh. "It's Ginger. She's working herself into the ground making up for lost time after her accident. She hasn't been home until after ten o'clock the last two nights."

He glanced at the clock and saw it was nearly nine. "She's still not home?"

"No. I'm worried about her dozing off as she's driving. Could be a deadly mistake with this cold snap, especially when the girl acts like she's in LA and refuses to wear proper winter attire. Which also made me realize it's time to change out the battery in the Mercedes, so I worry she'll have car trouble."

The image of Ginger huddled in her paper-thin leather coat, no gloves, wearing fuck-me stilettos, as she froze inside her dead car along the side of the road, shook Kane out of his sleepy state.

"Has she been out of contact with you? Because I could call Cam at the sheriff's office and have him start lookin'—"

"No. I know she's still at the office working. I spoke to her right before I called you. I hate to impose, but is there any chance you can check out her car and see if there's an issue with the battery?"

"Tonight?"

"Yes."

"Okay. No problem. Anything else?"

Another hesitant pause. "Could you check on her? I'm aware she's a grown woman, but she pushes herself to the limit."

If Kane didn't know better, he'd suspect this was the old man's attempt at matchmaking. "I can do that. You want me to call you after I check on her?"

"No. If I don't hear from you I'll assume no news is good news." Dash hung up.

Shep didn't budge when Kane got up from the couch. He

didn't wag his tail with interest when Kane donned his outerwear. He just blinked his eyes and went back to sleep.

Smart dog.

The thermometer in Kane's truck read twenty degrees below zero. Not an ideal night for a drive. But it'd be worse if Ginger called him at two in the morning because her car had crapped out.

Would she call you?

Yes. Who else did she have to call?

How about AAA?

He snorted. She'd rather walk home than admit to anyone in town, let alone that gossipy old tow truck driver Barney Troller, that she needed help. Damn stubborn woman.

The lights shone in her office. Her car remained parked in front. No streetlights, no easy access in case her battery was dead.

He parked beside her Mercedes and scaled the steps, two at a time. Kane got a little pissy when he walked right inside her office because she hadn't bothered to lock the front door.

He rapped on her office door four times. "Ginger?"

Footsteps on the other side, then the door flew open. "Kane? What are you doing here?" A stark expression crossed her face. "Has something happened to Hayden?"

"No. He's fine and your dad is fine." Kane understood he might have to cover Dash's butt. "I was in town and I noticed your office lights were on. Then I saw your car and wondered why the hell you're workin' this late on a Friday night."

Ginger lifted her eyebrows. "You just happened to be in the neighborhood? Bullshit. Did Hayden send you? Or my dad?"

Busted. Before she flew off the handle, Kane pointed out, "Dash worries about you, Red. He feels pretty helpless. He couldn't check up on you himself, so I volunteered to make sure you were okay on his behalf. It's damn cold out there tonight. Sub-zero." His gaze swept over her. She looked fantastic in a figure-flattering suit jacket and matching short skirt the color of coffee. Tan lace peeped from between the lapels of the jacket and her nylon-clad feet were bare. "Please tell me you brought more weather appropriate clothing to wear home?"

Those brown-green eyes narrowed. "Don't start on me."

Kane stepped closer. "Answer the question."

"And if I don't?"

"Such a sassy mouth. Damn, I missed it the last week."

Her face softened. "Kane—"

He fused his lips to hers, stopping her protest. He groaned softly at the dark, sweet taste of her and deepened the kiss.

Immediately Ginger melted into him. Both arms circled his waist as her mouth clung to his in a kiss that was both sweet and compelling.

When he went to touch her face, he realized he hadn't even taken his damn gloves off. He broke their lip-lock and studied her. "Where's your sling?"

"Off. Doc said I only have to wear it at night. I've actually gotten pretty proficient at attaching it myself." She pointed to her right calf. "The cast is gone too. No ligament damage. She was shocked about how fast I healed up."

Both of those bits of good news should've warranted a phone call. "No need for me anymore?"

Ginger flirtatiously kissed his soul patch. "You almost sound sad about that, McKay."

"I am." He let her think on it for a few seconds before he said, "You about done here so I can follow you home? Or am I takin' off my jacket and stayin' awhile?"

"Maybe you should take off your pants too," she teased.

"What would you do if I did?"

The humorous light left her eyes; they turned liquid with pure sexual heat. "I suppose I'd be forced to service your needs."

"Forced?" he repeated.

Her gaze dropped to his crotch, then returned to his eyes. "Last night I dreamt of you. We were at some party and you got this...hungry look in your eye, the same one you're sporting right now. You took me by the hand and led me to a bathroom. You locked the door, leaned against it and started to unbuckle your belt, all without saying a single word."

Holy shit. Kane swallowed the ball of lust stuck in his throat. "What did you do?"

"Waited until you gave me the signal. You put your hand on my shoulder and pushed me to my knees to suck you off. Then I woke up hot and bothered and pissed."

"Pissed? Why? Because of my highhanded behavior? Or

because you liked bein' obedient?"

"Neither. I was pissed because I was horny as hell. I knew if I'd been allowed to finish the dream you wouldn't have left me wanting." Ginger placed both palms on his chest. "You would've seen to my needs."

"I can still see to your needs, sugar," he said with a silken drawl. "Right after you see to mine." Kane tugged off his gloves and threw them aside. His coat hit the floor someplace behind him. Keeping his eyes locked to hers, he unhooked his belt buckle. He lowered his zipper. He dropped his jeans and boxers mid-thigh and pulled out his fully erect cock. "You know what I want."

Without hesitation, she lowered before him. She kissed the head of his penis, grabbing it at the base with her right hand. She stroked, and outlined the flared rim of his cockhead with her tongue.

Kane hissed in a breath. He about shot his load when Ginger gave him that vixen-like smirk and sucked him to where her hand circled his dick.

He let her play. Tease and retreat. Taking his full length into her heated mouth while she rolled his balls between her fluttering fingers. He had to clench his butt cheeks together a couple of times to keep from taking over and fucking that sassy, sucking mouth.

Ginger slid her hands around to cup his ass and stopped. She allowed his dick to slide free from her mouth. "Holy crap. Your butt is like ice."

"Told you it was cold out there," he murmured.

She tongued the tip and smiled cheekily. "But it's nice and warm right inside here." She canted her head and swallowed him to the root.

Kane thrust his hands into her hair, keeping her head in place as a not-so-subtle reminder that he was in control.

Their eyes met. The surprise he saw reflected in hers morphed into heat. She knew. She handed him the reins.

He released the tight grip on her head and pulled back, thrusting in, showing her his preferred rhythm. This blowjob wouldn't take long. Between her sexy-ass dominant dream and the fact she'd dropped to her knees—well, he was hard and ready and that pretty much guaranteed he'd be quick on the trigger.

When Ginger started sucking him harder and squeezing his ass, Kane grunted as his balls grew tight. His cock lifted in anticipation of release. Instead of driving deep and feeling her throat muscles working him, he withdrew halfway, resting the sweet spot on her tongue.

"There it is. Goddamn." He let his head drop back, keeping a firm hold on her head so she couldn't move. Spurt after spurt fired out and he felt her swallow every time his dick contracted. The pleasure was so potent his legs began to shake, rattling the loose belt buckle around his knees.

Then he felt a humming sensation, which he attributed to her laughter.

As he eased out of her mouth, he warned, "Two can play at that game." He cupped her left elbow and helped her to her feet. His mouth enclosed hers in a forceful kiss. A primitive noise escaped when he tasted himself on her tongue.

"Take off your nylons. Those ankle-breakin' heels you prefer are around someplace?"

"Under the desk."

"After you take off the hose, put them shoes back on."

She ditched the hose and waited for his instruction, which quite frankly, shocked the crap out of him. He half expected the lawyer inside her would point out they weren't in a bedroom, so technically, he wasn't in charge. He yanked up his pants, zipped and buckled. "Sit in your office chair and slip on your heels."

Ginger sat like a lady and inserted her feet into the pointy-toed brown patent leather pumps.

Damn damn damn. That was one smoking hot image. Kane spun the chair so he could drop to his knees, half under the desk.

"Kane, what are you doing?"

"Hike up your skirt and put your feet on the desk. Just like that. Now angle your hips...perfect." Then his mouth was on her, his tongue separated her soft, pink folds. He loved how she was already wet. As he licked and lapped at her slick sweetness, his cock hardened. This woman fired him up in no time flat.

Her hips began to lift and he noticed the death grip her fingers had on the arms of the chair.

He raised his head. "Ginger, look at me."

Passion-glazed eyes met his. "Why? You planning to torment me with that talented mouth, cowboy?"

"Depends." He flattened his tongue and dragged it up her wet center. "On." He reversed course, zigzagging his tongue back down. "You." A long, slow lap up. "Saying." A meandering flicker of just the tip of his tongue as he made his way to the entrance to her body. "Yes."

"Yes to what? I'll say yes to anything if you just make me come right now."

Kane grinned and blew a stream of air across her engorged tissues. "Anything, counselor?"

"I believe what you're doing is called 'leading the witness' and my God, this time I won't object. Please, Kane."

He let his thumbs glide up, mapping the outer swells of her cunt, until they met at the top. He gently separated the pliant skin, exposing her clitoris and lightly grazed his teeth over it.

Ginger jerked against his mouth with a gasp.

Then he formed a circle around the nub with his lips and sucked while his tongue flicked back and forth.

"Oh, yes, I'm already so close..."

His belt buckle dug into his abdomen and his cock probably had permanent zipper marks, but Kane didn't move. He remained fully focused on proving how much he loved to be between her thighs. Her taste coating his tongue. Her wetness dampening his mustache and goatee. And the squeaking moans she only made when his mouth was on her like this.

Her legs trembled and her hands went from gripping the armrests to gripping his head. "More. Suck harder. Like that. Yes! Yes! Yes!"

At the peak of her orgasm, a burst of wetness coated his chin and he wanted to burrow into her completely.

As the pulses slowed, then faded, her grip on his head loosened and she ran her fingers over the stubble.

With one last soft smooch, he pulled away.

The sated, dazed look in Ginger's eyes made him want to roar, the alpha male who'd pleased his mate. He circled her ankles and put her feet on the floor.

"I don't know if I should be scared of that twinkle in your eye, McKay."

"Too late, you already said yes to anything I want,

remember?"

"I was under duress," she half protested.

"Uh-huh." Kane stood and moved behind her. "How's about you move outta this chair and sit on the desk, facing me." He nibbled on the shell of her ear. "Lose the skirt."

"Why do I have the feeling I'll be losing my shirt too?"

"Because you are one smart cookie." Kane toed off his boots, shucked his pants and underwear and plopped in her chair. "Nice. The material feels good against my bare ass."

Ginger whirled around after her skirt and panties hit the carpet. Her eyes narrowed on his cock, sticking straight up like a flagpole. "You *are* hard again."

"Your fault."

She smirked. "And on my honor, I'm not one bit sorry. But if I'm totally naked, you'd better be too." Her fingers slipped under the first button on his shirt. She undid them all and made a disgruntled sound when she saw he wore a T-shirt.

"Some of us know how to dress for the weather."

"Some of us like to play with your chest as much as you like to play with mine."

Kane brushed a curl from her forehead. "Next time, you can play all you want. This time, you're gonna be facin' forward." At her perplexed look, he said, "Reverse cowgirl style."

"I don't know if I've ever done it that way."

"This position definitely has its charms. Lemme show you." He turned her around. "Brace your hands on the desk and spread your legs." He rolled the chair closer. "Now scoot back, that's it, keep your legs wide. Hang on a sec." Kane lowered the chair arms, allowing her thighs to straddle his.

"Kane. I'm not sure—"

"I am. Trust me. Lift your ass a bit. Damn do I love this ass. I cannot wait to grind my cock into it and feel how tight you squeeze me with those muscles."

Ginger looked over her shoulder at him. "I figured you'd like anal."

"Why's that?"

"Because you like everything else."

"Smart mouth." Then he thrust into her pussy to the hilt.

"Oh Lord, you could've warned me."

"You should've been payin' attention, not thinkin' so hard

about how much you want my dick in your ass."

She laughed. "Bastard. Stop talking and fuck me."

"You're gonna hafta do some of the work, sugar. Push back into me. Yeah, just like that."

He cupped her tits, feathering his thumbs across her nipples. They built a rhythm without words, letting their motions do all the talking. Sweat dripping, skin slapping skin, sighs, moans, the squeak of the office chair.

Ginger centered her left hand on the desk and her right hand disappeared between her thighs.

"Are you touchin' yourself?"

"I need direct contact with my clit in order to come."

When her stroking fingers accidentally brushed where they were joined, Kane's balls drew up. Knowing she was pleasuring herself did it for him in a big way. He kept playing with her nipples and brought her upper torso back so he could scatter kisses across her back. "Come on, Red," he whispered. "Send yourself over the edge and take me with you."

"God, your voice is like sandpaper on my nerve endings. I love that husky rasp. Keep talking to me."

Kane pumped his hips and licked the slope of her shoulder.

"I wanna mark you here." He sucked and felt the goose bumps rise on her skin. "When I see you all fancied up in your suit and fuck-me heels, I'll remember this. Me fucking you in your chair, you bent over your desk, touchin' yourself. No one will know that always-in-control Ginger Paulson, lets me, a simple rancher, have her any way I want. Any time I want."

"Kane—"

"Take us there. Now." He sank his teeth into her nape and pinched her nipples hard.

She started to come. Her muscles clamped down on his dick and he was done. He came so hard and fast he was damn glad they were sitting because he doubted his shaky legs could hold them up.

Kane placed a kiss on the teeth marks on her shoulder before he slumped back into the chair.

Ginger emitted a soft sigh. Then she rested against him, wrapping her arm around the back of his neck. "You were right."

"About?" He nuzzled her head above her ear.

"That position does have a certain charm."

He chuckled. "You hold all the charm for me. Doesn't matter what position we're in or where we are."

"Were you upset that you didn't hear from me since last week?"

"Maybe a little."

"I sort of figured. I just...don't know what we're supposed to do now, Kane. I'm not ready to..."

"I understand why you're wary and want to keep 'this'—whatever it is—on the down low."

"You do? And you don't mind?"

Hell yes, I mind. Kane wasn't keen pretending he was cool with it, but he wasn't willing to sacrifice time with Ginger to save the sting to his pride. "I like bein' with you. You already know that. You've got enough pressure in your life and I won't demand more than you're willin' to give me." Because he wanted it all. He kissed her neck. "We'll figure it out as we go along, okay?"

"Okay."

As Ginger donned her winter clothes, Kane shook his head.

"What?"

"You really don't have any snow boots?"

"No. Every pair I've ever seen are butt-ugly."

"So are frostbitten toes. They turn black and fall off. Then how would you wear them sexy-assed heels you're so fond of?"

She waved him off. "I'll be fine."

Kane counted to ten. "Give me your keys."

"Why?"

"Because it's twenty degrees below zero out there and I want to warm up your car so your damn legs don't freeze. Plus I need to check your battery."

"Oh." She offered him that smile that would've gotten her anything. "Thank you. What would I do without you?"

"Maybe the question oughta be—what would you do with me if you had me all the time?"

Before he acted even more like a lovesick fool, asking foolish questions, he stomped outside.

Chapter Eleven

The basement of the community center was absolute chaos.

Over the past two years Ginger had attended plenty of Little Buddies events, so her bout of nerves baffled her.

You know exactly why you're nervous. Two words: Kane McKay.

She and Kane hadn't been together in a crowd and she wondered if people who knew them both would notice a difference in their dealings with one another.

Maybe Ginger had been a bit disappointed last night when Kane admitted he was fine sneaking around with her. Part of her wanted that public acknowledgment.

Her gaze was drawn to him like a magnet. His dark head was a contrast to Hayden's blond one as they bent over the model on the table. Their concentration was absolute. She hung back, content to watch them together.

It'd been a sticky subject when her father had suggested Hayden needed more hiking, hunting, fishing—Wyoming type of outdoor activities to supplement the boy's tendency to bury his nose in a book. And it'd pained her dad to be handicapped because he couldn't share his love of the great outdoors with this only grandson.

Ginger had been skeptical of signing on for the Big Buddies/Little Buddies program. She suspected half the single or divorced ladies in the tri-county area had signed up hoping to snag a husband. It'd given her a sense of relief that many of the volunteers were married men. Fathers whose children had grown up. Men who wanted to give back to the community by providing a positive example to boys who didn't have a consistent male influence in their young lives.

She hung back, content to watch them together. But Ginger wasn't the only one watching Kane. Four mothers hung on the periphery as their sons' Big Buddies helped with the model cars. None of the other male volunteers garnered the type of interest Kane did. Because he was sexy as sin and single? Partially. But she suspected the other reason Kane held appeal was because he didn't appear to be paying attention to any of those hungry-eyed women. An aloof man was a trickier target, and therefore, more prized if obtained.

She supposed it wasn't really Kane's fault women flocked to him. He was a striking man, with his dark good looks and easy grin. His Built Ford Tough body was definitely sigh-worthy, as were those stunning blue eyes.

The next thing she knew, that intense blue gaze was directed at her.

A delicious warmth unfurled as Kane studied her from beneath lowered lashes. No one else could tell he was watching her. But Ginger knew. When that secret smile played around the corners of his sinful mouth, the smile indicating he'd been conjuring raunchy sexual images, her mind flashed to last night's sexcapades.

It'd been easy to let go with Kane. To be the sexual woman she'd forgotten she could be. To hand the reins to him, knowing he wouldn't abuse her trust. Knowing he was as helpless as she to ignore the passion that exploded between them. Anytime, anyplace.

And this is definitely not the time nor the place to be thinking about sex with Kane McKay.

She forced herself to look away.

"Ginger?"

She spun around and faced Stacy, the director of the program. "Hi! Looks like you've got a great turnout."

"Better than last year, which hopefully means more fundraising profits." Stacy smiled. "I'm surprised to see you here."

"Really?"

"You tend to...let Hayden and Kane do their own thing."

"Is that bad? Is there more I should be doing?"

Stacy patted Ginger's arm. "No, not at all. In fact, I wish some of the other mothers would follow your lead. Some women have to tag along at every event, and quite frankly, that defeats

131

the purpose of the organization."

Ginger's gaze returned to Hayden and Kane. "Can't you point out the obvious to them?"

"No. We've always maintained an 'open door' policy for our members. Anyone can come to any event that involves their child."

"This program has been good for Hayden."

"Glad to hear it. And between us, consider yourself lucky you ended up with Kane McKay. There are lots of mothers requesting him as their son's Big Buddy."

There was that flare of unexpected feeling of jealousy. "Do you take that into consideration when pairing boys with mentors?"

Stacy shook her head. "Mostly we have to work around how many boys each Big Buddy can handle. Some guys do well with three or four boys. Others only have time for one. Since we're short on volunteers, our priority is not to overload the volunteers we have. The only solution is to put prospective Little Buddies on a waiting list."

The question *How many boys does Kane oversee?* danced on the tip of Ginger's tongue, but she knew Stacy couldn't give her that information.

She squinted at the table. Another boy, younger than Hayden, sat next to Kane. Her gaze moved to the woman with her hands on the back of boy's chair. She appeared to be chattering away to Kane.

"Excuse me," Stacy said and drifted off.

Ginger headed toward her son and his mentor, deciding at the last second to cut behind the bank of tables behind Kane and Hayden. That way she could eavesdrop and neither would be the wiser.

"That's great, son," the stacked blonde cooed. "But maybe you oughta let Kane show you how to paint that stripe a little straighter."

"You're doin' a fine job, Lock."

"But—"

"Leave him be, Daphne," Kane warned softly. "Maybe you oughta go get a glass of punch and let us finish up."

"I'll stay. I'm not really very thirsty."

"Mom! I didn't see you standing there," Hayden said.

There went her great eavesdropping plan. Ginger smiled. "I didn't want to interrupt you guys."

"Come and look at this. Kane helped with the design, but isn't it cool?"

Ginger angled over Hayden's shoulder. "Very cool, very creative. I love the silver flames. What happens when you're finished with it?"

"There's a contest. First place gets a big blue ribbon."

She was acutely aware of Kane's gaze on the back of her head and of Daphne's air of hostility. She glanced up and met the woman's eyes.

Daphne sent her a tight smile. "You must be Hayden's mom."

"Yes, I'm Ginger Paulson. And you are?"

"Daphne Martin. My son Lock is also Buck's Little Buddy." She draped herself over her son's chair, closer to Kane. "Maybe now that Hayden is almost finished, Buck can finally help you?"

Kane's eyes never strayed to Daphne's cleavage, which seemed to have its own gravitational pull toward Kane's face. "Sure. What's left to do?"

"That whole side is messy," Lock said glumly. "Maybe I oughta just paint over it."

"Only this section. The rest is good," Kane offered.

Hayden rose up on his knees to watch. Kane glanced up and smiled at him. "Hang tight, sport. We'll get that last stripe on in a second."

"So Buck, are you gonna stick around for the after party?" Daphne asked.

"I usually do. Why?"

"I wondered if I could talk to you about a couple of things." *In private* wasn't said, but it was heavily implied.

Ginger curled her hands around the back of Hayden's chair, instead of into fists. Unhappy with the urge to publicly remind Kane what they'd done in private last night.

Hayden said, "We're staying for the after party, right Mom?"

Her gaze hooked Kane's and his blank expression felt like a punch in the solar plexus. "I'm not sure."

"Aw, please? That's when we watch a movie and eat popcorn and stuff. Buck sneaks us candy too."

"We always have such a good time with the boys, don't we,

Buck?" With saccharine sweetness, Daphne said, "If you have other plans, Hayden is welcome to sit with us. He usually does since he always seems to be here by himself."

Ooh. Snap.

"Please?" Hayden pleaded.

Kane said not a word.

"We'll see."

"But Mom—"

"I said we'll see. Excuse me." She spun on her heel and dodged kids on her way to the punchbowl. Her hand shook as she poured the creamy lime green goo into a plastic cup. She grabbed a brownie.

Ginger hadn't attended many of these functions, believing, probably mistakenly, that Hayden needed guy time, whether it was with Kane or with the other boys in the program. Now as she looked around, she saw she was in the minority. Most mothers were here with their sons.

Did people think she didn't show up because she didn't care? Or she was too busy? Did they think she used the Little Buddies program as a daycare service?

Oh. God. What if people assumed she thought that her participation in the program was beneath her? She'd run into that lawyers-are-idiots mindset many times. Or worse, lawyers-are-money-grubbing-charlatans. Or lawyers talk above everyone else. Even Kane had made a couple of cracks about not being on her intellectual level.

Normally she couldn't give a rip what other people thought about her, but it bothered her to think they were feeling sorry for Hayden because of her actions—or lack thereof.

"If you have things to do today, Red, I can run Hayden home after the movie. No big deal."

No big deal. Maybe not to Kane, but it was to her. Rather than snapping at him, Ginger stuffed the entire brownie in her mouth. She chewed. And chewed.

And chewed.

Dammit. It hadn't looked that big on the napkin.

Kane stepped in front of her. "What's wrong?"

She pointed to her mouth and chewed. Then she took a swig of the punch and about gagged. She hated lime sherbet and mixed with 7-Up? It tasted like pond scum. She swallowed the sticky lump, but she still had to clear her throat several times. "Thanks for the offer, but I'm taking Hayden with me."

"Why?"

"I don't have to explain my reasons to you, Kane."

"Yes, you do, when he's looked forward to this movie day for the last couple weeks."

Why hadn't she known that about her son? Ginger hated to be on the defensive and her first response was always to lash out. "I'm Hayden's parent, you aren't."

His blue eyes turned ice cold.

But she'd stepped in it too deeply to back down. "I've been working late nights this week. I've barely seen him so I planned something special for the two of us. Besides, it seems you've already lined up an after-party movie date with Lock and Daphne. I wouldn't want Hayden to be a third wheel."

"Don't punish Hayden for your jealousy."

"Me? Jealous? Please."

"Daphne is an annoyance to me. That's all. But you? You, are..." He snarled, "If I wasn't tryin' so goddamn hard to keep my cool right now..."

"You'd what?" she taunted.

His voice dropped to a low rumble. "I'd throw you over my shoulder, take you home and spank you."

The gleam in his eye suggested his idea of spanking would only have the slightest playful edge.

Something warm and liquid pooled in her belly, despite the anger still lingering in the air between them.

Kane stepped back and rubbed the bridge of his nose. "Look. Whatever you decide to do, at least let Hayden stay for the contest announcement winners."

"Fine."

"And, counselor?"

"What?"

His gaze landed on her mouth. "You've got brownie in your teeth."

Damn man. At least he hadn't pointed out her food avoidance tactic again.

After a quick trip to the bathroom to remove the brownie evidence, Ginger struck up a conversation with Hayden's first grade teacher. She ignored Kane McKay, although it was difficult with the way Hayden was practically hanging off him.

Maybe Hayden had gotten the idea from Daphne.

Ooh. Double snap.

The announcement of the contest winners quieted the room. Hayden won third place and a red ribbon. Two older kids took the top spots. A lot older. How long were boys allowed to remain in the Little Buddies program anyway? She'd never thought to ask and wow, did that make her feel even more out of the loop.

Hayden bounded over, waving his ribbon, Kane meandering behind him. "I got third!"

"I see. That's awesome. I'm proud of you. Grandpa will be excited for you too."

"Are we staying for the movie?" he asked.

"No."

"But—"

"If you argue, maybe I won't take you to Spearfish."

His eyes widened beneath his glasses. "I didn't know we were going to Spearfish."

Neither did I. "That's because it's a surprise."

Hayden looked torn. He glanced at the volunteers setting up the movie screen and the chairs, then at Kane. Then back at her.

Kane put his hand on Hayden's shoulder. "Go on and have a good time with your mom. She mentioned she'd worked late all week and she was lookin' forward to spendin' time with you. We can catch the next movie, okay?"

"Okay. Thanks, Buck. See you later."

"Drive safe and have fun," Kane said to her and walked away. Back to Daphne.

And whose fault is that?

Ginger let Hayden pick out a new model airplane at the hobby store. She'd also bought him a new Xbox game. The kid's athletic shoes were too small. While Hayden tried on every pair in the store, she browsed the snow boot section. She found a pair that weren't...hideous. Would Kane be happy she'd taken his warnings about frostbitten toes seriously?

He'd probably be happier if you owned up to the fact you were consumed by the green-eyed monster today and probably deserved the spanking he's threatened.

Why did the suggestion of Kane's big hand connecting with her bare ass cause her belly to flutter? His growling challenge brought out a strangely submissive need—another new feeling for her.

"Mom?"

She focused on her son. "Sorry. What did you say?"

"Can I buy this for Buck?"

The ball cap in his hand was the same midnight blue as Kane's eyes. Above the bill was a patch that read *Superstar!* in red, white and blue lettering.

"He likes to wear ball caps when he plays poker with his cousins. He told me the luck had run out of the last one. I think this one would bring him good luck."

"It's very nice you're thinking of him."

"He's always bringing me cool stuff and I never give him nothin'—"

"Anything," Ginger automatically corrected.

"I never give him anything, well, except the stuff I've made for him."

Did Kane keep the Lego cars and airplanes, and robot inventions Hayden gave him? Did he display them around his house? Or hide them in a drawer?

You'd know if you'd ever been to Kane's house.

That jarred her. She knew he lived in a trailer on McKay land off of Highway 14A. Hayden had spent time out there, considerable time in the summer. Which was why it seemed weird she'd never picked her son up at Kane's house. Kane had always brought Hayden home.

Maybe it was time she went to him. She owed him an apology anyway—she *had* been jealous.

"Come on, Mom, let's go."

Hayden fell asleep on the way home. Ginger's thoughts were as scattered as the patches of snow blowing across the interstate. By the time they reached home, it was after eight and they were both starving. After a quick supper, she was still restless.

Her father's interest in model airplane building had rubbed off on his grandson. They conspired on the best way to start this newest project and Ginger knew they'd be engrossed all

137

night.

She rarely went out on the weekends. Definitely never just happened to "drop by" a man's house more than twenty miles away. She slipped on an emerald green cashmere sweater with a deep "V" in the front that showcased her cleavage. She shimmied on a pair of western jeans. She fluffed her hair. Touched up her makeup. And put on her new sheepskin-lined snow boots.

Her father noticed her improved appearance, but didn't comment. But Hayden said, "Hey, Mom, where you going?"

"Out for a little while. Grandpa's in charge, so when he says go to bed, I expect you to listen to him." She kissed the top of his head. "See you in the morning." She bussed her father's cheek and whispered, "I have my cell if you need anything. Don't wait up."

Her nerves nearly got the best of her when she pulled up to Kane's trailer and saw four other pickups parked in the drive. Was he having a party?

What if one of those trucks was Daphne's?

She stomped up the steps and pounded on the aluminum screen door.

The porch light went on. The inner door opened. A tall, lanky and deeply dimpled cutie poked his head out. "Please tell me that you're the surprise entertainment. And you'll be actin' out the, 'I'm havin' car trouble and these winter clothes are *so* constricting' fantasy."

"No pasties under my coat. But I can come back later if this is a bad time?"

The kid was jerked out of the doorway and Kane opened the screen door. "Ginger? What the devil are you doin' here?"

Not good. "Sorry to disappoint you. Sounds like you were expecting a stripper?" she said tightly.

"For Christsake, Dalton, what the hell did you say to her?" Kane shook his head at whatever was said behind him. "Ignore my bonehead cousin and come on in."

All of a sudden this seemed like a really lousy idea. "I didn't mean to crash your party."

"It ain't a party. Just a poker game and...Jesus Christ. Are you wearing...snow boots?"

She swiveled her toe in the snow. "Yes. That's why I came

over."

His intense gaze didn't waver from her eyes. "You drove all the way out here to show me your new snow boots?"

"Yes, since you nag at me for not wearing proper winter wear, I thought I'd prove that I do listen to you. You are a smart man, who's usually right, and I am an idiot."

Kane continued to give her an inscrutable look.

"Shit. Sorry. Dumb idea. I'll go."

Then he was right in her face. "You take one step off the porch, Red, and I'll tackle you in the snow and drag your ass inside my house by the heels of your new snow boots."

Oh. Wow. That caveman growl was sexy as hell.

"What the fuck, Kane? I know your mama raised you better than to let a beautiful woman shiver outside in this frigid weather. Come on in, darlin'. I'll warm you up."

Laughter.

"You touch her, I break your hand," Kane snarled.

Really Neanderthal behavior. Really hot behavior.

Kane grabbed her by her coat sleeve and led her inside.

Four guys—all dark-haired, ranging in age from early twenties to late twenties—grinned at her and crowded around her, despite Kane's back-off vibe.

"Hey, Ginger, nice to see you," Bennett McKay said. "You're lookin' fantastic as usual."

Kane made a growling noise.

"Thanks, Ben."

Brandt McKay leaned forward. "I ain't gonna offer my hand, bein's psycho here—" he pointed to Kane, "—would probably cut it off. But I'll echo Ben's sentiments. You are lookin' mighty fine tonight."

"Thank you, Brandt. Is every one of you McKays born with a silver tongue?"

"Absolutely," the cute, lanky one said. "The more we use our tongues the better we get with them." He held out his hand. "Dalton McKay, at your service."

Ginger bit back a smile the same time Kane reached around and cuffed the impudent Dalton in the back of the head. "Dalton, don't make me grind you into dust."

"Always with the violence, cuz. Do you want Miz Ginger here to think we're all as uncivilized as you?" Tell McKay winked at her. "Some of us do have manners."

Ginger had grown up surrounded by hot guys in California. Surfer types. The All-American types. The brooding types. The small town sports hero wannabe Hollywood-star types. But the Wyoming McKays were in a class by themselves. Talk about an irresistible natural charm. Lord. No wonder every woman wanted a piece of them.

"Speaking of bad manners, I'm sorry I interrupted."

Kane said, "No, they were just leavin'." He stared at each one of his cousins hard.

"Ah, yeah. Right. Poker night is over at...ten o'clock on a Saturday night?" Ben said, glancing at his watch.

"I'm tired of givin' all my money to Dalton anyway," Tell complained. "Let's hit the Golden Boot."

"Hell yeah," Dalton said. "I'll buy the first round."

"You guys do what you want. I'm out. I'm headin' home," Brandt said.

"Home?" Dalton repeated.

Brandt glared at him.

"Dalton. Let it be," Tell warned.

"The fuck I will. We both know he ain't goin' home, bein's she called less than ten minutes ago." Dalton sneered. "Forget about her—"

Both Brandt and Tell cuffed their younger brother upside the head, shutting him up. "Thanks for the game, Kane. We'll see you in church tomorrow mornin', right?"

"Get the fuck out."

Amused male laughter.

Ginger ducked her head to keep from joining in.

Four men donned boots, hats and outwear, taking their own sweet time, bullshitting among themselves, trying to engage her in conversation, while Kane folded his arms over his chest and glared at them.

Finally the trucks roared off and they were alone.

Kane began to stalk her with that look in his eye. The look that told her when he caught her, he'd do all sort of naughty, wicked things to her, without apology, and probably, without her permission.

Ginger stopped.

Kane didn't until he crowded her against the wall. "Why are

you really here?"

Damn, he smelled good. Even with whiskey on his breath. His body heat permeated her clothing, seeping into her skin, setting her needs on fire. She wanted to lick him up one side and down the other. Bury her face in his neck. His chest. His groin.

"Ginger?" he prompted. "Are you gonna answer the question?"

Question. Right. Refocus. "Umm. I'm here because you were right today. I lied. I was jealous of Daphne. Really jealous and I feel stupid about it because that's never happened to me before."

He offered her a feral smile. "A lawyer recanting? Sugar, you sure your license to practice law ain't gonna be revoked?"

"Funny."

"What else?"

"I wanted to tell you I'm sorry for acting like a jerk to you. And I'm also sorry for the snotty way I pointed out that I'm Hayden's parent, when you've been so good for him, Kane. I see you with him and I—"

"Red," he said sharply.

"What?"

"Shut up."

But she couldn't seem to stop babbling. "I'm sorry I broke up your poker party too. And. Well. Umm. That's it. I should be going."

"Like hell." Then Kane crushed her lips beneath his and rocked her world with a tongue-thrusting kiss.

Then his hands were tearing at her clothes. Coat. Gone. Shirt. Hanging open. Jeans. Unbuttoned and unzipped. Kane's hand followed the curve of her belly over the rise of her mound. He slipped one finger between her wet folds and plunged it inside her pussy.

She gasped, breaking the kiss.

Kane nestled his face in her cleavage, rubbing his beard across the tops of her breasts. "Take them off."

A little dazed, she said, "What? The boots?"

"The boots, the jeans, your panties. All of it. Off. Now."

"You'll have to quit finger fucking me."

His mouth brushed her ear and he removed his hand. "I

love it when you talk dirty. I love it more when you *act* dirty."

Ginger pushed him back a step and kicked off her boots. Her hands weren't cooperating and she struggled to peel off her jeans. Once she was naked from the waist down, Kane pressed her against the wall again, plastering his chest to hers. His cock dug into her belly.

She realized he'd only lowered his Wranglers past his knees. But he had unsnapped his shirt so she could run her hands all over him. Thoughtful.

"Spread your legs."

The instant she widened her stance, his fingers were pushing inside her again. He fucked in and out while using his teeth on her nipple. Then he pulled his fingers free and held them to her lips with a guttural "Lick them."

Keeping her eyes locked on his, Ginger parted her lips and sucked his fingers inside her mouth. The taste of her own juices on the roughness of his skin sent a spike of desire straight to her core. She felt her pussy soften. Moisten.

He tugged his fingers free and traced the damp digits down her chin, her throat, between her breasts and right back into her pussy. He thrust harder, deeper.

The friction only made her eager for the thicker, longer length of his cock to fill her completely. "Kane—"

His mouth cut off her protest. The wild, desperate kiss had her whimpering, clawing at him.

Kane's tongue and fingers slid free from inside her body simultaneously. His hands circled her waist. "Jump up and wrap your legs around me."

Ginger was too far gone to care about him bearing too much of her weight. Those big, strong, wonderfully rough hands grabbed a handful of her ass, holding her in place as his cock impaled her.

"Jesus, you feel amazing." He rammed into her hard. "Wet."

"More."

"Hang on."

She wreathed her arms around his neck, scattering kisses and little love bites wherever her mouth landed.

Kane made sexy, masculine groans and grunts as he fucked her like a man possessed.

Harsh breathing, the scent of sex, the rapid pistoning of

Kane's pelvis spun Ginger out of control. She flew apart on his next thrust, digging her nails into his back, arching hard for more contact on her clit, squeezing her legs, her ass, her pussy, trying to make the orgasm last as long as possible.

And it did.

Kane followed her over the edge. She swallowed his surprised shout in a blistering kiss, holding on as he came.

He slowed his frantic thrusting, then stopped moving entirely, gentling the kiss. Ginger knew she made mewling, whimpering moans, but she loved his surprising tenderness in the aftermath of their no-holds-barred passion.

Wetness trickled down the inside of her thigh as Kane brought her back down to her feet. Luckily the wall held her up because her legs were wobbly.

They were both still breathing hard.

Kane strung a line of kisses from the hollow of her throat, across her jawline to the section of skin in front of her ear. "That was the very best apology I've ever received."

She laughed. "So I'm forgiven?"

"And then some." He nuzzled her cheek. Her throat. Her hair. "I wish you could stay with me tonight."

"Me too." She slid her hands down from around his neck and framed his handsome face. "Come over tomorrow. Eat with us. Hang out with us."

"You're sure?"

"Yes. I know Hayden would love to see you."

"Just Hayden?"

"No." Ginger pecked his frowning mouth. "I'd love to see you too."

"Good to know."

After they helped each other dress, Kane insisted on walking her out to her car. Just before she pulled away, he knocked on her window.

"Thanks for showin' me your snow boots."

She smiled all the way home.

Chapter Twelve

How many times had Kane knocked on Ginger's front door in the last two years? If he averaged once a week, the number would be over a hundred.

Why was he nervous now?

Because everything had changed last night when Ginger had come to him. Her invitation to spend the day with them hadn't been issued lightly. Neither had her apology.

And what an apology it'd been. The sounds she'd made. Her utter lack of inhibition. The wet clasp of her pussy around his cock and the greediness of her kisses.

Jesus, McKay, that's just what you don't need—to sport a goddamn erection when Ginger opens the door. She already believes you're some sex-starved beast who ruts on her the instant she's within grabbing distance.

While Kane wrestled with getting his libido under control, Hayden answered the door with a huge grin. "Buck! What're you doing here?"

"Thought I'd swing by, see what's up since you left early yesterday. You busy?"

"Nope." Hayden grabbed his coat sleeve and dragged him inside. "I've got something for ya. It's in my room."

"Hang on. Lemme get my boots off so I don't track snow all over your mama's floor."

"I'll go get it. You stay right here. Don't move," he warned and disappeared around the corner.

Kane ditched his gloves, coat and boots. When he glanced up, Ginger was inclined against the wall, smiling at him. Damn if he didn't grin back at her like a lovesick fool. "Hey."

"Hey, yourself." Her gaze encompassed his body with blatant appreciation, ending at his black cowboy hat. "So the boots come off but the hat stays on?"

"Yes, ma'am."

"You might want to rethink that."

Hayden raced back into the foyer, skidding to a stop in his sock-clad feet. He held something behind his back, and wore an enormous grin. "Ready?"

"Yep."

He whipped out a ball cap. Navy blue with *Superstar!* emblazoned on it. "I got you a new cap since you said your other one was unlucky. This one looked lucky."

That little shit. That little, sweet shit. Kane took the ball cap, keeping his face shadowed beneath the brim of his cowboy hat. Not only was it a thoughtful gift, it proved Hayden listened to him. Sometimes with kids, he wasn't sure how much they tuned out.

"Do you like it?"

"It's perfect." He removed his cowboy hat and handed it to Ginger. He adjusted the cap and smiled again. "Fits great. Thanks, Hayden. My cousins better look out. I'll be winnin' piles of money from them the next poker night."

The boy still grinned. "Cool. So you wanna play my new Xbox game?"

He looked at Ginger. "Is it okay if I hang out for a while?"

"Sure. Would you like to stay for supper?"

"It depends."

"On?"

"On whether you're makin' liver and onions." He winked at Hayden. "If that's the case, I'll pass."

"I'm making beef and noodles."

"It's my favorite," Hayden inserted. "It's really good."

"Then I'd be happy to stay." His gaze strayed to the living room. "Where's Dash?"

"Taking a nap. Why?" Ginger asked.

"I'm thinkin' I'll challenge him to a game of poker later. See if my new lucky hat can break my losin' streak with him."

Any awkwardness vanished as the afternoon flew by. Hayden beat him three games out of four on the Xbox. He won seven out of ten hands of poker with Dash, but Kane suspected

Dash let him win, so Hayden could see the ball cap was indeed lucky.

The beef and noodles were delicious. It surprised him that Ginger was such a great cook. The few professional women he'd dated couldn't cook worth shit. Then again, having a child with food allergies changed everything.

Dash seemed strangely subdued and retired to his room shortly after they'd eaten. Ginger disappeared for a few minutes as she helped Dash settle in. Kane remembered Dash's embarrassment the nights he'd stayed here and helped Dash into bed. It'd been no big deal for Kane, holding the wheelchair steady as Dash pulled himself onto his mattress.

It'd taken a lot out of Dash, so the next night, Kane had just picked the man up without asking. Luckily Dash hadn't rolled out of bed on his watch, but Kane suspected if they installed folding hospital rails, Dash wouldn't fall out of bed at all. Since Kane wasn't family, he didn't feel comfortable bringing it up with either Ginger or her father.

Hayden yawned and asked his mother if Kane could tuck him in. Kane sat on the edge of the bottom bunk. "So your mama don't read you stories before she tucks you in?"

"Not anymore. Sometimes I let still let her." His eyes looked so much bigger without his eyeglasses. "Did your mom read to you?"

"If she had time or if me'n Kade weren't in trouble. Truth is, my dad liked to read us."

"He did? What did he read?"

"Adventure stories he'd saved from the magazines he'd had growing up."

A somber expression settled on Hayden's face.

In that instant he looked exactly like Ginger. "Something wrong?"

"What's it like to have a dad?"

He'd taken classes through the Big Buddies program on how to address this question, but faced with it now, he couldn't remember a damn thing on how he was supposed to answer. "Well, since I've always had one, I guess I've never really thought about it."

Hayden's small fingers pleated the dark green comforter. "You look like your dad."

Jesus. Kane knew what was coming before Hayden opened his mouth.

"Do you think I look like my dad? Because I don't look like my mom."

"Says who? I was just thinkin' that you look exactly like her. Especially when you're thinkin' hard. You both get this little crease between your eyebrows. And you definitely have your mama's eyes." Nervous, Kane tugged the sheet into a straight line. "Lookin' like someone else...well, that ain't really a picnic, to be honest. I look exactly like my brother. But neither of us looks anything like our mama."

"She is kind of...little."

"That's one thing me'n Kade aren't, is little. Genetics are a weird thing. If I mate a Hereford cow, the ones with the reddish-orange bodies and the white faces? With a Black Angus bull, the calf will have a white face and a black body. It don't look nothin' like its mama or its daddy. But it don't matter none to the mama cows because it's their job to protect and care for their babies, no matter if they look like them or not. Kinda reminds me of your mom."

Relief replaced Hayden's somberness. "Yeah, I guess you're right."

Kane brushed the hair out of Hayden's eyes. "Now, get to sleep. If you ever need to talk about anything, you can call me. You know that, right?"

"Really?"

"Absolutely. I'll see you sometime this week, okay?"

"You won't be here in the morning?"

I wish. "Nope. I'm headed home shortly."

"Night, Buck."

"Night, sport."

After Kane left Hayden's room, he slumped against the wall in the hallway. Had what he'd said made a lick of sense to the boy? Should he tell Ginger her son had asked about his father? Or would mentioning it violate Hayden's trust? As he listened to Ginger doing dishes in the kitchen, he wondered why Hayden had brought it up tonight.

Maybe it came about because you're in his house, hanging out with him, his mother and his grandfather. Wouldn't that make him wonder what it'd be like to have that life all the time?

Probably. Because as Kane sat at the dining room table tonight, he let himself imagine, just for few minutes, this *was* his life. A beautiful, smart, sensual wife. A great kid. An old timer to keep things in perspective. The only thing missing in the picket-fence scene was a dog.

Was it ironic the dog was the only thing Kane had in his life right now?

"Kane? Is everything all right?"

Ginger had poked her head around the corner.

"Yeah. Great. I should probably be goin'."

"Now that we're finally alone...you're bailing on me? I thought we could make out on the couch for a little bit."

"Good plan." He towed her into the living room, tugged her onto his lap and smothered her squeak of protest with a kiss.

She melted into him, running her hands up and down his arms. "God. I want to touch you everywhere."

He dragged his wet lips across the smooth expanse of her throat. "I want that too, Red, but I think we oughta talk."

Ginger lowered her head, her eyes connecting with his. "You're serious."

"Yeah." Kane threaded their fingers together and kissed her knuckles. "I want to keep seein' you. I realize you're in a tricky situation with Hayden and your dad."

Those expressive hazel eyes tapered to fine points. "Are you suggesting we sneak around?"

No. I want everyone to know we're a couple and you're mine. "Sneaking around sounds a little tawdry, don't it? How about if we call it a private preliminary test drive?"

"You sure you haven't had law classes?"

He slapped her ass hard. And wasn't that interesting? Ginger didn't yelp. Or protest. She sort of...moaned.

"I want to keep seeing you too, Kane, but the issue is where? I can't spend the night at your place. You can't spend the night here. It seems high schoolish to have you show up after Hayden and my dad are in bed. And as totally hot as it was for you to fuck me in my office, I do have clients show up unannounced during the day. I can't make them wait in the reception area while we're going at it on the floor."

He'd take the floor idea as a challenge for a future hook-up. "But you get a lunch hour, right?"

"I usually eat lunch at my desk."

"I could eat you at your desk," he offered with his best big, bad, wolf growl.

She whapped him on the bicep. "Stop derailing my train of thought with that suggestive tone, mister. Keep it G-rated tonight since XXX ain't happening."

"Sorry." But he wasn't. Kane smoothed her hair over her shoulder. "Our nighttime options are limited, Ginger."

"So are our daytime ones, especially since my dad is here during the day."

"Not every day," he pointed out. "There's always my place. It's further out, but it'd be more private." Kane placed a kiss on the hollow of her throat. "Or we could meet halfway and do it in my truck."

She giggled.

Damn her and that charming, girlish giggle.

"I've never done it in a pickup before."

"As a dedicated, lifelong pickup owner, it's my sworn duty to show you the kinky pleasures of the flesh that can be performed in a pickup, while tryin' to avoid bangin' your head into the steering wheel, and smackin' your ass into the dash." He grinned. "It'll be all kinds of fun poppin' your pickup cherry, sugar."

"Okay. Lunch. Tomorrow. Here. We'll save the truck rendezvous for another time. Will one o'clock work?"

"Be here with a hard-on." He pulled her closer and teased her mouth with his until her lips trembled. Then he kissed her soundly and released her. "I've gotta hit the road."

At the door he switched out his ball cap for his cowboy hat. He rolled up the cap and stuck it in the inside pocket of his coat.

"Hayden was pretty insistent you needed a new hat. I'm glad you liked it."

"I like everything he gives me. He's thoughtful. Not many kids his age are."

Ginger smooched his chin. "You are thoughtful too, Kane McKay."

"Must be because mine and Hayden's mamas raised us right."

"Such a silver tongue. See you tomorrow, cowboy. Drive

safe."

"Night, Red."

On Monday, Ginger had been so frantic to get her hands on him that Kane had found himself flat on his back, in the middle of her bed, with Ginger going to town on him like a Pony Express rider—almost before he'd even said hello. He went with it, because hey, there were worse things than a smokin' hot woman moaning his name and bouncing on his pole until he came. But she seemed to have forgotten his "in charge" rule and he intended to remind her on their next lunch date.

So Wednesday, he brought his handcuffs. At first Ginger balked at being bound, even slightly. He'd waited for her to accept his control by spending several long minutes just kissing her bare arms. Sucking on her fingers like he sucked on her nipples. Once he'd earned her trust and promised not to tickle her, she relaxed.

Kane spent half their allotted time toying with her breasts, just because he could, just because it made her crazy, made her wet. After he'd wrung one orgasm from her, he straddled her chest and fucked those luscious tits, sliding his dick in the tight valley until he couldn't hold back. He finished by jacking off on her chest and belly, fighting the urge to roar with male satisfaction at seeing her marked with his seed. Then he settled between her legs and sucked on her clit until she screamed.

Yeah, the counselor was a little late getting back to the office that day.

On Friday, Kane had walked into Ginger's house and saw her naked on the living room rug, getting herself off with a vibrator. After witnessing the live floorshow of her oh-so-sexy act of self-pleasure, he stripped and fucked her, right there on the floor. Twice.

Then he'd confiscated her vibrator, knowing the weekend loomed without the prospect of another naked lunch. He informed her that if he wasn't getting off, neither was she.

Lunch was becoming his favorite part of the day.

When five o'clock rolled around the following Friday, Ginger gathered her paperwork and separated the piles into appropriate folders.

A knock sounded and her assistant, Rissa, poked her head in. "I'm going. Need anything else?"

"I'm good. Have a great weekend."

"You too."

She sagged deeper into her chair. She had another splitting headache. The other symptoms had been building all week and she faced the truth. The little sniffle she'd noticed last weekend wasn't a simple cold; it'd morphed into a full-blown sinus infection.

She'd never suffered from allergies as a kid, nor as an adult, and she'd gone through the various allergy tests along with Hayden, mostly to allay his fears that the tests didn't hurt. Her tests had come out negative. Since sinus infections were a recurring problem, Dr. Monroe suggested the dry air and higher elevation wreaked havoc on her sinuses because the infections surfaced after she'd relocated to Wyoming.

Ginger called DeWitt's Pharmacy and ordered the two-week cycle of antibiotics Doc Monroe had left on file for her. She was so damn tired. She wanted to go home and crawl in bed. Heck, she'd felt so out of it today she'd sent Kane a text message canceling their lunch date.

Kane McKay. Lord, that man had turned her into a stick of dynamite—one smoldering look or one heated touch from him and that fuse fired. She'd spent the week in a sexual daze. When she wasn't in the throes of experiencing the combustible, amazingly hot sex, she was thinking about it. Constantly. After he'd confiscated her vibrator, she'd wondered how Kane would kick up the sexual scenarios the following week.

Woo-boy. Kick them up he had.

Monday's lunch menu consisted of an appetizer of sixty-nine, a position she'd rarely enjoyed until Kane showed her the delicious benefits of mutual pleasure. She'd barely caught her breath from her orgasm while his cock was buried in her mouth, when he flipped her over and fucked her from behind. He'd kept one hand gripped in her hair, holding her head in place, and the other hand curled around her hip, ordering her to rub her clit until she came. His sexual aggressiveness allowed her to unlock a side of herself she'd been too tired, too afraid to access. Kane didn't exploit that compliant part of her; he used it to take her—them—to new sexual heights.

Although they hadn't been scheduled for a lunch date on Tuesday, Ginger had been so...frantic to experience the feelings of sexual empowerment he'd aroused in her, that she'd driven out to his place and surprised him in the barn. She'd dropped to her knees, willing—eager even—for him to take her mouth without any thought to her pleasure, only to his own. Kane had been a little rough, but she'd loved it. Loved that he trusted her with a side of himself that was more animal than man.

And after he'd roared his climax loud enough to spook the horses, he'd taken her into the cab of his pickup. While the heater warmed the frigid winter air, and country tunes drifted from the radio, Kane slowly, thoroughly made love to her. Face to face, as she straddled his lap. He'd worshipped her breasts, knowing how wild it made her, whispering erotic, raunchy words in her ear, across her skin. He coaxed two orgasms from her before he'd allowed another one for himself. As she'd pulled back onto the highway, headed for town, he leaned against his pickup door, snow swirling around him, watching her go with a big smile on his face.

Wednesday, she'd marked off two hours for lunch. Kane was already in her bedroom, already naked, a rope dangling between his fingers. The spike of uncertainty increased when she'd noticed the bottle of lube on the bed.

When she saw his wicked, wicked grin, she actually turned and ran out of the room.

He chased her. His laugh resembled a pleased growl of intent. When he caught her, Ginger gave herself over to him entirely.

Kane stripped her, bound her wrists behind her back with the rope, and centered her on her bed. Then he kissed her everywhere. The sensation of his firm lips, wet tongue and the scrape of his facial hair was mind-boggling. Every single inch of her skin was subjected to Kane's questing mouth. Her first orgasm, courtesy of his tongue flicking her clit, hit her from out of left field. The second orgasm built with each drive of his cock into her pussy until they'd sailed over the edge of the abyss together, silent besides their labored breaths, body plastered to body by sweat.

Without the use of her hands, Ginger was entirely at Kane's mercy. She missed touching him, mapping those work-defined muscles with her fingertips. Digging her nails into his ass as he pumped into her. Because she was bound, he took extra care to ensure her comfort. He verbally admired the way the position straightened her shoulders, thrust out her tits, and showcased her toned arms. He smoothed and petted her, murmuring erotic words that would've been enough to keep her primed.

Then he'd cracked open the container of lube and said, "This sweet, sweet ass is mine today." He'd kissed her while he'd prepared her, gently, but she didn't suspect that would last long. Kane's eyes had darkened with feral intensity. His movements were quick. Sure. Demanding. Impatient.

When Kane determined she was ready, he hiked her hips up. He gripped the backs of her thighs, spreading her legs wide, leaving her balanced on her bound arms and shoulders. The slick head of his cock prodded the puckered entrance. Once. Twice. On the third jab, the thick crown popped past the rigid ring of muscle and he pushed his cock into her anal passage to the hilt.

Ginger wasn't a virgin to anal sex, but that first stroke hurt. She bit her lip and held her breath, hoping the pain would ease and give way to that hazy feeling of floating.

Kane's focus wasn't on her, and strangely that didn't bother her—rather, it turned her on. The visual of his cock balls-deep in her ass must've been an erotic sight; he couldn't tear his focus away from where they were intimately joined. He pulled back, coming completely out of her ass, the tiny hole rippled open again as his entire shaft slid in. And back out. And in again. Harder. Faster. Deeper. And as Kane fucked her ass, she felt a thrilling sense of his possession. No other man had touched her the way he had, physically, emotionally.

The knowledge freed her. The bite of pain as his hard length scraped her delicate tissues became an exquisite ache—a welcome ache. She countered his thrusts, meeting his urgency. His need. Silently encouraging him to take.

His climax rolled through them both, his hot ejaculate burst against her inner anal walls. As soon as his dick softened, he eased out. He scooted down the mattress and circled his lips around her clit, suckling strongly until she came against his mouth.

There hadn't been much to say after that. He'd unwound the rope from her arms, rubbing until the circulation returned, kissing her shoulders, nuzzling her nape, brushing her nipples across his forearm. He understood the rasp of his body hair on the tips was almost an orgasmic experience itself.

They'd kept the silence as they'd dressed, even after he'd kissed her with a lover's surety and a whispered goodbye. She listened as his truck roared off, with her forehead pressed into the doorframe, completely undone.

Ginger's cell phone buzzed on her desk, startling her out of her sexual flashback. "Hey, son. What's up?"

"Are you coming home soon?"

"Pretty quick. I have to make one stop first. Why?"

"Grandpa says to tell you we're out of cereal and bread. He's making fish sticks for supper and they smell gross. Now he's mad that I don't wanna eat his food, but I'd rather starve."

"Did you tell him that?"

"Yeah. That's why he's mad."

As many times as she'd told her father he didn't need to help out in the kitchen, every once in a while he got it in his head that he could cook. Never mind his culinary skills were limited to heating prepackaged frozen entrees, canned soup and dishing up ice cream. Even Ginger admitted the thought of eating fish sticks turned her stomach. "What would you rather have for supper?"

"SpaghettiOs."

"I'm leaving the office now."

By the time Ginger picked up her prescription and stopped at the grocery store, her head pounded with such force she felt her eyeballs pulsing.

Playing intermediary between her son and father didn't help her headache. Once she'd finished kitchen duties, she downed her pills, crawled in bed with a box of Kleenex and a hot compress on her sinuses and was dead to the world.

Chapter Thirteen

"I'm out."

"Jesus, Chase. That's like the fifth hand in a row," Bennett complained.

"And I'm still up more than you," Chase pointed out. "I'm playin' smart."

"For a professional bull rider, you're playin' it awfully safe."

Kane watched his cousin Tell sweep Chase's cards into a pile. Then Tell looked at him. "How many?"

"Two."

Tell dealt then faced his brother Brandt. "How many?"

"Three."

"He's bettin' on a pair, boys," Dalton announced.

"Shut your pie hole," Brandt grumbled.

Dalton, the youngest McKay of the group, just grinned. "I'll be takin' three cards myself, bro," he said to Tell.

"Fine. I'm takin' two. Kane, bid's to you."

Kane knocked back a sip of his Budweiser. Full house. Threes and queens. Maybe he could bluff his way into winning the pot. "I'll raise three."

All around the table, trash talking ensued between the brothers and cousins. These biweekly poker nights had become a tradition in the last year. Kane didn't kid himself it was his great planning that brought them together. Things had always been somewhat strained between his Uncle Casper and his three brothers, Carson, Charles and Calvin, hence a strained relationship existed between the McKay cousins from that branch. The original McKay homestead had been equally divided between the four brothers, which meant they were tied together in the ranching business until one of them bought the other three out. With the value of the ranch, no one had that kind of cash, and the McKays were beyond stubborn so the chances of that ever happening were slim to none.

Uncle Carson had quadrupled the size of his holding, and that didn't include the pieces of land his sons had purchased. Kane's dad had added to his original section too, but not as substantially. He only had Kane and Kade to help him work it, not four or five sons. Uncle Charles had added acreage in the last few years when he'd turned over the majority of the ranch responsibility to Quinn and Bennett. Chase returned to Wyoming and helped his brothers when he wasn't on tour with the PBR. Except it seemed Chase's return home lately was to avoid the tabloids. Kane admitted pride in the kid, for taking the bad-boy, hell-raisin' McKay reputation to a whole 'nother level—a national level.

But the biggest reason for them spending time together, besides the fact they were all still single, happened after Luke McKay's death.

The remaining sons had a falling out with their father, a rift that still hadn't healed. Uncle Casper had a bug up his ass about something, and he'd further alienated his brothers and nephews. It made for awkward conversation when dealing with ranch business. Especially since Brandt, Tell and Dalton purchased a tract of land on their own. As their father was the only McKay descendant who hadn't added on—it'd always been a bitter point of contention for Uncle Casper and he'd taken it out on his sons.

Yeah, they were just one big happy fucking family.

Kane knew this type of poker game wouldn't have happened in his younger years, when he was in the same age group as Brandt, Tell, Dalton, Bennett and Chase. At almost thirty-seven, Kane was the old man in the group. Uncle Casper and Aunt Joan had started their family later than his brothers, and had four boys in six years. Luke had been just turned twenty-seven when he died. Brandt had just turned twenty-five; Tell had turned twenty-four and Dalton twenty-one.

On the Charles McKay branch of the family, Quinn was going on thirty-four. Bennett was twenty-nine and Chase had passed the quarter-century mark and turned twenty-six.

Why did age—his and his other family members'—matter to

him?

Because all Kane's male cousins had been married by his age. Most married with families. And he wasn't enjoying the bachelor lifestyle these days, not like he had when he'd lived at the Boars Nest. Hell, he hadn't even missed having an active sex life. He avoided the bars, knowing he'd run into a woman or fifteen he'd fucked at some point in the last two decades, usually a woman he'd fucked over. The sad truth was, Kane had been with so many women...he didn't remember all of them.

Talk about great husband and father material. Jesus. No wonder he was single.

His thoughts drifted to Ginger. At times, he believed they could make a good life together. But other times, he wondered why she'd want him long-term. They were already getting it on every chance they had. He was already a father figure to her son. She wasn't looking for security or a provider. Hell, she probably made more money in two months than he made all year. He knew she wasn't looking to take this to another level.

And that sucked.

"He's thinkin' about bein' on his knees in front of some big biker dude with a pierced cock, wearin' leathers, holdin' a whip."

Kane's focus zoomed back to the present and he stared at his cousin Tell. "What the hell were you talkin' about?"

"You. Dreamin' of your new boyfriend," Tell answered.

Chase made kissing noises.

Laughter.

"Fuck off. All of you."

"Just sayin'...we tried to get your attention, but you were off in dreamland. We're all mighty curious to know whatcha were thinkin' about."

"I was thinkin' about all the ways I'm gonna spend the money I win tonight when I kick your pansy-asses."

"Bring it." Tell pointed to Kane. "No one raised after you, so show your hand."

"Full house. Threes over queens."

Bennett threw down three kings.

Dalton had a flush, all spades.

Tell showed a straight, ten high.

Brandt spread out a full house, aces over jacks, and grinned. "Kitty pay me."

Boos, fuck yous and cards flew. Chase passed out another round of beer. And they settled in to the next game.

"So Chase," Dalton drawled, "which buckle bunny hottie you bangin' this week?"

"Maybe you oughta ask him which buckle bunny he's runnin' from this week," Bennett said slyly.

Chase took a long pull of his beer. "Neither. I've given up women for Lent."

Guffaws broke out.

"No, I'm serious."

"Right. We ain't Catholic and it's a goddamn long time until Easter."

"True story, I swear. Since that tabloid shit went down with Vivica, my publicist said to cool it. And my buddy Marshall bet me I couldn't go four months without sex. So cousins, I'm sittin' here before you, a man who hasn't fucked a woman since New Year's Eve."

Silence. Then laugher.

"You've got to be pullin' our leg," Tell said.

Chase shook his head. "Ten thousand dollars is on the line."

Dalton's eyes widened. "Christ, cuz, you bet that kinda money on keepin' your dick in your pants?"

"It ain't a cash bet. If I can do it, Marshall's givin' me a quarter share in this up and comin' buckin' bull named Atomic Fireball." Chase pointed his beer bottle at the guys at the table. "So you all need to be getting some serious ass to make up for my lack of it."

Tell and Dalton high-fived, and Tell said, "We've got ya covered."

"With who?" Brandt demanded.

"The Sweeney twins. Kristol and Marisol. And here's the kicker." Dalton leaned in. "They wanna play musical brothers. Hell, when we go out, we ain't ever sure which one we'll end up with that night." They high-fived again.

Kane shifted in his seat. He remembered those days. Mostly. Quite a few days, even a few months were a blur, but he'd been in plenty of threesomes with Colt and their woman of the night. Funny thing was, he couldn't recall the faces of the female players.

But he could recount every freckle on Ginger's skin.

What did that say about him?

You're pussy-whipped, boy. Big time.

"How about you, Bennett?" Chase asked.

"I've got a hook up whenever I want it." He shrugged. "And gentlemen don't kiss and tell."

"Since when are the McKays considered gentlemen?" Dalton volleyed back.

Laughter.

Kane expected the question to be directed at him next, because none of his cousins had uttered a peep about Ginger showing up on his doorstep two weeks ago. And it'd been apparent the only briefs he and the fiery redhead had intended to discuss were the ones on his body.

Brandt's phone rang.

Tell and Dalton exchanged a look before Brandt picked up.

"Jessie? Why're you—" He stood abruptly. "No. It's okay. I can be there in twenty-five minutes. Come on, Jess, calm down. I'm on my way." Brandt clicked his phone shut. "Sorry guys, I've gotta go."

"What's goin' on this time?" Dalton asked. "Is her kitty-cat stuck in a tree?"

"And big, brave, Brandt is the only one who can rescue her poor little pussy?"

Kane sucked in a breath. Talk about harsh.

Brandt stiffened. "Fuck off, both of you. Jessie had a pipe freeze in her trailer."

"So have her call a plumber," Tell said.

"Tomorrow," Dalton added.

"Why you guys bein' such a dicks about me wantin' to help her?" Brandt demanded.

Tell leaned back and crossed his arms over his chest. "Because she's always needin' your help, bro. And every time she calls, you drop whatever you're doin' and go to her."

"Run to her is more like it," Dalton corrected.

"Do you need me to remind you that dad kicked her off the place she shared with Luke? Left her damn near destitute?"

"No. It's the reason we all took a stand against Dad." Tell

spit tobacco juice into an empty beer can. "Look, we get that you have feelings for her, Brandt. And without bein' an ass, she ain't reciprocating those feelings or else you'd be together."

"Luke's been dead a little over a year," Brandt snapped. "She ain't hardly had time to get used to bein' a wife and then she was a widow. So yeah, maybe I feel guilty for what Dad done. Hell, I feel guilty for what Luke done to her. What am I supposed to do?"

"Say no," Dalton said quietly.

Brandt whirled on him. "What the fuck did you say?"

"You heard me. Say no."

"She's usin' you. Knowin' Jessie, she ain't even aware she's doin' it."

Tell nodded and Dalton kept talking. "In the year before Luke died, she'd started callin' you when she couldn't rely on Luke to get anything done. Don't deny it."

Kane's gut twisted. Brandt carrying a torch for Jessie would only end badly. But he admired Brandt's brothers for addressing something that'd been building for a long time.

"We all care about Jessie. But there comes a point where you've gotta man up."

Brandt sagged against the wall as he pulled on his boots in angry, jerking movements. "Meanin' what?"

"Let her know you don't wanna be her handyman. If she ain't interested in bein' with you, walk away." Tell's voice dropped. "Me'n Dalton see how it's rippin' you up. Seein' her everyday... We're all still hurtin' about Luke. Seein' her makes it worse."

"For some of us more than others." Brandt stomped his feet into his boots and clapped his hat on his head.

"What the fuck's that supposed to mean?" Dalton demanded.

"Grieving over Luke hasn't stopped you and Tell from getting all the pussy you possibly can every goddamn weekend, has it?"

Tell and Dalton stood simultaneously.

"Just cause you can't get the pussy you want—Jessie's—don't mean you can take it out on us," Dalton said hotly.

"There are plenty of women around here who'd take you on if you'd take the fuckin' blinders off," Tell said.

"Like the skanky bar rats you two are screwing on a regular basis?" Brandt shot back. "No thanks."

"Fine. Jack off all alone in your trailer until your goddamn hand falls off, thinking about your precious Jessie. But I can guaran-damn-tee she ain't sitting around home, thinking about you," Dalton sneered.

Kane intervened. "Enough. Everybody sit down and calm down."

"Shut up, Kane. This don't concern you," Tell said.

"The fuck it don't. I won't sit here and watch brothers cut each other down to the bone just because you can. Just because you're all hurtin'. Jesus. I can't imagine what it'd be like to lose Kade." He gestured to Bennett and Chase. "I'd bet they feel the same way about Quinn. For Christsake, our fathers can still turn on one another in a heartbeat. Don't make their mistakes. Don't do something or say something you can't undo."

Silence.

Dalton spoke first. "Will you at least help us talk some sense into him? Bein' at Jessie's beck and call ain't good for either of them. Jessie needs to learn to do things herself."

Kane looked at Brandt, slumped against the door. "Come clean, cuz. Do they have a reason to be concerned about this?"

"Do we have a reason to be concerned about you and Colt takin' cheap shots at each other every chance you get? Jesus. What's goin' on with you two?"

I don't know. They'd never gone this long without trying to patch up their differences. Kane pointed at Brandt. "This ain't about me. So I'll ask you again. Do your brothers have a reason to be concerned?"

Brandt didn't answer immediately. Finally, he said, "I don't know how to say no to her. The hell of it is, I don't want to say no to her. I wanna be there for her because Luke never was. I fuckin' hate that she only sees me as the guy who'll change her battery, or help her haul feed, or fix her goddamn pipes. I shouldn't care about her so damn much. She's my brother's wife."

No one corrected him that she was now Luke's widow.

"Your brothers are right," Bennett said. "You have to find out how Jessie feels. Maybe part of the reason she's callin' you all the time is because she wants you. Havin' you do 'man stuff' for her is the only way she can get you to come over."

"You really think so?" Brandt asked.

Heads nodded. None of them really believed it, but they were too conscious of Brandt's difficult position to point it out.

"Look, sorry I was a dick. I appreciate your concern and I'll think over what you said." He gave his brothers an apologetic look. "All of you."

Then he was gone.

Beer was consumed in the quiet. Kane changed out all the poker chips on the table for real money, just to have something to do.

"Well, that was fun...*not*," Tell said.

"Good strategy, bringing it up in front of witnesses when we weren't out feedin' cattle or something," Dalton said to Tell. "He'da put us both on the ground and beat the livin' shit outta us."

Chase looked back and forth between them. "Seriously?"

"Uncle Carson's kids ain't the only ones to settle sibling matters with their fists." Tell drained his beer. "Christ. Brandt and Luke used to get into a knock-down, drag-out fistfight at least once a month. Me'n Dalton let them have at and stayed on the sidelines. It never solved a damn thing anyway."

Yeah, Kane understood that reaction but it'd never seemed to matter to him or Colt. They tended to let fists fly first and then worry about the talking bullshit afterward.

"Were their fights about ranch business?"

"Sometimes. But mostly, in the last year, they were about Jessie."

"I tell you what. I ain't ever gonna be at the beck and call of any woman."

"Amen, brother." Dalton and Tell high-fived. As did Bennett and Chase.

Fools. He'd love to be at Ginger's beck and call. He'd just be goddamn happy if she called him at all. It'd been two days since he'd heard from her.

Dalton stood. "I ain't really in the mood to play poker anymore."

Tell followed his lead. "Me neither. Thanks, cuz. Keep the beer cold for next time, huh?"

"You got it."

Chase and Bennett were also donning their winter clothing.

"That was a bit of a buzzkill," Bennett said.

"Chase, you gonna be around in two weeks?"

He shook his head. "Hitting the event in Memphis."

"Good luck."

"Thanks."

After he picked up trash and shoved the remaining beer in the fridge, he plopped on the couch. Too early to hit the hay. He snagged the remote and started flipping through channels. About ten minutes into mindless surfing, his cell phone trilled. He looked at the caller ID. It read: private caller.

Ginger.

Kane answered on the fifth ring. "Hello?" His smile dried. "No, it's okay. I told you to call me. I'll be right over."

By the time Brandt reached Jessie's trailer on the outskirts of Moorcroft, he'd lost the edge of rage his clueless brothers' comments had invoked.

Few people knew about his temper. Brandt took great pains to keep it hidden, as it was an embarrassing trait he'd inherited from his father. He scowled. He'd rather have male pattern baldness than sudden bouts of fury with no outlet besides taking it out on the people he cared about.

He sat in his truck and counted to one hundred before he got out.

Jessie answered the door in pajamas. Not sexy ones. Flannel. No lace. No frills. Which described Jessie to a "T". She still looked damn sexy. It made Brandt feel like a fucking pervert to wonder if Jessie had worn skimpy lingerie in the two years she'd been Luke's wife.

"Brandt. Thank God you're here." She stepped aside and waited for him to remove his outerwear and boots before heading down the hallway. "It's in the bathroom. I turn on the taps for the shower and nothing happens."

"How long has it been like this?"

"It worked fine when I showered yesterday."

"Got water in the kitchen?"

"I did for a while, but now it's tapered off to nothing."

Brandt scratched his chin. "To be honest, it sounds like a

major problem. If the entire system is frozen, you'll have to crawl under the trailer and see what section froze up and try to thaw it with a torch. Chances are good if it's broken and leakin', it's caused more freeze ups down the line."

"Oh." Her pretty face fell and she absentmindedly batted a stray strawberry-blonde hair from her face. "Would it help if I held the flashlight when we crawled under there?"

Jessie just assumed he'd crawl under her trailer? At ten o'clock at night? With the temp stuck at three degrees?

Not likely. Not even for her.

She's using you. She's using your guilt about Luke.

"Whatever's wrong is gonna have to wait until mornin' and you can get a plumber or another qualified professional out here to take a look."

"I assumed you could fix it."

"I can't fix everything, Jess." Brandt sidestepped her and returned to the living room.

He paced in front of the pictures—dozens of them, all of Jessie and Luke. The room wasn't a shrine, but as far as he could tell, it was awful damn close. Thing was, he didn't blame her. He dropped onto the couch, too keyed up to relax into the puffy cushions.

"Would you like a beer?" she offered.

"Soda, if you've got one, bein's I have to drive back."

Jessie handed him a Diet Coke.

It didn't help matters that she sat close enough to him he could reach out and touch her. He cleared his throat. "So, you heard anything from your dad lately?"

She frowned. "He called me from some podunk rodeo in Oklahoma. We didn't talk long. Why?"

"Just curious. Chase is back for a spell and it reminded me that your dad is still traveling the circuit."

"Chase does a lot better as a professional rodeo cowboy after just a few years than my dad has in his entire rodeo career."

Brandt sipped his soda. "How's your mom?"

"Good, I guess. She's working at a coffee shop in Riverton."

"Pretty place, Riverton." *Lame, Brandt.*

"She invited me to visit."

"You should go." Pause. "So, you guys busy at Sky Blue?

Or is January as slow there as it is everywhere else?"

The space between her eyebrows puckered with confusion. "What's up with all the questions, Brandt?"

He bristled. "What? I can't ask you about your family? Or your job?"

"It's not that... it's just—"

"You prefer to keep the conversation focused on my dead brother? Or whatever chore or 'favor' you require of me?"

Her face turned as red as a radish and Brandt felt like a total heel. But his brothers had been right about one thing: it was time to fish or cut bait where Jessie was concerned.

"If you hate helping me out so much then why are you here?"

Brandt locked his gaze to hers. "You know why I'm here."

Jessie blushed even more furiously. She started to get up but Brandt clamped his hand around her thigh, keeping her in place.

"Are you drunk?" she demanded.

"No. Are you blind?" he countered.

"Wh-what?"

"Why do you think I run right over here every damn time you call me? Because I love fixin' wiring or haulin' shit around in my truck? No. I come here to see you. And the only time I can get your attention is when I'm helpin' you."

"Brandt—"

"We can talk about this later. At my place."

"But—"

"No buts. You're out of water. I want you to come home with me tonight."

Awareness of the strings to his offer flashed in her eyes. The color drained from her face. "Why are you doing this?"

"Because it's past time, Jessie." He brought her hand to his lips. "I care about you."

"That's what you came all the way out here to tell me?"

"No, I cut short my poker game because you called me and begged me to come. I had time to think on the way over. Time to get up my courage to ask about you and me...if there *is* a you and me. Or even a chance for a you and me in the near future."

Her eyes fairly shimmered with tears. "You thought that you and I..." She swallowed hard. "Brandt, I think of you as my brother."

Holy fuck that stung.

"I couldn't imagine us being..."

Jesus, Jessie, just say the fucking word.

But she didn't.

Brandt snapped, "You can't imagine us bein' lovers?"

She shook her head. Vehemently.

Direct hit. She could imagine him crawling under her goddamn trailer house, but couldn't fathom him crawling into her bed?

Grief, so raw and debilitating, nearly doubled him over.

Enough.

After what seemed an eternity—but was probably only a minute—Brandt managed to stand. He didn't say a word to her as he slipped on his boots and outerwear.

"I'm sorry," Jessie blurted. "I just don't want to give you false hopes."

Too late.

"It's not you, it's—"

He whirled on her. "If you say it's not you, it's me, I swear to fuckin' God I'll punch a hole in this cheap-ass paneling."

Jessie was taken aback by his violent outburst. "I wasn't gonna say me. I was gonna say...it's Luke."

"He's dead." And again, Brandt felt like a fucking heel for making her flinch.

"I know. But even after more than a year, neither one of us has really let him go, have we?"

Brandt froze.

"You're upset, I understand. I've spent the last year and a half upset."

"Jessie, I'm—"

"Sorry? Yeah, me too. Go home, forget about this, and we'll talk later, okay?"

He wanted to tell her it was all or nothing. He couldn't be just friends and her errand boy anymore.

The words stuck in his throat.

"Drive safe, Brandt. I'll call you."

And Brandt knew she would. Probably tomorrow.

But he also knew the next time Jessie's number flashed on his phone, he wouldn't pick up.

Chapter Fourteen

Kane made it to Ginger's house in record time. Hayden stood at the door waiting for him, his face pale.

"She's awful sick and I thought she'd get mad if I called 911."

"Where's your grandpa?"

"He's having one of his away weekends..." The boy's voice broke and his chin trembled.

"Hayden. It's okay. You did the right thing callin' me." Kane shed his winter clothing. "How long's she been sick?"

"Since she came home from work yesterday. She got up when the senior bus picked Grandpa up this morning. And after he left, Mommy went back to bed."

Hayden had been fending for himself since this morning? "What've you been doin' all day?"

Guilt colored his cheeks. "Playing Xbox."

At least the kid didn't lie. "Tell you what. How about if you let me check on your mama and then we'll figure out what to do."

"Okay." But instead of staying in the living room, Hayden clutched Kane's hand and followed him down the hallway to Ginger's bedroom.

Kane didn't bother knocking. Ginger was sprawled in the middle of the bed in a skimpy nightgown, but he didn't allow his gaze to linger on her generous, nearly naked attributes. The tangled covers were an indication she hadn't been resting peacefully. He glanced at the window. She had to be feverish to crack the window open when it was nine degrees outside.

"Is she gonna be okay?"

"If she needs to go to the hospital I'll take her myself. We'll both take her."

Hayden leaned against him, pressing his face into Kane's rib cage.

Poor kid. Kane gave him a one-armed hug and moved to sit on the bed. He placed his hand on Ginger's forehead. Damn, she was burning up. "Do you know where your mama keeps the thermometer?"

"Uh-huh. Want me to get it?"

"Please." Kane watched the uneven rise and fall of Ginger's chest. Choppy breathing. Flushed face. Sweat soaking her skin. He swiped away a few stray tendrils stuck to her damp neck. "Ah sugar, what am I gonna do with you? You still won't ask for help when you need it." He ran the backs of his knuckles down her cheek and murmured, "I'm stickin' around to take care of you, whether you like it or not."

Hayden returned and handed him the thermometer.

Kane hadn't a clue how to use it. "How does this thing work?"

"You hafta put it in her ear. Probably she should be awake." Hayden stood in front of Kane and shook Ginger's shoulder. "Mommy?"

No response.

Hayden whispered, "I couldn't wake her up before, either."

It pained him to do it, but Kane pinched the underside of her arm.

"Ouch. Stop." She mumbled, "Leave me alone," and attempted to turn away.

"Mommy?"

She rolled flat, blindly reaching for Hayden's hand. "I'm here. Just give me a sec."

"We need to take your temperature."

Her eyes opened. She blinked at Kane as if he was a hallucination. "Kane?"

"Yep. Let's get you upright." He supported her with a hand on her back. "Hold still." He pointed at the thermometer. "Why don't you do it since you know how it works."

Hayden inserted the plastic tip into Ginger's ear. "Is it in?"

Ginger adjusted his hold on it. "Okay. Now it's in."

Click. Pause. Then a drawn-out beep.

Hayden studied the digital read out. "It says 102."

"I'm so hot. And I can't keep my eyes open."

"Have you taken anything to drop your fever?"

She shook her head. "Just antibiotics. I get these nasty sinus infections and sometimes I get a fever and sometimes I don't. This time I did."

"You want aspirin or Tylenol?"

"Tylenol. It's in the middle drawer in my bathroom vanity."

"I'll get you a glass of water," Hayden said and took off.

Kane shook out two pills and handed them over when Hayden returned with the water. "Bottoms up."

After Ginger drained the water glass, she rolled back down on the mattress. Her eyes were still cloudy with fever as her gaze flicked between Kane and her son. "How long have you been here?"

"About ten minutes. Hayden called me because he was worried about you."

"What time is it?"

"Almost eleven."

She squinted at the window. "Eleven...at night?"

"Uh-huh."

Shock flashed across her face. She looked at Hayden. Her eyes glazed with tears. "Oh, baby. I'm sorry you've been alone..."

"I'm okay. But when I couldn't wake you I called Buck."

"And I am mighty glad you did, sport. Why don't you head to the kitchen and figure out what you wanna eat? I'll be there in a sec."

Hayden laid his head on his mother's chest. "We'll take care of you, Mommy. Just like me'n Buck did last time."

"Thanks."

Ginger broke down the second Hayden fled the room. "I am the most horrible mother on the planet." Tears streamed down her face. "Leaving an eight-year-old boy to fend for himself while I was sacked out in my room? What if he'd gotten hurt? What if he'd locked himself outside? What if—"

"Stop. C'mere." Kane gathered her in his arms. "He's fine. He's a smart boy."

"Oh God, Kane, don't be nice to me. I don't deserve it." She muffled her cries against his chest and he felt the heat of her feverish skin through his shirt.

"Ginger, sugar, cut yourself some slack. You can't help bein' sick."

"But I'm never sick. And even if I am, I can still take care of my kid."

"This might be what you lawyers call 'extenuating circumstances', doncha think?"

"That's not a good excuse for neglecting my child."

Kane rested his chin on top of her head. "Nothin' I say will ease your guilt?"

"N-no," she stuttered.

"How about the fact Hayden played Xbox all day while you were conked out?"

She made a sobbing laugh sound. "Really?"

"Yep. Probably was a good thing he let you sleep because you must've needed it. But don't you dare rat me out."

"I won't." She tipped her head back and looked at him. "Thank you for coming over."

"Anytime." He smoothed the tiny wild curls springing up from her hairline. "You hungry? I can fix you something while I'm makin' Hayden a snack."

"No, thanks."

Ginger gave him such a somber look his heart sank. Was she throwing him out, now that she was awake?

"What?" he said, a little testily.

"Are you tired of coming to my rescue?"

Never. Kane smooched both her cheeks. "Nope. I like playin' the part of the brave knight who saves the beautiful damsel in distress. Besides, lookin' after you and Hayden ain't exactly a chore, Ginger. I like doin' it. A lot."

"Why?"

"Honestly? My whole life Kade's been seen as the responsible one. The stand-up guy. And I've been seen as the good-time guy. No responsibilities beyond ranch work. People around here assume I prefer bein' a bachelor and tryin' to score with every hot chick...rather than look harder to see the real truth."

"What's the real truth, Kane?"

"I want the life everyone thinks I'm tryin' so hard to avoid. It don't matter how much I've changed... they see me as they want." Kane traced the indent in her chin. "It means a lot that you see me differently. I know you want my help even when it nearly kills you to ask for it when you don't think you need it. I like that you let me take care of you. Even when it's hard as the dickens to admit you *like* me takin' care of you. You trust me with your son. You trust me on a level no one ever has, Red."

"You've never given me a reason not to trust you."

"Good. I hope that don't ever change." He resettled her on the pillow. "Need anything before I continue my knightly duties?"

She shook her head and closed her eyes.

Would Ginger remember that he'd basically poured his heart out? He sure hoped so.

In the kitchen, Hayden sat at the counter eating a bowl of Oreos cereal. Kane frowned. "I thought I was fixin' you something to eat."

Hayden shrugged. "I like cereal."

"What have you eaten today?"

"Cereal."

Kane rolled his eyes. "Fine. But tomorrow, you're eatin' real food. No cereal."

"Not even for breakfast?"

"Nope."

"Aw, man." Hayden looked up at him and shoved his glasses back in place on his nose. "Are you staying over?"

"I think it'd probably be best, don't you? In case you or your mama needs something during the night?"

Hayden nodded. "Where are you sleeping? Cause I've got Lego junk on the bottom bunk."

"I'll crash on the couch."

"Or you could stay in my mom's room. I bet she wouldn't mind. I wouldn't mind either."

Nice, the other male in Ginger's life gave him permission to share her bed. He fought a smile. "We'll see."

When Hayden started to yawn, Kane let him check on his mother before he started his bedtime rituals. Then Kane tucked him in the upper bunk.

Kane cleaned up Hayden's mess in the living room and the kitchen. He locked the doors and debated on switching on the TV, but the chance to watch Ginger while she slept had a stronger pull than mindlessly flipping through channels.

In her bedroom he stripped down to his T-shirt and boxers. She didn't move when he crawled onto her bed. He straightened out the quilt and sheet that'd twisted into a ball because Ginger had kicked them off in her feverish state. He left her half of the covers in the middle of the bed and tucked the other half around himself.

As many times as Kane imagined spending the night—the whole night—in her bed, he hated she was sick and hurting. He reached for her hand, wanting to offer her comfort, wanting to assure her that he was right beside her if she needed him. He strummed his thumb across her knuckles, content just to touch her.

She emitted a satisfied-sounding sigh, threading her fingers though his.

A few hours later, the bed started to shake, instantly putting Kane on alert. He touched her arm to wake her. "Ginger? You all right?"

"No. I'm c-cold. Like I have ice in my veins c-cold."

"Your fever must've broken."

"Great." Her body shook.

"C'mere. I'll warm you."

She scooted beneath the pile of covers, pressing her cheek into his chest, curling into him—nearly on top of him. Her skin had gone from fiery to clammy. He pulled her more tightly against his body, trying to stop the worst of the tremors.

"You're as toasty as a furnace," she murmured.

"Just hot-blooded, I guess."

"In many ways."

He smiled, stroking her back.

"I'm glad you're here."

"Me too."

"I'm really glad you don't mind taking care of me, Kane. I'm glad you don't think that makes me weak, or clingy or needy."

"Red, you are the strongest woman I know."

Kane thought she'd fallen asleep, but she spoke again very softly. "Do you know I haven't slept in the same bed, all night, with a man...since I was about twenty-four?"

"Can't say as I'm unhappy to hear that."

She rubbed her face on his pec. "You've pretty much ruined me for any other man."

"How's that?"

No response.

"Ginger?"

She'd fallen asleep.

When Ginger woke up alone, she assumed she'd dreamt of Kane cuddled up to her all night. He'd been so warm and solid. Sweet. Comforting. Saying such loving things. Showing his vulnerable side while offering reassurance he didn't see her as weak.

Had to've been a dream.

She'd scooted up to rest against the headboard when Hayden tiptoed in. "Mom! I came to see if you were still sleeping."

"I'm awake now. Has Grandpa fixed you breakfast?"

Hayden frowned at her. "Mom. What are you talking about? Grandpa's in Deadwood, remember?"

But...if that was the case, who'd been watching Hayden?

Kane sauntered in and set his hands on Hayden's shoulders. "Mornin', Red. How're you feelin'?"

Like a total idiot. Like I lost an entire day in a fever-fueled daze. "So it wasn't a dream," she muttered.

Kane frowned. "Excuse me?"

"Never mind. I feel like I've got cement in my sinuses. My body aches. And I need a shower."

"Anything I can do?" A tiny gleam shone in Kane's eye. He was probably recalling how thoroughly he'd washed her back, her front and everything in between the last time he'd "helped" her shower.

"No. Thanks. I can handle it."

"When you're all scrubbed clean, we'll be in the living room."

She stayed in the shower until the water ran cold. The steam helped her sinuses. With her hair combed, her teeth brushed and a layer of her favorite scented lotion applied, Ginger almost felt human. She debated on wearing jeans, but chose comfy, fuzzy sweats instead.

Maybe she'd expected Hayden and Kane to be playing Xbox, but Kane's dark head was bent close to Hayden's blond head as they worked on a jigsaw puzzle spread out on the portable card table.

Kane sensed her immediately, leaving Ginger no time to dissect the warm feeling of rightness as she watched the two of them together. He smiled the charming, sexy grin that made her heart skip with joy.

"You look better."

"Thanks." She crossed the room to look over their shoulders. "How goes the puzzle project?"

"Slow." Hayden sighed. "I don't ever wanna put another one of these together."

"Why not?"

"It's fun for a while, but then it's boring. I'd rather play with my Legos or do something else." Hayden wormed his way out of the chair. "You wanna work on it?"

She opened her mouth to decline, but Kane rather chivalrously pulled the chair back. "Have a seat."

After she sat, she watched her son open the closet door and start dragging out his winter clothes. "You going someplace?"

"Out to shovel."

Her mouth dropped open. "What?"

"Buck said I'm old enough to do chores because you shouldn't have to do everything around here."

Ginger faced Kane. "Is that so?"

He shrugged, but wariness entered his eyes. "You already do plenty. All kids need chores so they learn how to do basic stuff. Shoveling was Hayden's idea of how to pull his weight."

"And then I'm gonna have big muscles just like Buck."

The door slammed behind Hayden. About three seconds later Ginger slapped a hand over her mouth to stifle a giggle. It didn't work. She kept giggling, quietly.

Kane got the strangest look on his face.

"Sorry. It's just..."

"I love to hear you laugh, Red." He angled closer and smothered her next giggle with his mouth. The kiss wasn't a tonsil scratcher, but decisive—as if Kane had made his mind up about something and this kiss sealed the deal.

Ginger smiled at him and set her hand on his cheek. "Thank you for everything."

"Aw, shucks, ma'am, I's just bein' neighborly." He turned

his head until his mouth connected with the corner of her palm. "Now let's see if we can't make some progress on this puzzle."

When Hayden returned inside, his cheeks red, his eyes shining, nearly busting his buttons with pride, Ginger realized Kane understood the things Hayden needed that she didn't, not because she was a bad mother but because she was female.

How much different would her son be if Kane hadn't come into his life via the Little Buddies program?

Maybe you should ask yourself how great it would be if Kane was a permanent part of your life as well as your son's. Not as his Big Buddy but as his father.

"That'd be totally cool, huh Mom?"

Ginger's focus snapped to Hayden. "Excuse me?"

"If Buck and I went out on the ATVs in the snow."

"That would be very cool." She didn't add, *If you wore a helmet and the proper safety gear, and carried a GPS tracker*, knowing he'd accuse her of treating him like a baby, especially in front of his hero.

"You guys ready to eat?" Kane asked.

"I'm starved," Hayden said. "Chores really make you hungry, huh?"

Kane fixed grilled soy cheese sandwiches and sliced up carrots and apples. Ginger stuck with hot tea and soda crackers. The antibiotics upset her stomach and half the time she felt like barfing—not that she'd mention that to either of them. She stayed at the table with them while they ate.

"Surprised me that Dash is off to Deadwood," Kane said.

"The Sundance Senior Group goes twice a year. Deadwood caters to an older crowd so there are plenty of handicapped-accessible rooms. He has a blast. Plus, the coordinators look after him so I don't worry."

"No wonder he whupped my butt at blackjack if he's been playin' the tables in Deadwood," Kane grumbled.

"Last time he was the big winner at the Silverado. He took the entire group out for steak and crab legs."

"Grandpa says that's why they tolerate an old wheelchair cripple like him on those trips, and at the senior center."

"Why's that?"

"Because he has money."

Ginger frowned. She knew her father donated to the

Sundance Senior Group and to the senior center, but surely he didn't believe that was the only reason they kept him around?

"I think your Grandpa was pullin' your leg, sport. I bet they'd let him go along on those trips for free." Kane mock-whispered, "I've heard redheads are really wild. Ol' Dash is probably the crazy man of the bunch and the life of the party, even when now he looks like a mild-mannered white haired old man."

Hayden's eyes widened. "You think so?"

"I know so, but it's probably best if we don't let on we know his secret," Kane said.

Her son grinned.

After lunch, her sinus headache returned. She tried to hide it and act normal, but Kane was very attuned to any change in her.

"Ginger, you're lookin' a little peaked again."

Lie and tell him you're fine.

No. Give him a reason to stay.

"I'm back to feeling like my head wants to explode."

Kane was by her side in an instant, his hand on her forehead. "You feel hot. You need to take some Tylenol and get back in bed right now."

"Should I salute too, Mr. Bossy?"

His eyes narrowed. "I don't care if you flip me off as long as you do it while you're layin' down."

Once she'd taken her pills and crawled in bed, Kane checked on her. Retucking the sheet, setting a glass of water on the nightstand, restocking her Kleenex supply. Touching her. She loved the way he touched her, as if he couldn't get enough of her.

"I'm thinkin' I'll need to stay another night, since you still ain't your chipper, contrary self yet."

"I'd like that."

He feathered his lips across her forehead. "Good. Get some rest, counselor."

Ginger was faking it.

Not orgasms. God knew she didn't ever have to fake those with Kane. She was faking being sick. Although she still didn't

177

feel one hundred percent, she could've sent Kane on his merry way.

But she didn't want him to go. She liked having him here.

After Kane tucked Hayden in, she heard him rattling around in the kitchen. Then the house became quiet. Thirty minutes passed.

What was the man doing?

Don't you mean: what's he doing that's keeping him out of your bed?

Ginger donned a robe and tracked him down. He wasn't watching TV; he was working on the puzzle. His forehead wrinkled in concentration, his fingers sifting through the piles of pieces.

"You determined to finish that tonight?"

Those indigo eyes locked onto hers. "No. Actually, the more I work on this the more I agree with Hayden. It *is* boring."

"Then come to bed."

He lifted an eyebrow.

"I'm not up for anything more than us just sharing sleeping space."

Kane eased his chair back and stood. He took her hand and led the way to her bedroom. Undressed, under the covers, wrapped in each other, any tiredness vanished. They talked for a good hour about everything from Hayden to TV shows and his large family before she yawned.

The next morning, while still in the realm of sleep, Ginger felt Kane's hands on her. Hiking up her nightgown. His lips trailed the curve of her jaw with light, yet insistent kisses. Her back arched of its own accord as his mouth hit all the good spots, spots he'd already memorized.

"Sugar, I'm wantin' you real bad. Let me have you."

"You're asking me? This must be a dream."

He sank his teeth into her earlobe. "You must be feelin' better if you're bein' contrary first thing." His warm breath drifted across her cheek. "Say yes, Ginger."

"Yes, Ginger," she teased.

"There's that smart mouth I've been missin' something fierce." He kissed her, sealing their lips together.

Clothes disappeared. Kane pushed inside her on a long, smooth glide and her body was ready for him.

He made love to her sweetly, passionately. The intimacy of being cocooned in their own little world in the predawn hours amazed her. Body to body, heart to heart, face to face.

When his pace increased, it sent them spiraling into the abyss of pleasure together.

More dreamy kisses. More feather-light caresses. He whispered, "Go back to sleep, sugar. No reason for us both to be up." He headed for the shower as she snuggled into the sheets that smelled like him.

Ginger awoke an hour later. She saw Kane's wristwatch on the nightstand and knew she hadn't been dreaming.

"And then Buck came over. We took care of Mom and we worked on the puzzle and we played some games. And he made me do chores! So when Mom napped we went to Buck's house to check on his dog and other ranch stuff," Hayden added.

Ginger sipped her tea and watched her father's reaction to the news Kane McKay had spent both nights here while he'd been out of town.

Her dad smiled. "Sounds like you had a great time while I was gone."

Hayden nodded but Ginger saw the hint of sadness in her dad's eyes. "For some of us, it wasn't a great time. I still don't feel back to normal."

"You should go in and see Doc instead of self-medicating."

"I will. If I'm not better by the time I'm done with this cycle of antibiotics." She stood and started clearing supper plates. "Who wants a brownie?"

"Me!"

She looked at her dad. "How about you?"

"No thanks."

Odd. Brownies were his favorite dessert.

Hayden stuffed his entire brownie in his mouth and raced away from the table.

"Something on your mind, Dad?"

"Is it me?"

"Is what you?"

"The reason that you don't feel comfortable having McKay in the house overnight while I'm here?"

Her face flamed. "It's not that. Kane wouldn't have been here if I hadn't been sick. *I* didn't call him. Hayden did." She pointed at him. "And you don't get to act pissy about Kane showing up to help out, because if I recall, *you* called him and insisted he check up on me at my office."

He sighed. "True. It's just...it seems..."

"What?"

"Forget it."

"No, Dad, tell me."

His voice dropped. "I don't care that you're sleeping with him, Gigi. You're a grown woman. You've sacrificed your personal life for both Hayden and me the last few years. While I appreciate it, I don't want to be an excuse for you."

Confused, she said, "An excuse for what?"

"For you to act like you don't need the happiness that only comes from an intimate relationship. While your mother and I were mismatched from the start, when I met Linda, it was like the clouds had lifted and I was finally standing in the sun."

Ginger reached for his hand. Her dad rarely talked about the woman he'd married after moving to Wyoming. Ginger had only met Linda once, but she'd made her father happy. She knew it wasn't a coincidence that his arthritis had taken a turn for the worse the year following Linda's death from cancer. That'd also been around the same time Ginger had given birth to Hayden. Her father had reached out to her and she'd grabbed for him with both hands and hadn't looked back. She couldn't imagine her dad not being in her life.

"What I'm saying is I've had my happiness. I'd never stand in the way of yours."

He pushed away from the table and left her staring after him, wondering if that was his stamp of approval as far as Kane McKay went.

Chapter Fifteen

An unexpected winter storm blew in. Ginger paced, watching the snow pile up outside her office window. At one-thirty she sent Rissa home before the Wyoming Highway Patrol closed the roads. At three she called the Sundance retirement home, making sure they had room to keep her dad overnight. The change in accommodations didn't bother him; he'd dealt with unpredictable Wyoming weather much longer than she had.

Hayden's school field trip to Casper caused her the most concern. The potential for fifty kids and four teachers stranded in an old school bus out in the middle of the prairie? Not good.

When she heard on the radio that I-25 had been closed from Casper to Wheatland, she knew Hayden wouldn't be coming home, which alleviated her safety worries. She just hoped he wouldn't eat dairy, or shellfish, or strawberries. She hoped he wouldn't run around like a madman and need to use his inhaler. If she could just talk to him, tell him she loved him, tell him to be careful, maybe she could stop wearing a hole in the carpet in her office.

At four o'clock the principal called and assured her the kids were fine, tucked away in a hotel in Casper. Here she was freaking out and Hayden was probably having the time of his life, hanging out with his buddies with no parents around.

Still, she worried because Kane hadn't texted her back. So much of his time was spent out in the elements, in places where no one could get in touch with him. Hopefully he was hunkered down in his trailer with his dog, riding the storm out.

Ginger had no choice but to outwait the blizzard in her office. She checked the food situation. Four packages of instant oatmeal, six packages of Cup o' Noodles, half a package of Fig Newtons, two protein bars and a Snickers. She ripped open the candy bar wrapper. Her first course would be chocolate.

And truthfully, it wouldn't be bad being snowed in. She had a couch and a blanket. She could work as late as she wanted without guilt about neglecting her family. If she got bored, she could watch TV shows on Hulu. If she got lonely...no cure for that. She spent so little time by herself in recent years she really didn't know what to do.

She'd just tossed the empty Snickers wrapper when a loud bang sounded at the front of the building. The strong gusts had probably blown the door open. She left her office and started down the stairs only to see a large hooded figure lurking in the foyer. She screamed.

The head whipped around and the hood fell back. Kane snapped, "Jesus, Ginger. You scared the hell out of me."

"*You?* What about me? I'm here alone and then I see the abominable snowman lurking in my foyer!" His sheepskin coat was coated with snow, as were the coveralls and snow boots.

"Yeah, well, the wind's whistlin' a little too loud for me to knock politely."

"What are you doing here? The roads are terrible, or closed, according to the radio."

"I had to get a couple of portable propane tanks in case something freezes. I saw your car and wondered what the devil you're still doin' here."

"The Mercedes isn't exactly an all-terrain vehicle. Plus I was waiting to hear about Hayden's class, and I had to verify the folks at the retirement home are keeping dad tonight."

"So once again you worried about everybody except yourself."

She folded her arms over her chest. "I'm safer here than trying to get home. I decided to stay put."

"Smart cookie. But I have a better idea." He gave her the hot grin that could've melted polar ice caps. "Why don't you come home with me?"

"You're going back out in this?"

"No choice. This close to calving I've gotta check cattle in the mornin', even if it's still blizzarding. So what's it gonna be, Red?"

"But Hayden—"

"Is in Casper. Cam told me about Anton, Kyler and Hayden getting snowed in on the school field trip. They won't be back until tomorrow at the earliest, and if Hayden needs to get in touch with you, he'll call your cell anyway, right?"

He had a point.

"You and me, spendin' the whole night together. Alone. You gotta admit this chance ain't gonna come along very often."

Wow. She hadn't considered that. Cuddled up to Kane all night, instead of camping out on the lumpy office couch? "Okay. Let me get my stuff."

"Quickly. And bundle up. I'll wait here so I ain't draggin' snow all over the carpet."

Ginger shut down her computer. She shoved her cell phone and the charger in her purse and switched out her low-heeled pumps for snow boots. Coat on, hat on, scarf on, gloves on, she turned off the lights, grabbed her bag and returned to the foyer. "Ready."

His critical gaze stopped at her knee length skirt. "Don't you have pants?"

"No. This is it."

"Let's hope we ain't gotta walk anywhere far."

Kane's big truck plowed through the snowdrifts in town. Once they were out of town, visibility was nearly zero and their progress slowed considerably.

The sky remained a pitch-black backdrop as the truck's headlights cut through the swirling flakes, which weren't falling softly—en masse the flakes became a blur of pure white. Wind whipped icy crystals with enough gale force they created a pinging sound against the windshield. The truck bumped over piles of snow blocking the road. A couple of times she caught sight of drifts several feet high before the truck broke them into a powdery spray that floated away on the wind.

Ginger stayed quiet throughout the drive. She had no idea where they were or how far they'd gone. Nearly forty-five minutes had passed since they'd left Sundance.

The truck slowed. Stopped. Kane leaned forward and squinted. "Can you see any light out there?"

"Like a yard light?"

"Exactly."

"Maybe if you cut the headlights."

Kane clicked the lights off, even the interior lights.

Talk about dark and spooky. Ginger focused on the blackness out her window. A snow squall faded and she caught a fleeting glimpse of light. "There. Straight ahead."

"You sure?"

No. "Yes, I'm sure."

"Hope you're right, Red. If I run over a fence, you'll be out here fixin' fence with me early summer."

"I know how to wield a pair of wire cutters, so bring it, cowboy."

Kane gunned the truck. For a second it felt as if they were airborne. They landed hard and Ginger held onto the support strap hanging from the top of the doorframe.

"Sorry." Snow covered the windshield as they annihilated another drift. The wipers whisked away the remnants in a rapid *slap slap slap* and they skidded to a stop.

"We're here."

Ginger made out the faint orange glow of the porch light. Snow had drifted in front of the screen door up to the door handle.

"Looks like I'm gonna hafta shovel again before we can get inside. Sit tight. No reason for you to be out in this." Then he bailed from the truck.

She watched him shoveling snow until he'd created a pile as high as the deck rails beside him. Despite the freezing-ass weather, something warm moved through her. Clearing a path for her through the snow was akin to him throwing his coat over a mud puddle. But Kane had proved himself thoughtful and chivalrous to the core numerous times. For the first time they'd be alone tonight—all night—and they could do whatever they liked.

Ginger had a few specific things she'd like to do with him.

Kane returned to the truck, killed the engine and pocketed the keys. "Need help getting out?"

"I'm good." She grabbed her bag and hopped down. The snow reached her knees and completely filled her snow boots. She trudged to the steps and Kane was already there, holding the door open.

She moved aside to give Kane room as they ditched their

winter clothing. He hung both sets up on pegs that resembled fossilized feet. "Interesting pegs. Are those chicken feet?"

"Turkey feet. My buddy Ash, over in Lingle, is a taxidermist and he makes 'em."

She stepped off the small square of linoleum. Her wet nylons clung to her legs. Shep was stretched out on the floor, eyeing them with "you poor suckers" canine smugness.

Even Kane noticed it. "Shep, you better get out there and get your business done before it gets any worse."

Shep scooted behind the chair.

Kane laughed. "Lazy damn dog."

Ginger tossed her bag on the coffee table and looked around. The last time she'd been here, Kane had literally thrown her up against the wall and fucked her. Then she'd left.

The kitchen and living areas were in the front of this trailer. She assumed the bedrooms and bathroom were down the hallway. From where she stood she could see the tidy kitchen and the dining room alcove, which boasted a felt-topped gaming table instead of a traditional dining room set.

A half shelf divided the rooms, but all the spaces screamed bachelor. No knickknacks, no artwork, no colorful rugs or extra throw pillows. The furniture consisted of one long black leather couch, one oversized black reclining chair. A chrome and glass coffee tabled piled with mail. A fifty-two-inch flatscreen TV mounted on the largest wall with AV equipment stacked beneath it.

Ginger glanced at Kane, who watched her taking stock of his place. He'd set his jaw in a hard line as if he expected her to pass judgment.

Silly man.

She closed the distance between them, wrapping her arms around his waist and placing a kiss on his neck. "Thank you for inviting me into your home, Kane."

"It ain't much."

"But it's yours and that's all that matters to me."

Kane kissed the top of her head. "You hungry?"

"Cold. I hope you've got some sweat clothes to lend me because this is all I have."

"Sure. I can hook you up with something." He snagged her hand and towed her down the hallway.

"Wait. I'll need my phone in case Hayden calls." She grabbed her phone from her bag, expecting Kane to protest, but he didn't. Again, she realized she should stop making assumptions about this complex man.

His bedroom was bigger than she imagined, with a king-sized bed covered in a puffy navy blue comforter, and yet another big TV atop a dresser. On the opposite side was a simple desk with a lamp and a laptop.

"So this is your bedroom." *Way to be obvious, Ginger.*

"I hope you weren't expectin' a swingin' bachelor pad. It's just a basic bedroom. Nothin' fancy."

Ginger slid her hands up his chest and trapped his face between her palms, looking him straight in the eye. "Stop. Do you really think I care that you live in a trailer?"

"I don't know. Hell. It's just...not what you're used to."

"What? Clean and quiet?"

He laughed softly.

"I am unbelievably happy to be here with you, so please don't think I'm looking around and finding anything lacking. Because really, when I'm with you? All I see *is* you."

Kane pressed his lips to her forehead. "You undo me sometimes, Red." His lips drifted down her hairline. "I know we just got here, but the truth is, if I see you takin' your clothes off in my bedroom? Well, sugar, I'm gonna want you to leave 'em off for a bit."

"Is that so? But won't I be cold if I'm naked?"

"I'll keep you warm." Kane's mouth grazed the top of her ear. "Very warm. Hot, even." Moist lips meandered down to the spot on her neck below her ear. The spot that caused her knees to buckle and made her panties damp. "I'm dyin' to touch you."

"What a coincidence. I'm dying to have you touch me."

Kane ate at her mouth as he unbuttoned her white blouse. His rough hands skated over her arms as her shirt slid to the floor.

Drugged by his kisses, Ginger let her head fall back as Kane removed her bra and unfastened her skirt. He snapped the waistband of her pantyhose. "Take these off while I get nekkid."

"Just as long as you get nekkid fast."

"That ain't gonna be a problem."

Ginger shimmied her pantyhose off and pulled back the covers on his bed. She sighed deeply when her skin touched the flannel sheets.

"I like the sound of that sigh."

"I like your flannel sheets."

Kane crawled across the bed toward her. "I really like the look of you in my bed on my flannel sheets."

"You don't have to use that sweet-talk when I'm a sure thing. Crawl under here with me. It's toasty."

"Aren't you the bossy one? In my bed, no less."

She blushed. "Am I in trouble?"

"I knew you were trouble the second I set eyes on you." He nuzzled her cheek. "Stretch your arms above your head."

Ginger pushed the pillows aside and placed her palms flat against the headboard. "Like that?"

"Perfect." He trailed kisses down the center of her torso, stopping briefly to suckle her left nipple, then her right. His tongue dipped into her belly button and followed in a straight line over her mound. When his tongue probed her folds, she spread her legs and arched into him. His fingers squeezed her inner thighs. Ginger realized that was one of her favorite things about oral sex with Kane—the feel of him holding her in place. Holding her steady to receive the pleasure he gave her. His tongue flicked her clit, teasingly, precisely, but always with unbridled passion.

Kane took his time tasting her, not in a teasing manner; he just slowly, thoroughly feasted on her pussy. When the telltale contractions started, Kane fastened his mouth to her clit, bringing her to climax with soft, gentle nibbles interspersed with butterfly licks as she came with a soft wail.

Right after the last pulse, Kane's cock was driving inside her still-throbbing tissues, immediately bringing her to the verge again. He buried his mouth in her throat, thrusting into her, making this bonus orgasm last.

Soon as her head stopped spinning, she opened her eyes and smiled at him. "Wow."

"The wow factor is always a good sign." Kane slid his hands up her arms and threaded their fingers together. "Look at me while I'm lovin' on you, sugar. See exactly what you do to me."

Something big shifted between them in that small moment.

Ginger molded her mouth to his, desperate to taste his passion as well as feel it. The kiss never veered out of control. It stayed as easy and steady as the way he made love to her.

When his thrusts became faster and his hands squeezed hers, she wrapped her legs around his waist and bowed into him.

Kane threw back his head and groaned, eyes closed, neck taut, mouth slack, absolutely beautiful in the moment that he let everything go.

He blinked at her, as if clearing the fog away, and smiled an endearingly shy and somewhat boyish smile.

That's when she knew what the elusive something was: love.

She loved him. Holy crap. She was in love with him.

"Why so serious?" he murmured.

Instead of blurting out, *Because I just realized I love you and I've never been in love and it's scaring the living shit out of me*, Ginger hedged. "I seriously like looking at you. You are one hot hunk of cowboy manflesh, Kane McKay."

Kane blushed. "Dammit, Red, knock it off."

"You can't take a compliment any more easily than I can ask for help." She framed his ruggedly handsome face in her hands. "I say, 'you are gorgeous' and you say, 'thank you'—go on let's try it. Kane, you are gorgeous."

"I am *not* gorgeous," he said through clenched teeth.

"Yes, you are. And you are one of those men who looks better as he ages. You are beautiful. Not just here." She stroked his cheekbone with her thumbs. "Inside too."

He kissed her then. With such sweet surrender she felt tears prickling the back of her eyelids. She felt him get hard again. He rocked into her as he kissed her. Their mouths weren't apart for any longer than a second or two, as they remained locked together, lost in each other. The waves of pleasure didn't crash over them, but built slowly, sweetly, until they were swept away.

After lolling in the moment, Kane withdrew and rolled to his back. He kept holding her hand and kissed her knuckles. "So you warmed up?"

"Uh-huh. And sleepy."

"We've got nowhere to be. Go ahead and take a little nap if

you want."

Ginger snuggled into him, resting her head on his chest. "Will you stay with me?"

"Yep."

"Red. Wake up. Hayden's on the phone."

She jackknifed, completely disoriented. "What?"

"Your cell rang and I answered it. Hope you don't mind but I didn't want you to miss the call." He handed her phone over.

"Hello?"

"Mom? Guess what? We're snowed in and the hotel has a pool and an elevator and me'n Anton and Ky are in the same room! And tomorrow morning there's breakfast and this is such a blast!"

She smiled and slid up the headboard. "You're okay? You're not scared of the storm or anything?"

"Mom. I'm not a baby."

"I know. But I was scared when I heard your class was stuck in Casper."

"But it's totally cool. Mrs. Dunnigan let me use her cell phone to call you and I gotta go so Anton can call his mom and dad next." His voice dropped. "Love you, Mommy."

"Love you too," she said to the dial tone.

"So Hayden's all right?"

"He's having the time of his life."

Kane sat on the bed. "Are you all right?"

She liked that he sensed her melancholy. "I guess. I'm not away from him very often. Kind of makes me..." She didn't know what it made her. Not the type of parent who lived vicariously through her kid.

"Makes you an awesome mother. Are you hungry? I heated up some chili."

"Sounds good. But I need clothes."

Kane handed her a pair of black sweat pants, a plaid flannel shirt and a pair of white athletic socks. "Here you go, but there is one condition."

"Which is?"

His fingertip trailed across the tops of her breasts. "No bra while you're wearin' my shirt."

"Why not?"

"I like the idea of bein' able to pop these buttons anytime I want and putting my hands on them. Or my mouth on them."

"That is a good idea." Ginger dressed and found Kane in the kitchen, talking to his dog. She leaned against the doorway to the living room. A pang of loneliness spiked in her gut. She had two people to come home to every night. Kane had his dog. Was he lonely?

Aren't you sometimes? Even when you're rarely alone?

He turned toward her with a sheepish grin. "And yes, before you ask, Shep does answer me back." He looked at the dog. "Shep. Speak your mind."

Shep barked.

"See?"

Ginger laughed.

After they ate and finished the dishes, Kane gave her a considering look.

"What?"

"Anything in particular you wanna do tonight? We are sort of limited for entertainment options. I doubt the satellite is workin' in this weather, so TV is out."

"Could we just hang out and watch a movie? Make some popcorn?"

Kane frowned. "You sure?"

"Actually, it sounds heavenly. I never get to watch the types of movies I want because Hayden is too young for them and Dad doesn't like anything with explosions, car chases or romance."

"Do I have a selection for you. Action movies are about all I own."

Cuddled up to a sexy, sweet man, sharing a bowl of buttery popcorn, a few intensive make out sessions snuck in between the movie action scenes and Ginger was in heaven.

No, silly, you're in love.

Ginger in his bed was too big a temptation to resist.

Kane woke up in the middle of the night wanting her. As he touched her, she murmured sleepily, clinging to him, letting him know with her body that his attentions were welcome. And in the aftermath of sating his need for her, she curled back into him and fell asleep.

Kane wanted this. Ginger in his arms every night, seeing her beautiful face first thing every morning.

Because he was an early bird, he got up and checked the weather. He'd intended to let her sleep in, but the aroma of coffee brought her into the kitchen.

"Mornin'. How'd you sleep?"

"Like a rock. A warm rock cuddled up to another warm rock. And I had this amazingly vivid dream."

"Was I in it?"

"You were the star, Mr. McKay."

"What a coincidence. I had the same kind of dream. Only in mine, *you* were the star, counselor."

She smiled coyly as he handed her a cup of coffee.

"Damn, woman, you look much better in that flannel shirt than I do."

"Can I keep it?" she cooed.

"Hell no. Every time I wear it from here on out, I'm gonna think of how perfectly the material hugged those tempting tits of yours."

"Flatterer."

Kane grinned.

"Thanks for leaving out the extra toothbrush."

"You're welcome. I need to head out and check cattle."

"When will you be back?"

"Dunno. Depends on if I run into any problems."

"Do you always check cattle by yourself?"

"I do when both my Dad and Kade are snowed in."

Ginger set down her cup. "I'm not comfortable with you going out there alone, Kane. I'll come with you."

He opened his mouth to protest, but really, he'd appreciate her company. Even if she didn't say a single word. "Okay. Let's find you all the gear you'll need to bundle up." He dug through the closet, coming up with an extra pair of coveralls, an extra coat and a pair of hiking boots.

She dressed without complaint until she was covered from head to toe. "I look like Ralphie from *A Christmas Story*."

"Since we'll be on the ATV you'll be grateful for the layers, trust me." Kane crouched down and spoke to Shep. "You wanna come along?"

Shep just gave him a baleful stare.

"Guess not."

It'd quit snowing, but the wind still blew like a bitch. He'd opened the gate before they'd gone in the barn to fetch the ATV.

The path he usually followed to the cattle shelter and stock tank was impossible to see, so he drove along the fence line, keeping an eye on the odometer to gauge how far he'd gone. He knew this ranch like the back of his hand, but blizzards fucked up everything and he could get turned around ass-backward in a helluva hurry if he didn't pay attention.

Kane cranked the wheel to avoid getting stuck in huge drift that resembled a foamy, curling ocean wave. Ginger's arms tightened around his midsection when they caught air.

Then he saw the wooden shelter, which really wasn't any more complex than a snow fence. Except they kept bales of hay stacked on one side just for situations like this. The cattle were milling around, waiting for the food fairy to appear. He shouted over the howling wind. "I've gotta spread out some hay. Sit tight."

"Can't I help?" she shouted back.

"Sure. Come on."

They trudged through the snowdrifts until they were at the backside of the shelter. The structure offered some respite from the wind, but not much. Kane scrambled on top of the haystack and kicked away as much snow as he could. Then he hefted two bales to the ground. He hopped back down and took out a pocketknife. He sliced the twine on the bales and yelled, "Spread it out. Along the length of the shelter."

Without a word, Ginger spread out the hay and didn't panic with the cows started to surround her, looking for food.

Kane knocked down eleven bales. By the time he finished, there were only three bales left to break apart. Since Ginger was doing such a fantastic job, he headed to the stock tank.

Frozen. Dammit. The solar panel was supposed to store enough energy that this didn't happen, and it was the fourth time it'd happened this winter. He dug through the snow until he unearthed the crowbar he'd left for just this purpose. He broke the top layer of ice and yanked the biggest pieces out. Thirsty cows came to drink. While Kane tried to catch his breath, he counted cattle. Seventy-five. Two were missing.

He squinted across the horizon and saw nothing but acres of white. He hoped the cows were hunkered down someplace safe and he wouldn't find their bloated corpses come spring thaw.

Kane turned around and saw Ginger cornered by one of the more curious cows. He jogged back and came up behind it, slapping it hard on the right flank. The old girl's head swung round and she bellered at him. "Don't you be getting sassy with my girl, or I'll turn you into hamburger, you old sow." Then he reached for Ginger's hand and led her out of the tight mass of hungry cattle. "Let's go. We're done."

"Good. I'm freezing."

By the time they returned to the barn, over three hours had passed. And Ginger seemed grumpy. Maybe because the sky looked to be clearing up and their alone time was coming to an abrupt halt?

He'd just have to make the next couple of hours memorable.

First thing Ginger did after peeling off the layers of clothes was check her phone.

"Any news?" Kane asked.

"One message from Hayden's teacher. They're opening I-25 at two this afternoon, so that'll put them back at the school around five."

Kane glanced at the clock. Almost eleven. "That gives us a little time."

"All I want is time to warm up. I don't know if I've ever been this cold."

"Then you'd better strip them clothes off and crawl in bed."

"Kane—"

He was right in her face. "No arguin' with me. Do it. Now."

Ginger's hazel eyes sparked defiance for a second. But she whirled around and stomped to the bedroom. About halfway down the hallway, she tossed out, "This'd better be good, McKay."

Any leniency he might've had vanished with that challenge.

He snatched a bottle of lube and his other supplies from the bathroom. He locked the bedroom door and saw the outline of her body beneath the covers. "Ginger, I'm givin' you a choice. Handcuffs or rope?"

Slowly, the covers peeled back. Her hair appeared first, since it stuck straight up from static electricity. "You're serious."

"Yep. Choose or I will."

Ginger smoothed her hair back and studied him. "Rope."

Kane lifted his hand and let the length of rope dangle from his fingertips. "On your knees, arms above your head, palms on the mattress."

It might've surprised him that she turned over and assumed the position without argument.

He used a slipknot to bind her wrists, a binding that'd be easy to get out of, if she knew the secret. But if she didn't, well, that gave him more time to play.

"You look gorgeous, all stretched out before me."

She didn't respond.

"This is where you say, 'thank you'."

"Thank you."

"See? That wasn't so hard. Now widen your knees. That's good." Kane climbed behind her. He skimmed his hands over her body, starting at the crease where her ass met her thigh, and moving up her back. "You are cold." He levered his fully clothed body over her naked form. He placed a kiss on her nape, loving how quickly goose bumps bloomed across her skin.

"So warm me up." She remained with her forehead to the mattress, almost in a submissive manner.

Kane didn't give her a warning. His open palm connected with the center of her right ass cheek.

She gasped.

He smacked the left cheek.

Another gasp.

Then he went a little wild; the visual of his red handprint on her white skin brought out his primitive side. He peppered her ass with strategically placed swats, some hard, some playful, so Ginger never knew what to expect.

His cock was fully erect and digging into his zipper. Despite being chilled only ten minutes ago, his skin was on fire; he was actually sweating.

Kane smelled her arousal, saw the slightest movement of her ass pushing back, silently asking for more. He obliged her until he couldn't stand it. He had to feel that beautifully heated flesh on his face. He had to taste it.

He shoved back, first running his tongue down the crack of her ass. Then he rubbed his face over her flaming butt cheeks, letting his goatee tickle and tease.

Ginger whimpered. Her hands clenched into fists.

Kane used his tongue to bathe the red hand marks. Lapping. Licking. Leaving openmouthed kisses from the sexy dimples above her ass cheeks to the curve at the bottom. He lost his mind in the feel of her, the scent of her, her willingness to explore his kinky side without hesitation.

He gripped her lower body at the base of her thighs and lifted, using his thumbs to pull apart her cheeks, revealing that pink pucker and the glistening mouth of her sex. Kane plunged his tongue into her cunt and then dragged it up, over the bud of her anus. He flicked the very tip of his tongue over that tiny closed hole, painting it with his saliva. When he stopped, Ginger made a keening wail, sounding mighty displeased he'd halted his attentions. Then he rammed his tongue in deep and repositioned his hand so his middle finger could rapidly flick her clit.

She came with a half gasp, half scream.

After the orgasmic pulses stopped and she slumped forward, Kane released his hold on her, smoothing his hands across her still heated skin. He unbuckled his belt, freed his cock from the confines of his zipper and dropped his jeans and his boxers to his knees. He grabbed the bottle of lube and slicked up his shaft. Then he squirted the gel on his fingers and worked both fingers into her ass, preparing her with decisive strokes.

He leaned across her body, bracing his left hand by her left shoulder. "You okay?"

"Uh-huh," was her muffled response.

"I've decided since you've been so good, that it's time I give back your vibrator."

"Now?"

"Yes, right now." Kane nuzzled the back of her head, breathing in the lavender scent of her shampoo. "My cock pounding into your ass and your vibrator in your cunt. You'll be double teamed, but by one man."

"Oh God."

He didn't need to lube up the vibrator since she was

already wet and loose from her orgasm. He inserted the phallus completely into her pussy and turned it on.

Her body trembled, from her bound arms to her toes curled into the mattress.

Kane prodded her tiny entrance, slipping just the cockhead in past the contracting muscle, which tried to keep out the intrusion. Oh hell, between the tightness of her body, the vibration from her sex toy and his anticipation, this wasn't going to take long. He shoved into her ass until the root of his cock was pressed against her anal opening and his balls slapped against her pussy.

Ginger arched up.

He stopped, despite how fast his heart hammered. His body shook and it didn't have a damn thing to do with the vibrator. "How does that feel?"

"I can't even... It feels full. Really, really full."

Kane withdrew from her back channel, again letting just the tip remain inside her. He snapped his hips, bumping the vibrator into his groin as he plunged in completely. Then he set to fucking her like a man possessed, his fingers digging into the reddened, soft globes of her ass. The visual was hotter than fire, seeing that hole stretching to accommodate his dick, his big hands spreading her wide and holding her in place for his assault.

His sac was already drawn up. Kane craved the rush of sensation as his cock emptied, feeling those close-fitting anal walls clamping down, milking every ounce of seed ˙from his aching balls.

Now, now, now became the rhythm in his head, his blood, his body as he fucked her. He closed his eyes, lost to everything but the overpowering need. When that familiar pulling began at the top of his head, tightening every muscle from his scalp to his Achilles, he groaned. When the first spurt shot out the end of his dick, he gritted out, "Bear down on me, harder. Fucking Christsake that's good. So goddamn..." He reamed her one last time, letting the white noise of pure sexual pleasure in his head take over, if only for a minute.

The buzzing against the underside of his shaft roused him from that happy pecker place. Staying embedded in her ass, he reached down between them and slid the vibrator out of her cunt, rubbing it up over her slit.

"Kane—"

"Come for me, sugar." He nestled the rounded end on her clit and held it there.

Ginger bucked against him, dislodging the vibrator.

"Hold still. Let it happen."

Although she stopped wiggling, her breath remained uneven. Kane wanted to press his mouth between her shoulder blades and taste the perspiration dotting her skin. He wanted to lay his head there and hear her heart beating.

Then she tensed and the throbbing pulses from her orgasm constricted her anal passage around his dick, and he felt every spasm as she came.

Kane eased out and retreated to the bathroom to clean up. He returned, placing the cool cloth over her ravaged tissues and unwound the rope.

Ginger slid forward to rest on her belly and groaned.

Was that a good groan? Or a bad groan?

He reached for her hand, noticing the red rope burns on her wrists. Holy shit. What was she supposed to say when her clients saw those rope marks? "Oh, ignore those. My rough and raunchy secret lover likes to tie me up when he fucks me in the ass."

Maybe you should be more worried about what her son will say when he sees them.

Or her father.

Kane froze. What the fuck was wrong with him? Ginger wasn't some bar wench who was up for anything-goes domination bedroom games. Ginger was a well-respected woman in the community. A mother. A daughter.

A classy broad too good for the likes of you.

No kidding. No wonder she didn't want to go public with their relationship. She probably never would. And once again he was reminded of the chasm between them. How much longer would she be willing to play the dirty-rancher-seduces-the-horny-lawyer bedroom games? Chances were pretty good once she caught sight of the hickeys and rope marks on her body it'd be over.

He lifted her arm, tenderly kissing the red marks. "I got a little rough."

No answer.

Her cell phone rang. Since she didn't look like she had the energy to pick it up—or maybe she was too embarrassed to look at him—Kane handed it to her without a word.

She rolled onto her back. "Hello? Hey, Hayden. Really? I can't wait to hear about your adventure. Tell Ms. Dunnigan I'll come and get you. Okay. Bye." She tossed the phone on the bed. "I need to go to the office right now. I hope the senior bus can deliver Dad home. I really don't want to dig my car *and* our van out of the snowdrifts."

"I can help you do all that. But first..." Kane captured her mouth, intending to give her a possessive kiss, but changed his mind at the last second, trying to keep it relaxed.

Ginger pulled away immediately. "Enough, don't you think?" She rolled off the bed, snagged her clothes and shut the bathroom door with a decisive click.

Yeah. The word *enough* summed up everything he was feeling—and none of it was good.

Chapter Sixteen

Brandt's cell phone buzzed in his front shirt pocket for the fourth time. He ignored it, knowing it was her. Knowing she was having some other crisis and desperately needed his help.

Sad thing was he was so desperate for the sound of his brother's widow's voice he almost answered it.

What if she needs you? What if it's something serious?

He ground his teeth. In all the times she'd called him in the last year, nothing had been earth-shatteringly important.

Every time he and Jessie had connected in the last two weeks, he'd managed to keep the phone call short. He wondered if she'd noticed. Then in the last week he'd stopped answering her calls altogether.

Goddammit, cutting Jessie out of his life hurt like a son of a bitch. He'd realized the night he'd raced to her rescue that she'd never see him as anything but the helpful brother of her dead husband. Hell, she'd even told him she considered him like a brother.

Brandt grunted. His feelings for her were so goddamn far from sisterly it wasn't fucking funny.

"Brandt. Buddy, you're up."

He took the cell phone out of his pocket and set it on the table. He grabbed his cue and lined up his shot, trash talking with Tell, Dalton and Ben as they finished up their weekly pool game. After he scratched on the eight ball, he grudgingly gave both his little brothers ten bucks, and listened to Ben grumble about his shitty pool playing as they returned to the booth.

The waitress swung by just as his cell phone vibrated on the tabletop again. Brandt looked up at her and smiled. She was sort of cute.

That's because she reminds you of Jessie.

He'd been tempted for about two seconds to ask for her number. *Scratch that idea.* "I'll have another Coors."

Dalton plopped down across from him. "Make it three. Nope, better make it four, Tell's gonna stick around for one more."

The phone continued to buzz.

His youngest brother frowned at him. "Ain't you gonna get that?"

"Nah."

"You sure?"

"Yep. It's nothin' important."

"Your phone's been ringing a lot tonight."

"You're right. This'll fix it." Brandt reached over and shut the phone off.

Jessie McKay paced in the kitchen in her tiny rented trailer. "Come on, pick up," she muttered as she switched the position of her cell phone to her other ear. Voice mail clicked on for the fifth time and she snapped the phone shut.

"Dammit, Brandt. Where are you?" She'd had a lousy day and needed someone to vent to. Brandt never minded listening to her complain, but he'd been pretty scarce since the night he'd invited her home with him. She'd chalked up his uncharacteristic moon-eyed behavior to the fact he'd been drinking before he showed up. The poor man was probably embarrassed for making a pass at her.

She took the pot pie out of the microwave and dropped it on the lace placemat on the table. One placemat. On days like today, when it seemed like everything in the world had gone wrong, seeing that lone placemat, when there used to be two, could bring on a fit of tears like nobody's business.

Don't be a crybaby, Jessie.

How many times had she heard that? From her father? From Luke?

Too many to count. But really, who'd know if she sobbed at her dinette table like a lost little girl? She felt like one most days. It wasn't as if she had friends to confide in since moving to Moorcroft. She'd started to make friends with the women she worked with at Sky Blue, but that wasn't a good way to cement a friendship, by whining about how sucky her life was.

Jessie didn't have family to count on either, unless she counted Brandt, but he was Luke's kin, not hers, and then she was back to wondering why he'd started ignoring her calls.

Maybe because you call him all the time.

So? Her surly side countered. *He's my friend. Friends call each other.*

Yeah? How many times has your "friend" called you?

Jessie frowned. Brandt had called her...hadn't he? Curious, she flipped open her phone and checked received calls. Two calls from her boss at Sky Blue. Twenty-seven from Brandt in the last month.

See? He calls me.

All the calls were in response to you calling him first. How many times have you called him?

She scrolled down to the Dialed option. One hundred fifty-two outgoing calls. In the last two months... Holy crap. Only ten of those calls had been to someone other than Brandt McKay.

She'd called him one hundred and forty-two times in the last two months.

Hot mortification rolled through her like acid. My God. Why had she called Brandt that many times?

Because you're lonely. Because you know that Brandt is missing Luke too.

So why was it Luke didn't come up in their conversations very often?

He does. It's one-sided on your part. You insist on extolling Luke's virtues, you talk about how much you miss him and Brandt just lets you ramble.

A little dismayed by that thought, she recalled the last few times she'd seen Brandt.

He'd helped her unload hay.

He'd helped her deal with the dead battery in her truck.

He'd helped her fix the broken door on the barn.

He'd helped her unload more hay.

He'd shown up when she'd had plumbing issues.

Except he'd refused to do anything. And yeah, maybe she'd been a little upset about it at the time, his reluctance to fix the problem for her lickety split. But when she'd thought it through the next day, she understood Brandt wasn't a miracle worker with everything.

That was the first time that'd happened since Luke died; Brandt McKay encountered a problem that he couldn't fix for her.

Or maybe it was one he *wouldn't* fix?

Jessie grabbed a beer from the fridge and started to pace again. Angry at Luke for dying. Angry with herself for doing exactly what she'd sworn she wouldn't the day Casper McKay had kicked her off their land: rely on a man. And worst of all, the man she'd come to rely on was another McKay.

Would she never learn? She slumped against the wall and swallowed a big gulp of beer. The aftertaste made her shiver with disgust and she looked at the bottle. Why the hell was she still drinking Coors? She didn't even like Coors—it'd been Luke's favorite beer, not hers.

Poor, pathetic doormat Jessie. She hadn't even mustered the guts during her marriage to buy the kind of beer she liked. She'd gone along with whatever Luke wanted because...

Why? She thought he'd love her more if she never rocked the boat? She was afraid he'd leave her, like her father had left her mother? Her "Yes, dear" attitude hadn't mattered one whit. Luke had left her anyway—maybe not bodily, but the last six months of their marriage had been sheer hell because he'd never been around. Too busy shacking up with some bimbo. Probably she'd stocked Luke's favorite beer, too, in hopes of keeping him around.

Hah. That hadn't worked for her either. Luke was dead to both of them.

A burst of anger surfaced and she threw that half-empty bottle across the room and it shattered against the wall.

Her dog whimpered and hid behind the easy chair.

You are the clingiest girl I ever met. Jesus, Jessie, can you just let me do some things on my own? We ain't joined at the hip. We don't gotta do everything together just because we're married.

Yeah, that mindset had worked out well for him, especially since he'd encouraged her to dump her "lowlife" friends after their wedding, promising they'd make new friends. Couple friends.

That'd never happened. Why? Because Luke never allowed

it to happen. Luke had called all the shots from day one. And she'd been so freakin' happy to have Luke McKay's attention that she would've danced naked around the Sundance flagpole if he'd asked her.

More fury raced through her.

Let it go, Jessie. No man wants a wife who's a shrew. No man wants a wife who nags, yells, cries and whines all the damn time. No wonder I'm not here as much as you like. You're drivin' me away.

Funny, how whenever she'd stuck up for herself Luke considered her a shrew, but if he put his boot down and ended the discussion, he was just being the man of the house, not a controlling asshole.

Something inside her shifted and shattered.

"You fucking self-centered prick. You set this all up from the beginning, didn't you? Having the perfect little doormat wife at home, cooking your meals, washing your clothes, making nice with your asshole father, doing your ranch chores, trying to get pregnant to birth your babies. While you were out fucking any woman that looked your way."

Jessie slid to the floor and started to cry. Not tears of grief for a change. Granted, it wasn't the first time she'd shed tears over Luke—not even the first time today, but goddammit, it'd be the last. As she cried, the rage built to the point she tipped her head to the ceiling and screamed, "I'm done with you, you cheating bastard! You hear me? Done. You and your whole rotten goddamn family can go straight to hell."

She sobbed. Lexie slunk next to her and licked her hand. That made her cry harder. Bringing Lexie home as a surprise gift was the one nice thing Luke had ever done for her.

Eventually her cries quieted. Her eyes dried because she literally had no more tears. She'd cried herself out. Jessie dragged herself up from where she'd curled into a ball on the floor. She ate, showered and decided to wear her nicest jeans and her favorite shirt, rather than lounging around in ratty sweats. She styled her hair, put on makeup, feeling foolish because really? Who would see her tonight besides her dog?

Don't make yourself look good for a man. Make yourself look good for yourself for a change. You can change.

Whoa. That was a new voice inside her head offering advice. Good advice.

She'd just sat and turned on the TV when her cell phone rang on the kitchen counter.

Her first thought: *Finally! Brandt called me back.*

Her second thought: *He can suck it. I'm done with him.*

Jessie sighed and stood, promising herself she wouldn't answer if it was Brandt. But it wasn't. The caller ID read: Keely McKay.

She smiled. She adored Keely. The woman was fun, funny, smart, sweet, sassy and she didn't take shit from any man, especially none with the last name McKay. Although Jessie knew Keely had been beyond busy in the last year, Keely always made a point to check in with her to see how she was holding up.

"Hello?"

"Jessie! I was hopin' you were around. What are you doin' right now?"

Sitting around all dressed up with no place to go. "Not much. What's up?"

"Well, I'm in Moorcroft with a few members of my new dart league team. Guess what? We just kicked the crap outta the Moorcroft Deadly Tips dart team, and we are seriously in the mood to celebrate. And I thought, Jessie lives close, I'll see if she's in the party mood."

"Where are you?"

"Ziggy's. Come on down. It'll be fun."

"You surrounded by hot cowboys?"

Keely laughed. "Absolutely. And I've even got a designated driver lined up so if we get shitfaced, we have a ride."

Jessie froze. Sometimes Keely cajoled her McKay male cousins into helping her outwit her five older brothers, since they continued to treat Keely like a twelve-year-old girl. She also knew Brandt had gotten roped into being Keely's cohort on several occasions. "Who's lined up as your DD?"

The phone rattled as Keely spoke to someone else. "Hey, darlin', what's your name again? Robbie? My new friend Robbie," Keely cooed, "has a tryout early tomorrow morning for a team ropin' event, and he's not drinkin' tonight, so he'll be our DD as long as we dance with him until closing time." Keely whispered, "He's hot, Jess, like really freakin' hot, and he loves to dance as much as you do. You should come and check him out."

She hesitated.

"Please? I haven't seen you in forever. I'm only in town this one night. When was the last time you went out and had fun?"

"It's been a long damn time, Keely."

"Then I say you're past due to cut loose."

Years past due. Jessie glanced at her reflection in the window glass above the sink. She didn't look half-bad for a twenty-six-year-old widow. She wasn't ready for any kind of intimate relationship, not even a one-night stand, but it'd do her good to make friends in the community. It'd do her good to start her life again.

If you don't grab this opportunity, you'll regret it.

Every journey started with one step. It was past time to stop living in the past.

"Okay, you convinced me. But you're buying the first round."

Chapter Seventeen

Two weeks later...

More snow.

Kane sipped his coffee and stared out the window to the sea of whiteness. He'd promised Colt he'd pick up a load of cake—supplemental cattle feed—before they all got busy with calving season. Best to wait to see if the road conditions improved before he loaded up the trailer.

On his way to the bedroom, he nearly tripped over Shep, stretched out in the middle of the floor. Shep slunk toward the door.

"Ready to go out?"

His tail thumped.

Kane petted his head. After the dog lumbered outside, Kane started his computer. Might as well get something accomplished besides pining for Ginger.

Man. He was so whipped over that woman. Seriously fucking whipped. It was a no-brainer they both enjoyed their explosive sexual chemistry, but they'd clicked out of bed too. Things had changed between them since they'd gotten snowed in. Sure, they'd kept up their lunch dates during the week, but two out of the four times they'd been together, they hadn't even had sex. They'd had...lunch.

And the hell of it was, he hadn't minded. He liked talking to her. Laughing with her. Making sandwiches with her. Ginger hadn't invited him over for supper again, but she'd tagged along when he'd taken Hayden to the rodeo, although the twisty drive had made her sick. They exchanged text messages several times a day.

As much as Kane wanted to push their relationship to the

next level—telling family they were a couple—in some ways, he liked romancing her in secret.

He focused on updating the cattle records. By the time he'd finished and glanced at the clock, he realized two hours had passed. Kade would be along soon.

Shit. He'd forgotten about Shep. Kane returned to the living room and opened the front door, seeing one set of tracks leading away from the house, but he couldn't see beyond the carport. Feeling guilty, he donned his winter weather gear and trudged outside.

First place he checked was the barn. "Shep? Come on out. I know you're probably pissed off and hungry." He checked the stalls and the tack room. No sign of the dog in his usual spots. Kane checked them all twice.

Although the sun wasn't shining, the white reflection of the snow made everything blindingly bright. After he retrieved his sunglasses from his truck, he followed the tracks leading away from the house. They were scattered pell-mell as if the dog had sniffed everything in sight. Around the tractor, to the gate leading to the pasture, to the stock tank. But no sign of him.

Kane hunkered deeper into his coat against the icy blast of wind. He would've worn his Carhartt coveralls if he'd thought he was going on a wild dog chase.

He called out, "Shep?"

No answering bark.

The tracks morphed into a straight line, rather than the random sniff and explore variety he'd been seeing. Snow eddied around him, cutting visibility. He hurried. He'd have to find the dog before the elements erased the tracks.

Kane stopped to catch his breath and looked back to see how far he'd gone. He was maybe a quarter mile from his trailer. He spun back around, taking in the dark outline of the lone cottonwood tree, an anomaly out here on the high plains. The big tree towered above the gnarled scrub oaks clustered in ravines. A creek popped up in the spring and trickled through the shallow gouge in the earth before summer heat returned it to a dry creek bed again. It'd always been one of Shep's favorite places. He'd lounge in the shade while keeping an eye on the cattle drinking at the stock tank.

He squinted, focusing on the base of the tree.

Was that a black lump?

Shit.

He ran, the snowdrifts slowed his progress and he felt as if he wore cement shoes.

By the time Kane reached the tree, he was out of breath. And when he saw his dog, curled up in a ball, he knew he was too late.

"Goddammit, Shep." Kane dropped to his knees in the snow. Shep's head rested on his front paws, as if he'd just laid down for a brief rest. His eyes were even closed, which was uncommon with his always-alert dog. His fluffy tail was tucked under his nose. The wind ruffled his black fur, blowing away the crystals of snow that'd accumulated on his still form.

He flashed back to the first time he'd seen Shep. His dad's buddy Walt Collier had suffered a stroke, forcing him to move into the Sundance nursing home and give up his dog. Old Walt had owned Shep since he was a puppy. Around that same time Kane had moved into his trailer and was feeling a mite lonely. When Kane's dad asked if he'd be interested in taking the dog, he'd immediately said yes.

The first month had been rough. Shep mourned Walt. He hadn't shown much of an appetite or interest in tagging along with Kane out on the range. Kane had begun to wonder if his company wasn't even fit for a depressed dog.

But one afternoon when the cattle came in from the pasture to drink from the stock tank, a couple of calves raced off. Shep gave chase, snapping at them, driving them back to the herd where they belonged. After that day, Shep had been a great cattle dog and a great companion.

"Damn, dog. Had to make a dramatic exit, didn't ya?" He'd seen things like this happen too often on the ranch to chalk it up to coincidence. Animal instincts never ceased to amaze him.

Kane stayed crouched down, his gloved hand absently petting Shep's head. He hadn't realized he was crying until he couldn't move his face, which had become covered in frozen tears.

"Kane!"

He didn't turn around at his brother's shout. He'd come out here anyway.

Kade stopped behind him, huffing and puffing after trudging through the knee-deep snow.

"Kane, what the hell are you doin'... Oh shit."

Kane didn't say a word. Couldn't speak around the lump lodged in his throat.

"Aw, man, I'm sorry. Really fuckin' sorry." Pause. "How long...?"

"He went out this mornin' and didn't come back so I went lookin' for him." More tears fell and he didn't bother to swipe them away. "Damn dog."

After a bit, Kade clamped his hand on Kane's shoulder. "This just sucks."

"Yeah." Kane stood and shivered. "I'm gonna head back to the barn and get a shovel. The ground'll be a bitch to dig since it's so fuckin' frozen, but I ain't gonna just leave him out here as buzzard and coyote bait..." Kane's voice broke.

Kade squeezed his shoulder. "Lemme take care of this for you, bro."

Kane looked at his twin, knowing the sunglasses masked his red eyes, but also knowing Kade didn't need to see his eyes to know he'd been crying. "Thanks for the offer, but I should—"

"No man oughta hafta bury his own dog, Kane. I've been around Shep a lot too. This is the least I can do for you and for him."

No sense arguing. Kane said, "Thanks. I'll get the shovel."

"I know where the shovels are. How about if you head to town and get that cake loaded? Then I'll meetcha at Dewey's for lunch."

Kane nodded. They plodded through the snow in silence. Kade cut to the left toward the barn when the buildings came into view, while Kane went straight for his truck. He loaded the trailer. He hadn't meant to look back, but just as he started down the driveway, he glanced in his rearview and saw his brother traipsing through the snow, dragging two shovels.

He cranked on the radio for the drive into town, but he flipped it off when Blake Shelton's "Old Red" came on.

At the feed store he wasn't in the mood to make idle chitchat with Denny, but this was a small community, and Kane had been trying like the devil the last few years to overcome his previous brusque reputation. Once he and Denny finished jawing about the weather, the Broncos' lousy season, the rash of new McKay babies and the upcoming calving season, Kane was ready to load up.

It took forever to load, which was odd because it wasn't a

full order. Kane wasn't happy with only half the amount of cake they'd ordered. When Kane questioned why, Denny informed him Colt had already been by to pick up the other half for the McKay Ranch account.

That pissed Kane off. If Colt had intended on getting the cake all along, why had he made such a big deal about Kane picking it up right away? It incensed him further when he saw Colt's rig—loaded with the other half of the cake—parked across from Sandstone Building.

Probably wasn't the smartest thing, storming into the Sky Blue and India's Ink in his present mood, spoiling for a fight. But Kane scaled the steps and burst through the door anyway, sending the cowbell door chime clanking. Not even the sweet scent of lavender that Ginger favored calmed him down.

Colt looked up from the magazine he was thumbing through. He yelled over his shoulder, "It's just Kane, Indy."

Just Kane. He fought a sneer.

"So what brings you by, cuz?" Colt asked as he strolled from behind the counter. "Lookin' for some sweet-smelling potion to lure the ladies into your lair?"

"Fuck off."

Colt froze. His eyes narrowed. "Jesus. What crawled up your butt and died?"

"You. I get sick of your wisecracks like I'm still some horny fuckin' teenager."

"Lighten up. I was jokin'."

"Well, it ain't funny. And it hasn't been for years."

"Ain't you in a special mood? Why in the hell did you bust in here and decide to take it out on me?"

"You know goddamn good and well why I'm here." Kane pointed to the street. "Why'd you only pick up half the order of cake?"

"Because we're runnin' low."

"Who's we?"

When Colt didn't answer, Kane stepped closer. "Why didn't you pick up the whole order?"

"Are you seriously chewing my ass for this?"

"Yes. Because you made it clear I needed to get to town ASAP and pick it up. So after a spectacularly shitty morning, I finally get to the feed store and find half our order is missin'."

"It ain't missin', Kane, it's right there in the goddamn trailer."

"Oh yeah? So you're gonna deliver that half to the hopper out by the old Foster place?"

Colt stared at him coolly.

Which gave Kane the answer he needed. "You son of a bitch. You took half the cake for your separate cattle operation with the Glanzers."

"So? I didn't take it all. And for Christsake, it's supplemental feed. Not a big deal."

Kane glared at him.

"When the feed store told me they were gonna be temporarily out of stock for a week, I took what we needed."

"What about what we need?"

"What's the big deal? We'll get the other half next week when the Glanzers' order comes in."

"The deal is, you're more worried about your little side cattle deal with Trevor, Chassie and Ed than you are with what's goin' on with our herd right before calving."

Colt stepped forward, his eyes blazing fire. "That's bullshit and you know it."

"Do I? All's I know is you made a big hairy damn deal about havin' this cake order handled early and now you're tellin' me it don't matter? You're tryin' to cover your ass. Probably so you can pass off the really shitty stuff that needs done to me, Ben, Brandt, Tell and Dalton when the time comes."

"Don't you fuckin' lecture me about what needs done before them calves start droppin'. We own—"

"Don't you even think about sayin' that you guys own more than we do," Kane warned, "or I will punch you right in your smart mouth."

"The facts are the facts, Kane. Between me and my brothers, we own four times as much as of the McKay Ranch as the rest of you *combined*."

Kane reacted instinctively. He cocked his right arm and his fist connected with Colt's jaw with a loud crack.

Caught off guard, Colt staggered back. Before he recovered from the first punch, Kane drew his fist back again and nailed Colt in the eye.

"What the fuck?"

"I warned you. And this has been a long time comin'."

"Bring it, fucker." Colt jumped him. A blow landed on Kane's chin, then on the side of his head by his temple. He jabbed and connected with Colt's gut, and then quickly followed with a shot to Colt's ribs. When Colt doubled over, Kane used an uppercut on Colt's jaw and knocked him to the floor. Then he pounced on his cousin, fists flying.

Colt dodged the blows and bucked, throwing Kane sideways. But Kane recovered quickly only to feel a fist plow into his mouth. The taste of blood seeped through his teeth and ran down the back of his throat and down his chin.

He popped back up on his feet, only to see Colt do the same. They bobbed and weaved like prizefighters. Colt feinted left, catching Kane's eyebrow with his wedding ring.

The instant Kane felt the slicing sting, he roared and intended to leap at his dumbass cousin, but found himself immobilized.

"Jesus Christ. That's enough. Both of you."

When the hell had Kade shown up? He blinked trying to clear the blood dripping into his eye, and saw Brandt had a similar hold on Colt.

"Let me fuckin' go," Kane said.

"Yeah. Let him go," Colt taunted, "I ain't done kickin' his sorry ass."

"Too bad your lips ain't swollen shut like your eye is," Kane shot back. "But I can change that in about one second when I punch you in the fuckin' mouth."

"Shut up, both of you. Nobody's hittin' nobody. What the fuck happened?" Kade demanded.

Kane breathed hard and glared at Colt. Colt was having his own difficulty breathing. And yeah, maybe it was petty to see that Colt only had one eye to shoot daggers at him, but it made Kane happy he wasn't the only one sporting blood and bruises.

"They got into a fight about cake," India said.

Kane's head swung her direction. She stood behind the counter, white-faced, holding Hudson as he tried to scramble onto the counter.

Fucking awesome, Kane. Getting into a fistfight with your cousin in front of his kid. Way to be mature.

Talk about a stellar fucking start to his day.

He turned his head and spoke to his brother. "Let me go. I ain't gonna go after him again."

Almost reluctantly, Kade released him.

Kane picked up his hat. Adjusted his clothes. He looked Colt in the eye. "You think on what I said. Bottom line is I don't give a shit if their cattle starve. But I care if ours do."

He walked out of the store and hit the halfway point to his truck before he muttered, "Fuck it." He headed the opposite direction, to the one place Colt wouldn't track him down: the Golden Boot.

Looked like he'd be having lunch in town after all. A liquid lunch.

An hour later Ginger found Kane hunched over the bar in the far corner of the Golden Boot. Two empty shot glasses in front of him next to a bottle of Bud light.

So far he hadn't noticed her. He was engrossed in breaking the pretzels in the bowl in front of him into tiny brown pieces.

Her heart stumbled upon seeing his animated face so miserable. She wanted to put her arms around him and hold him tight. Comfort him and take care of him like he'd done with her.

So why don't you?

Before she even took off her coat, Ginger came up behind Kane. She rested her chin on his shoulder, close to his neck, and slipped her hands underneath his arms. "Hey."

Kane remained frozen for a second, then he turned his head and buried his nose in her hair. "Hey."

She squeezed him a little tighter.

"What're you doin' here, Red? Lookin' for a nip to get you through the afternoon?"

"No. Looking for you."

He grunted.

"Mind if I join you?"

"Please." He spun on his barstool to help her take off her coat. Even when he was distracted and miserable he showed her gentlemanly courtesies, not because he was trying to impress her, but because that was his way. Kane's gaze landed on her feet. "I'm surprised you didn't bust your ass wearin' them heels."

She placed her burgundy pump on the metal part of his stool, using it as support as she sat next to him. "Don't you like these shoes?"

"I didn't say that." He smiled, but it didn't quite reach his eyes. "What are you drinkin'?"

"Is it horribly lame if I say...ginger ale?"

"Nah. It's kinda cute." Kane waggled his empty bottle at Lettie and said, "And bring her a ginger ale."

Ginger looked around the bar. Completely empty. Which was unusual. She said, "Slow day, huh?" when Lettie brought her drink.

"We hit a few of those this time of year. We're actually closed for inventory today. But I made an exception for one of the wonder twins." She didn't stick around to chat with them— also unusual.

Or maybe it was the "don't fuck with me" vibe Kane was throwing off that sent Lettie scurrying away.

Kane sipped his beer.

She sipped her ginger ale. She caught their reflection in the bar mirror. From here she could see the door and the entire length of the bar. So he had known when she'd walked in.

"So, counselor, if you ain't here for a three-martini lunch, which one of my meddlin' relatives called you? Kade? Skylar?"

"India."

That shocked him. "India ratted me out?"

"Yes. She... Omigod, is that...blood on your face?"

"Probably. What'd India say?"

He didn't care he'd been bleeding? "India said you were here drowning your sorrows and maybe I ought to check on you. Then she gave me a message for you."

"This oughta be good," Kane muttered.

"She said Colt might be an asshole on occasion, but he was her asshole and she didn't appreciate you messing up his pretty face." Her eyes searched his. "Does that mean something to you?"

Kane smiled. "Yeah, she's not pissed off at me for getting into a fistfight with her husband."

"Wait a second. You and Colt got into a...fistfight?"

"Yep. Wasn't the first time, probably won't be the last."

Ginger stared at him, her mouth hanging open. "You're both grown men! Whatever would possess you to take a swing at one another?"

He bristled. "I don't expect you to understand. Me 'n Colt... Let's just say we're both just hotheaded. We get pissed, come out swingin' and then we're done. Fine. Back to normal."

"You're serious."

"India didn't tell you that Kade and Brandt had to break up the fight between me 'n Colt at Sky Blue?"

"No. She just told me that you'd had a bad morning."

"Indy thinks Colt is completely tamed. Sure, he hasn't been drinkin', druggin' and whorin' around for a few years. He's happily married to a woman he worships and now they've got this perfect little boy. But there's a dark side to him. A side that likes to inflict pain and receive it in return. Colt's brothers have never understood it. Kade never understood it about me, either. But me 'n Colt? We recognized it from the time we were kids and accepted that violent side. And it might sound barbaric, but every once in a while? We just need to beat the ever lovin' shit out of each other. Today was that day."

She honestly didn't know what to say.

"When Colt hears why I was a major asshole today, well, he'll probably show up at my place with a damn puppy. That's just the kind of guy he is."

Ginger placed her hand on Kane's thigh. "I'm so sorry about Shep."

"Yeah. Ah. Thanks." He swigged from his bottle. "Seems a little silly, cryin' in my beer over my dead dog. Jesus, I'm livin' the clichéd country song—my dog died, I had a knock-down, drag-out fight with my kin and now I'm at the local watering hole drownin' my sorrows about the suckage of my life."

"I imagine so," Ginger murmured. "But your woman hasn't left you."

Kane muttered something that sounded like "Not yet."

She wanted so badly to soothe him. Kane constantly touched her when they were alone together. Tender lover's caresses on her face. Running his work-roughened fingertips down her neck. Twisting sections of her hair around his fingers. Playing dot to dot with her freckles on her.

How could she show him the same loving care he'd shown her?

"Don't move. I'll be right back." Lettie happily supplied Ginger with what she needed. She returned to the bar with a washcloth and a bowl of hot water.

"What the hell's that for?"

"I'm going to clean you up."

"Can't stand to look at me with blood on my face?" he said curtly.

"Blood, swollen spots and bruises on your handsome mug does affix you with a sort of sexy, rugged meanness. But the truth is, I was hoping for one of your amazing kisses. The taste of blood might spoil it."

His stoic face softened. "I'll give you all the kisses you can handle, sugar."

"Good. Then hold still and let me play doctor." Her gaze zoomed to the broken skin below his lips.

"Turn 'bout is fair play, right?"

She didn't respond. She just gently dabbed the spots until all the blood was gone. There wasn't a damn thing she could do about the bruises, except offer them a healing kiss, which she did. On his mouth, his jaw, the cut by his temple, his cheek. She also pressed soft kisses on the section of his lips that weren't swollen.

"Ginger," he said huskily, nuzzling her hair, "You make me want..."

"I know. But right now, I want to dance with you, Kane."

"Why?"

Because I want an excuse to wrap myself around you and just hold you. "Because there's no one here to see my two left feet."

"Really?" he asked skeptically.

"Really. I fell down the stairs, remember? I'm utterly graceless. I've watched you with Hayden. You're a wonderful teacher. I figured if anyone could teach me, you could."

"Okay. But I get to pick the songs."

Kane hopped off the barstool and made a beeline for the jukebox.

She yelled, "No 'Honky Tonk Badonkadonk', Kane McKay. I mean it."

He laughed and started shoving in quarters.

Selections chosen, he stood on the edge of the empty dance

floor and held out his hand.

Ginger wasn't sure why she felt nervous; she just did. As she started toward him, the Eddie Arnold classic "Make the World Go Away" drifted from the jukebox. When Kane's rough fingers enclosed hers, the heat lingering beneath the surface sparked. When he enfolded her in his arms, that same spark ignited. She wanted skin on skin, mouth on mouth, wanted to feel him above her as his body sought the entrance to hers.

But this cheek-to-cheek, chest-to-chest, pelvis-to-pelvis position was a good temporary substitute.

They drifted together through the mellow song, not talking, just dancing. The second song kicked in, Barbara Mandrell's "Sleeping Single in a Double Bed" and Kane kicked up the pace, deftly swinging her into two-stepping. Just when Ginger thought she might have to take a breather, the third song started: Big and Rich's "Lost in This Moment". She sighed. How had he known she loved this song?

Kane barely moved as they slow-danced. Ginger was truly lost—in the solid heat of Kane's body, surrounded by his earthy scent, his hard muscles pressed against her softness.

"I like dancin' with you, counselor."

"Same goes."

"Wanna know a secret?"

"Ah. Sure."

"I love that you're tall. I don't have to crouch down to dance with you and wind up with a crick in my neck."

"Being an Amazonian throwback does have advantages."

"Wanna know something else?" he whispered, sending a tingle strait to her core.

"What?"

"You don't have two left feet. You just needed to be with a man who takes the lead."

"Who takes the lead in all things," she murmured.

He stiffened. "Complaints?"

"Not on your life, cowboy. You've been avoiding me since the blizzard."

"I've been busy."

"Hayden misses you." *I miss you too.*

"Good to know."

That was it? They weren't going to talk about the over-the-top, totally domineering sexual encounter in his bedroom? How she's sensed his regret as he'd untied the ropes and she'd been more pissed off by that than by his intensive use of her body? It'd scared her how much she'd liked it. How much she'd wanted it again. How easily she could give everything over to this man. That was what'd bothered her. Not his rough side.

Tell him.

No. It'd be better to wait. See how things played out.

The song ended too quickly.

Ginger tilted her head back to look at him. "Kane?"

His eyes opened. The sadness was still there. She hadn't expected that a couple of dances and some sexual teasing would erase the day's events, but his suffering distressed her nonetheless.

She framed his face in her hands. "Come home with me. Have dinner with us. I've already got a roast in the Crock-Pot and I'll even let tonight be Hayden's Xbox night. Please."

Gratitude swam in his eyes before he looked away and kissed the inside of her wrist. "I'd like that, Red. I'd like that a whole helluva lot."

"Good. I've got a couple of hours left at the office..." She stopped talking. "You know something? Nothing needs to be done today. It can wait."

That surprised him. "You sure?"

"Positive."

"So what now?"

"Let's stay here and dance a little longer." Ginger pressed a soft kiss to his lips. "But now it's my turn to pick the music."

Ginger rode along with Kane as he unloaded the cake. Although many of her clients were ranchers, she wasn't sure what their daily lives entailed. She appreciated the glimpse into Kane's life. No wonder the man was so muscle-bound; it appeared everything he did required strength.

They picked Hayden up from school instead of at the bus stop. During the ride home, her son was subdued. Maybe it hadn't been the brightest idea to tell him about Shep, but Hayden deserved to understand Kane's melancholy mood.

Her father sat at the kitchen table working on a crossword

puzzle. He gave no indication of shock at seeing Kane making himself at home in the living room. Most days Hayden and his grandfather shared an after-school snack, but today, Hayden left his snack untouched.

Ginger watched covertly as her son stood in front of Kane, shifting from foot to foot.

"Hey, buddy. What's up?"

"Ah, nothin'. I'm sorry about Shep. He was the coolest dog ever."

"Yeah, he was."

"You're gonna miss him, huh?"

"Yeah, I'm gonna miss him. Big time."

Then without another word, Hayden crawled right onto Kane's lap and rested his head against Kane's chest, curling his arms around Kane's neck.

Kane hugged Hayden back without hesitation. He closed his eyes and they sank into the couch cushions.

Oh God. Ginger had to turn away, lest she start sobbing. Her sweet baby boy had such a kind heart. Kane knew that. He celebrated it. And it was never more apparent they had a unique bond than when Kane openly welcomed Hayden's comfort.

She was totally in love with this man.

But she wasn't quite sure what to do about it. She wasn't certain if she'd been celibate so long that Kane's expertise in bed turned her feelings of lust into love. Not only that, if she confessed her feelings, would he think she was no different than the other mothers in the Little Buddies program, angling for a permanent piece of him?

She'd never want Kane to think she prized his potential as a father over everything else that made him such a good man. And she wouldn't put the weight of her confession of her feelings for him when his day had already been filled with emotional upheaval.

Ginger felt her father's curiosity as he watched the boy and the man still snuggled on the couch. Without a word, or even a look her direction, he refocused on his crossword puzzle.

She put her father's guarded reaction out of her mind and prepared supper. After they ate, her father pleaded a headache and retired to his room. She thought about finishing paperwork in her home office, but she was content to sit between Hayden and Kane as they trash talked, wielding battling game controllers.

When Hayden's bedtime rolled around, he hugged Kane before skipping off to his room with Ginger following to tuck him in.

She returned to the living room and saw Kane staring out into the darkness, his hands shoved in the front pockets of his Wranglers, his shoulders hunched almost to his ears. She slid her arms around his waist and kissed the back of his neck.

Kane made a pleased-sounding rumble.

She kissed him again. "Stay with me tonight."

His hands came out of his pockets and he turned around. "What about—"

Another longer, deeper kiss quelled his protest. She eased back to murmur, "I don't care. I want to be with you tonight. All night. You and me. In my bed. If you're worried about your virtue, you can sneak out before sunrise."

He playfully nipped her bottom lip. "You sayin' my virtue is safe with you?"

"No. But we'll come up with a cover story if Hayden wakes up."

"Deal."

Ginger undressed him slowly, loving the way Mr. Take Charge gave control over to her. She soothed him with a deep tissue back massage, relaxing him to the point he fell asleep. She rested on top of him, her right cheek pressed between his shoulder blades, her pelvis curled over his buttocks, their legs entwined.

Kane woke up refreshed, ending her control. But he didn't push her to that deliciously dark edge of sexual pleasure. He touched her everywhere, from the soles of her feet to the tips of her earlobes with such sweet possession she had to bite her lip to keep from crying.

"Ride me," he'd urged in that husky voice.

After she sent him soaring, she collapsed in his arms and fell asleep.

Kane's cell phone buzzed at five a.m. Groggy, he patted

Ginger's nightstand until his fingers connected with the plastic casing. Without opening his eyes, he said, "Yeah?" He listened. "No, Dad. Just wait. I'll be there as soon as I can."

"Something wrong?" Ginger asked.

"The first calf dropped about an hour ago. Then two more. Dad's got one lined up in the barn at my place that we've gotta pull."

He rolled to the side of the bed and gathered his clothes from the floor. He felt Ginger's eyes boring into the back of his neck. "Look, I know this is gonna sound like a brush off, but I ain't gonna be around much for the next three weeks." Kane faced her. "Not for our lunch dates, not on weekends, not even for the Little Buddies events. The cell service sucks, so don't think I'm avoidin' you or nothin' when I don't call."

"Calving is tiring?"

"Like you wouldn't believe. Sometimes I fall asleep standin' up."

"So when you're done, will you let me take care of you for a change?"

Kane had known he loved her almost from the start. Right then, Kane realized he had to stop playing it safe—they both did. This was real, this was forever. But there wasn't a damn thing either of them could do about it now.

"Kane?"

He kissed her. "I'm puttin' in my request for you to wear one of them sexy harem-girl outfits as you're hand feedin' me grapes and coolin' me down with palm fronds."

She held her hands in prayer position and blinked her eyes. "Anything else, master?"

"Yeah, see if you can't round up some of them nipple clamps on a golden chain. And a satin pillow." He grinned. "For your knees."

"As you wish."

Two weeks later...

Kane was having a devil of a time keeping his eyes open. He yawned, knowing it'd be another long night out in the cold and snow. But at least he had this place to crash in.

Two years ago, the McKay "boys", as their collective fathers called them, had all chipped in and built a bunkhouse. The structure wasn't anything fancy, just one room with three sets of bunk beds, a big conference-type table, an old refrigerator and a small counter that held a hot plate, a microwave and a coffee pot. For warmth during the freezing-ass winter months, they'd bought several space heaters. For cooling off during the hot-as-hell summer months, well, they could leave the door open. A gas-powered generator provided electricity, but there was no running water, just a water tank. No bathroom either, just an outhouse in the trees. As far as amenities, it was damn primitive. Although it was out in the boonies, it was centrally located on the ranch. They'd even had an old-fashioned barn raising, building a small metal structure where they could keep equipment, and a place for calves to spend a night or two, if needed.

He kicked his chair against the wall. He hadn't bothered to look at the schedule to see who he was working with tonight. The schedule was more or less a joke anyway. He was always here, Brandt was always here and Tell was always here. The others came and went whenever the hell they felt like it. Truth was, Kane didn't begrudge them. This time of year was exhausting, but he looked forward to the annual birth cycle in a way he couldn't explain without sounding like a sappy damn fool.

The door opened and shut quickly. But even so, Kane felt the rush of cold air. Boots stamped. Clothes rustled. He finally opened his eyes.

Colt stared back at him.

Fucking awesome.

So far they'd managed to avoid working with one another. It'd been a childish hope on Kane's part that the avoidance would last through calving season.

"So if you're gonna jump me again, I'd rather you got it out of your system now, instead of when we're elbow deep in a cow's birthin' canal."

Kane smiled, even when he didn't want to. "But I like the element of surprise."

"How well I know that," Colt said wryly, rubbing his jaw.

Be the bigger man. This can't go on with your cousin forever. Kane picked up his mug of nearly cold coffee. "Look. I was an ass that day. I'm sorry. You didn't deserve me comin' after you and certainly not in front of your wife and kid."

Colt poured himself a cup of coffee and refilled Kane's. Then he sat across from him. "Well, it was as much my fault as it was yours. And fuck, Kane, I'm really goddamn sorry about Shep. If I'da known..."

"You wouldn't have hit me back?" Kane supplied.

He grinned. "Oh, I wouldn't go that far. We both know that fight had been building a long time. That's what happens when we don't beat the tar out of each other on a regular basis. And lifting weights and hitting a punching bag is a poor substitute, ain't it?"

"Yep. Shocks people that we still like mixin' it up, don't it?"

"Which is why we've always done it in private," Colt muttered.

"We're supposed to be mature. Solve all our problems with words."

"I'm a family man, for Christsake. I should know better. But there are times..."

Colt didn't have to spell it out. Kane understood. There was no substitute for the real thing, nothing like bleeding and hurting that really made you feel alive. That's where they were alike. The only other person in their family who had that same impulsive, primitive need was Brandt and he'd always refused to talk about it. Kane knew it'd come to a head for Brandt one of these days, probably sooner rather than later.

"You were right," Colt offered. "I fucked up. I forgot to do a whole buncha shit that week, and it wasn't your fault. I took it out on you because I could. So it ain't an excuse, but I've been so goddamn distracted lately."

"What's up?"

Colt ran his hand over the top of his head. "Indy's pregnant again, for one thing."

"Congrats, man."

"Thanks."

"You don't sound too happy about it."

"I am. It's just... There's so much more to bein' a husband and a father than I imagined. It's like calving all the damn time." Colt shot Kane a dark look. "And if you ever repeat that to Indy I will beat you bloody."

Kane held up his hands in mock surrender.

"Just when I think I've got a handle on it all, the kid is sleeping through the night, the puppy is house trained, and I've got my sexy wife back...I find out I knocked her up again. And that day, when I looked at you, without all the damn worries about this family stuff, I was jealous of your freedom. It only lasted a minute or so, but it was there."

He shook his head. "You're a lucky man. Your life wasn't such hot shit before Indy, remember? And I'd give my left nut to have those kind of family worries."

"Speakin' of..." Colt pinned him with a look. "What's goin' on with you and the fireball attorney?"

"Who the hell knows? One day it's great. The next... I can't get a bead on her."

"Then it's probably the real deal and she's running scared."

"Yeah, I'm pretty sure I'm not the type of guy she thought she'd end up with," he said, hating he sounded like a fucking whiner.

Colt frowned at him. "What the fuck are you talkin' about? You feelin' like you're not good enough for her? So she's a lawyer. Big deal. That just means when you do something stupid and get your ass tossed in jail she can give you a helluva defense."

Kane laughed. "Asshole."

"Listen to me. Don't be a dumbass and waste any more time. Do the adult thing and quit mopin' around. It's annoying as hell."

"How the hell do you know I've been moping? You ain't been around."

"Like anything can be a goddamned secret for long in this family."

Before he could tell Colt to mind his own fucking business, the door blew open and a whole mass of people crowded in. Kade, Cord, Colby, Cam and Quinn.

Kade spoke up. "We're staging an intervention."

Kane glared at Colt. "Was this your doin'?"

"Yep." Colt smirked. "Payback's a bitch, ain't it?"

Unbelievable.

All the guys grabbed a cup of coffee and took a seat.

When he couldn't take their amused stares and total silence any longer, he snapped, "What?"

Evidently Kade was the designated spokesman. "We've all been where you are, so we're gonna give you the benefit of our experience." Kade leaned forward. "Buy a goddamned ring and marry the woman. Don't take no for an answer."

Heads nodded in agreement.

Kane looked at his relatives like they'd all gone insane, because the road to happily ever after hadn't been easy for any of them. "That's your advice? That's why you're all here?"

Colby exchanged a look with Quinn and Colt and said, "Partially."

"They're using this 'intervention' as an excuse to avoid their wives, since they're all pregnant," Cam tossed in.

"Fuck off, Cam," Colby said.

"But it's true," Cam argued.

"They're all pregnant?" Kane asked. "Did you guys plan that or something?"

"No. Blame the last blizzard," Colby said.

Quinn nodded.

Kade said, "Well, Skylar ain't pregnant."

Colt said, "And Indy was pregnant *before* the blizzard."

"Far as I know, AJ ain't pregnant." Cord grinned. "*Yet*, but it sure ain't for lack of tryin'."

Cam sighed. "As for why they're here tonight, they each told their missus that they had to talk some sense into you about Ginger. Which if they're anything like Domini, they're all teared up thinking we're the greatest guys in the world, looking out for you."

Kane snorted.

"As much as we do care about you finally strapping on that old ball and chain like the rest of us," Quinn said, "we are here for another reason."

"Which is?"

Colby crossed his arms over his chest. "Poker."

That jarred him. "What?"

"We know you're playin' poker regularly with Brandt, Tell, Dalton, Bennett and Chase. We're pissed you didn't invite us, and we want in."

"Seriously?"

"Yep. We admire the hell outta you, Kane," Cord said. "You've actually tried to fix the rift between our families and

Uncle Casper's. None of us could do it, even when we all wanted to. Hell, even when some of us tried."

"So the next poker game after calving? We *all* expect an invite," Cord said.

"Besides, if it was just supposed to be a gathering of the single McKays, then you're gonna get kicked outta the club pretty soon, anyway," Kade pointed out.

Kane muttered, "God I hope so."

Cam threw a deck of cards on the table. "We've got an hour before we need to check cattle."

"Love the way you said 'we', little bro, when you've got no intention of climbin' on an ATV when it's ten below outside," Colt said.

"Hey. I'm handicapped."

Boos rang out, followed by laughter and trash-talking.

Kade leaned over. "Seriously. Don't wait to tell Ginger how you feel about her until you think she's ready to hear it. If she's anything like Sky, and I suspect she is, she already knows how you feel. She just needs tangible proof."

"Thanks for the advice, but I ain't getting a tattoo."

"Oh, you'll be surprised what you'll do in the name of love."

"Are you two done sharin' hairdo tips and secrets so we can play poker?" Colt rubbed his hands together with glee. "I'm feelin' lucky."

That reminded Kane he was wearing his lucky ball cap. It also reminded him that he missed Hayden as much as he missed Ginger. Rather than dwell on what he couldn't change tonight, but what he was goddamned sure he was gonna change as soon as humanly possible, he readjusted his cap and grabbed the cards. "Ante up, boys."

Chapter Eighteen

Ginger missed Kane. It was an odd feeling. She'd never had a man in her life that she cared enough about to miss.

And it'd only been a week.

Despite feeling lousy, Ginger allowed Hayden to invite his friends Kyler and Anton McKay for a sleepover. The boys amused themselves, but seeing Kyler reminded Ginger of Kane. The boy was all McKay with his dark hair, blue eyes and boyish cowboy charm.

Week two didn't fly by any faster than week one had.

When Ginger threw up her breakfast, lunch and supper for three days straight, she knew she'd have to break down and make a doctor's appointment. It'd been a lousy winter regarding her health, between the accident and the sinus infection that'd dragged on for a solid month. Her immune system was slacking; she'd caught every virus that'd come down the pike. Grateful as she was that neither Hayden nor her father had contracted anything from her, she was damn sick of being sick.

Doc Monroe ordered a bunch of tests. The worst one was the influenza A test, when the nurse stuck a tube up her nose to gather mucus. Urine and blood work were a piece of cake in comparison.

She sat in the exam room, staring at her sock-clad feet. She'd felt so rotten and off-balance the last three weeks she hadn't even worn high-heeled shoes.

Ten minutes ticked by. She rolled down on the exam table. Even that simple movement sent her stomach churning. She curled into a ball, pulling the blanket under her chin. Maybe if she closed her eyes the room would stop spinning.

"Ginger?"

She jumped and sat up, completely disoriented. "Sorry, I fell asleep."

"It's okay. We're overbooked today."

Ginger rearranged the sheet across her thighs after she tugged down the hospital gown. She looked at Joely, flipping back and forth between pages in her medical chart. "So Doc, what's the prognosis? Influenza A?"

"No. You tested negative."

"Shit. Is it swine flu?"

"You tested negative for that too."

When Dr. Monroe set the clipboard aside and pinched the bridge of her nose, Ginger had her first feeling of alarm. "What's wrong with me?"

"A couple of questions first. You were on a ten-day cycle of antibiotics after your accident, correct?"

"Yes."

"And then, according to your patient's report, you filled a fourteen-day-cycle prescription of antibiotics for a sinus infection four weeks before that?"

"Yes. But it didn't seem to work, so I refilled it again a couple of weeks ago."

"First of all, you should've set up an appointment instead of getting a refill, an oversight I've corrected by canceling your standing prescription at DeWitt's. I'm curious to know the details of your sinus infection symptoms, and why you didn't feel the antibiotic worked."

Ginger frowned. "Besides my head being stuffy? I constantly have a headache. My equilibrium is off and I get motion sick very easily. So I'm nauseous and dog-tired all the time."

Dr. Monroe crossed her arms over her chest. "Ginger. You're a smart woman. How could you not read the warning labels on the drug information sheet? I know you got them. I know you scour them if it's Hayden's medication. But you don't do that for yourself?"

Not a good sign, getting her ass chewed by her doctor.

"Here's the CliffsNotes version of pharmacology. Antibiotics can render birth control pills ineffective, especially the low dosage type you're currently taking. I would've made a point of discussing it with you if I'd known you were sexually active—"

"This hasn't ever been an issue before because I've been a freakin' monk since I moved here."

"When did your abstinence status change?"

"After my accident. When Kane stayed with us. It just sort of...happened."

"So it was a one-time thing?"

Ginger bit her lip, tempted to lie. "No, it wasn't a one-time thing. God. He's become like this...addiction. We're doing it all the freakin' time. I can't keep my hands off him and Kane can't keep his hands off me. I've never felt this way about any man." Ginger inhaled slowly and steadily. "It's like my hormones have taken control of my life."

"Your hormones are in control, Ginger, because you're pregnant."

Her mouth dropped open and all the air emptied from her lungs. "What?"

"You honestly had no clue?" Dr. Monroe asked gently, but with a hint of skepticism.

She shook her head.

"Your last menstrual cycle ended...just after New Year's?"

"Yes." She paused and counted. "Oh. My. God. It's...March!"

"Which means, in my estimation, that you are eight weeks pregnant."

Holy hell. She'd probably gotten pregnant the very first time they'd had sex. Ginger's thoughts bounced like a million rubber balls. Her tears fell—part frustration, part relief, part fear. "How am I going to tell Kane? He's been calving for almost three weeks and he has limited cell phone service..." Not something she wanted to tell him over the phone anyway.

But Dr. Monroe didn't have any magical advice about how to break the news to the father-to-be. She helped Ginger sit up. "Eat small meals until the morning sickness passes. I'll give you vitamins. And obviously you can stop taking the pill."

"Funny." Ginger dressed. She ran her hand down her stomach. Was it her imagination or did she have pooch there? Already?

She dreaded going back to the office, so she wandered down the sidewalk and found herself standing in front of Sky Blue.

Coincidence?

The aroma of sage, lemongrass and lavender greeted her. Followed by the sweet scent of wild summer roses, the crisp, clean tang of freshly laundered clothes hanging on the line, and an earthy trace of newly mown grass.

"Ginger! Good to see you," Skylar said behind her.

She spun around. "It's been a while since I've been in to browse. There are so many new products."

"You should try the goat's milk soap. It's unbelievably creamy and the almond scent is to die for."

"When'd you start this line?"

"A few months ago. Kade's cousin Chassie raises goats and she has leftover milk from cheese making, so we experimented and came up with a few products. They've been very popular. We're working on a new liquid hand soap that'll infuse the scent of chokecherry blossoms."

Ginger set two bars of soap on the counter. "How do you do it all? Run a business and have time to experiment with new products while you've got a husband and three kids at home?"

Skylar rested her chin on her hand. "No clue. Some days it's easy. Some days I wonder when I decided to join a circus. A flea circus with all the damn strays Eliza drags home," she said dryly. "I imagine you have days like those, running a law practice, raising a kid and having your dad living with you."

"It's manageable. Or it was until I realized that I've got no backup plan in case something unexpected happens."

"Like your accident?"

Like the accidental pregnancy. "Yes."

"So you're fully recovered from your fall?"

With the exception of falling in love with your brother-in-law.

Man, she was punchy today. "So far."

"That's good. I'm glad Kane was able to help you out."

"He volunteered."

"A wise move on his part because I doubt you would've asked him."

Ginger met Skylar's eyes.

"It's hard to ask for help. Trust me, I get that. It's a continual struggle for me, even now."

"It's easier to deal with things myself."

Sky looked at her thoughtfully. "You're not talking about

your law practice, are you?"

Ginger shook her head.

"What's on your mind?"

"Tell me about how you and Kane met and how you ended up married to his twin."

If Skylar thought the question bizarre, it didn't register on her face. "I'm surprised you don't know all the gossip. My first date wasn't with Kade but with Kane. The man was a total asshole. Such an asshole, that when I saw him on the street a week later, I called him out on his horrible behavior. He blushed and stammered and was so contrite, that when he swore he'd make it up to me...I let him. We started seeing each other. Turned out the guy with the guilty conscience wasn't Kane, but Kade. And it was Kade I fell in love with, but it took me a long time to admit it."

"How long?"

"Not until Eliza was five months old. The abbreviated version—when I discovered he'd been lying to me, I broke it off. At that point I was already pregnant. Due to his responsibilities to the ranch, Kade left for a year and when he came back he learned he had a daughter."

"You didn't tell him you were pregnant?"

"I tried to get ahold of him after I found out, but it was easier to give up than to track him down."

"Was Kade upset?"

"Yes. And no. He just accepted Eliza, moved in and basically took control of owning up to his responsibilities."

That sounded exactly like something Kane would do.

"Know my biggest regret?" Skylar mused.

"What?"

"I didn't accept Kade at face value. There was no ulterior motive in him wanting to be with me. He wasn't like any other man I'd ever met and I was wrong to expect he'd disappoint me like every other man in my life. Kade was exactly the good guy he appeared to be. He still is. And every minute of every day I count my lucky stars that he's in my life. He is my life. Does that sound sappy?"

"It sounds heavenly, Sky. You are a very lucky woman."

"You could be lucky too, Ginger." Skylar pinned her with a look. "I suspect we have more in common than you'll admit."

Yeah, we both got knocked up by one of the McKay twins.

Ginger managed a wan smile. "Thanks for talking to me." She pointed to the lavender shampoo on the display wall and slid her credit card across the counter. "Before you total me up, I need a bottle of that."

"That's funny. Kane bought the exact same kind yesterday."

She froze. "Kane was in here? Yesterday?"

"Yes. He watched the twins for me in the morning for about twenty minutes when I ran to the bank. Then he said he had some errands to run. Why?"

Be cool. "Oh, I thought he was calving. He hasn't been around for any of the Little Buddies events for the past few weeks and Hayden's been asking me when Buck is coming back."

"He's been back a couple days." Skylar totaled up the sale and swiped Ginger's credit card.

So. Kane had been around for two days and he hadn't bothered to call her?

Maybe he has a good reason.

Or maybe three weeks away hadn't made Kane's heart grow fonder.

Can you blame him? When you won't acknowledge you're a couple?

But that'd been Kane's idea—to sneak around. She'd never suggested it, let alone demanded it.

Yet you've done nothing to change it, even after everything changed between you. What if you've waited too long? You waited after the blizzard to contact him because you didn't want to seem...needy. You never told him you loved his rougher edges when you knew he feared he'd stepped out of line. You didn't tell him you love him because you're waiting for him to tell you first.

Her stomach churned.

Dear God, no. Not now. She swallowed repeatedly against the bile rising in the back of her throat.

"Here's your card—my goodness, Ginger, are you all right? You're almost green. Maybe you'd better sit down."

"No. I'm fine. Thanks. I just need some fresh air." She quickly signed the slip and hustled out.

But once she was back outside in the frigid air, she had the same sense of displacement. She didn't want to go back to her office. She looked at her watch. Noon. She needed to compose her thoughts and she couldn't do it at Dewey's Delish Dish, where she'd be forced to make small talk with whoever crossed her path. Plus, she'd have to try not to barf in public.

Ginger she cut through the alley and entered the Golden Boot.

Lettie smiled at her after she plopped on the barstool. "What's your poison today?"

"A glass of Sprite would be great."

"Comin' right up." Lettie slid the glass in front of her. "Need anything else, just holler."

Ginger hunkered down and considered her options. She could call Kane and demand he come into her office so they could discuss this situation like rational adults. She'd be on her turf, in professional mode.

A surgically enhanced blonde sidled up to the bar. When the woman faced her, Ginger inwardly groaned. Of all the people she could run into today, did it have to be her?

Daphne frowned at Ginger prettily. "I know you. You're Hayden's mom, right?"

"Right. How are you, Daphne?"

"Thirsty." Daphne dropped a ten dollar bill on the bar top when Lettie asked for her order. "Vodka sour."

The woman was in the bar at noon, having a drink?

You're in the bar at noon, and if you weren't pregnant you'd be having a drink yourself.

Self-chastised, Ginger politely asked, "So wasn't it scary when the boys got snowed in?"

"Lock didn't go on that field trip since he and Hayden ain't in the same class."

"Oh. Sorry. I didn't know."

"I'd be surprised if you did, since Lock and Hayden don't run in the same crowd. Lock is a sports nut and he hates being in the classroom. He tells me Hayden is some kind of genius."

"I wouldn't go that far," Ginger demurred.

"Anyway, Lock has real trouble with his homework."

Ginger bit back her retort, "He's struggling in third grade?"

"School wasn't really my thing neither, so he probably gets that from me."

"What do you do for a living?" Ginger asked.

"I'm a nail technician." Daphne twisted a section of hair, bleached to blinding white platinum, around her index finger, which boasted a fake gemstone that nearly reached her knuckle. "How about you? You ain't from around here."

"I moved to Wyoming a few years ago to take over my father's law practice."

"You're a *lawyer*?"

Ginger almost laughed at the comical look on Daphne's face. She half expected Daphne to blurt, "But you don't look that smart!" Wouldn't have been the first time Ginger had heard that. "Yes, I am. Are you originally from Sundance?"

"Born and raised in Lusk. Moved to Sundance to be with Lock's daddy, but the man took off before Lock was born so it's just been me and him."

"Same," Ginger offered.

"Men. Only good for one thing. Since my daddy took off too, I wanted something different for my boy, so I signed up Lock for that Little Buddies program."

"It's been great for Hayden."

Daphne gave Ginger a curious once-over. "You mean *Buck's* been great for Hayden?"

"That too."

"Did you request Buck?"

"No. Hayden was assigned to Kane from the start."

"Well, I specifically requested him."

"Really?"

"Uh-huh." Daphne pursed her pink frosted lips around the straw and sucked. "Those dreamy McKay blue eyes, that hard, toned body, that sexy grin? The man is prime. And now that he's officially dropped out of the Little Buddies program? He's fair game."

All the air left Ginger's lungs. "What?"

Daphne smirked. "You didn't know Buck resigned from the program?"

Stunned, she shook her head.

"He called and left a message on our home phone yesterday. Supposedly to let Lock know he was quitting, but I can read between the lines." Daphne leaned closer and confided, "He was letting me know he's free. There's always been a spark between Buck and me, even when I knew he'd never act on it because of what'd happened with Brandi."

For Christsake. Who the hell was this Brandi person? And why did it seem everyone in town knew more about the man whose child she carried than she did?

"You don't know what happened with Kane and Brandi?" Daphne prodded.

"No." Ginger waited, expecting Daphne to confide in her.

But Daphne just gave her a smug smile and grabbed her drink. "See ya around."

Ginger huddled into her coat and left the Golden Boot via the side door. Arctic wind gusts blasted her face as she returned to her office, but she scarcely noticed because she was absolutely numb. Maybe Daphne wouldn't tell what the hell had gone on between Kane and Brandi, but she knew someone who would.

She dialed Stacy Lynnwood, director of Crook County First Start, which oversaw the Big Buddies/Little Buddies program.

Stacy's assistant patched Ginger through. "This is Stacy Lynnwood."

"Stacy. Ginger Paulson. How are you?"

"Great. Are you all healed up from your accident?"

All except for the accidental pregnancy. Ginger cleared her throat. "Yes, I am."

"I hope you're not calling me on an official legal matter?"

"No. A little more personal. Kane has been Hayden's Big Buddy for two years and I'm wondering why he resigned without warning. Was it his choice? Or was it a decision the board handed down because he'd violated the board's policy?"

A long pause ensued and Ginger assumed Stacy was mentally composing a brush off. Papers shuffled in the background.

"I've heard there's been disciplinary action taken against Kane before. Is that true?"

"Yes. I suppose it doesn't really matter now, anyway," Stacy grumbled. "Kane McKay was put on notice from his very first Little Buddy assignment. He almost got kicked out of the program."

"Why?"

"Inappropriate behavior."

Rather than jump to conclusions, she said, "Meaning what?

Inappropriate behavior on whose part?"

"One of the boy's mother's exhibited inappropriate behavior toward Kane. He immediately requested her son be transferred to another Big Buddy. The woman turned belligerent and accused Kane of punishing her son because she'd turned down Kane's sexual advances."

"What happened?"

"Kane was cleared because it was a lie. Several people substantiated Kane's side of the story. Sadly, the woman's son was banned from the program because of her actions."

Ginger paced in front of the window. "Kane's been in the clear since then? No misconduct?"

"He's been an exemplary mentor. We are very upset to be losing him."

Too bad for you, but I'm not going to lose him.

Ginger wasn't about to wait around for Kane to come to her. Screw that. For the first time in a long time she'd be proactive, instead of reactive. No more keeping her heart hidden, afraid that Kane might crush it or break it.

No, Ginger was going to throw herself on his mercy and hope like hell he wouldn't sentence her to a life of misery without him.

Chapter Nineteen

Although another vehicle was parked in the drive at Kane's place, Ginger gathered her courage, got out of the van and scaled the steps. But she didn't see a patch of ice on the top stair. Her feet went out from underneath her and she landed face first on the deck with a loud "Uff."

The door flew open and Kane skidded to a stop in his bare feet. "Ginger?" He dropped to his knees beside her in the snow and rolled her over. "Are you okay?"

With the wind knocked out of her, she couldn't speak.

"Goddammit, Red. Don't do this to me." He scooped her into his arms, as if she were a waif-like child, and carried her inside his trailer, shouldering past Kade who held the door open. Kane laid her on the couch and brushed the snow from her face and hair. He unzipped her coat.

Kane was oblivious to his brother standing behind him as he ran his hands all over her body with obvious familiarity. Starting at her neck and clavicle, down both arms to check her wrists and palms. Then down the center of her torso, individually poking her ribs, curling his hands around her hips to see if she winced. Venturing south, over her thighs, knees and shins. His hands stopped at the top of her fleece lined snow boots. He met her gaze.

"See?" she said. "It's not the ankle-breaking shoes that are the problem, it's me. I'm such a klutz and an idiot—"

He placed his fingers over her mouth. "Stop. Are you okay?"

She nodded.

"About gave me heart failure when I heard that god-awful crash on the deck."

"About gave me heart failure when I heard you've been

back and you haven't called me, but you managed to call Daphne."

Silence.

Kade cleared his throat. "Ah. I'll just be takin' off. Call if you need me, bro." The door slammed behind him.

"Did you come here to chew my ass?"

"Maybe." The instant she was upright, Kane began to pace, which was completely unlike him.

"Why did you resign from the Big Buddies/Little Buddies program?"

That stopped him in his tracks. "How'd you find out?"

"Daphne told me when I ran into her at the Golden Boot. Is it true?"

Surly, he said, "Why you askin' me? You already seem to have the answer."

Ginger wagged her finger at him. "You don't get to pull that bullshit evasion. I'm asking you to tell me all of it right now. Full disclosure, Kane."

His voice dropped lethally low. "We ain't in court, counselor. I ain't some witness you're cross-examining."

She threw up her hands. "Fine. You're right. I'm sorry. I found out because ninety percent of my job is research. After Daphne dropped the bombshell, I called Stacy."

"And she just told you?" he said incredulously.

"Yes. You are assigned to my son, so your resignation does affect me." She met his perplexed gaze head on. "I hated that you called Daphne and not me. I hated that Daphne acted as if she had a claim on you. After what's happened with us the last couple months, it pissed me off. I have a claim on you first, Kane."

Kane moved in and braced his hands on the back of the couch, forcing her to look up at him. "You have a funny way of showin' it."

"That's why I'm here."

"Because of Daphne? You thought... I told you once how I felt about Daphne. Dammit, Ginger. Do you think I fall in love with every woman whose son I mentor? You're the first. You're the only."

When Kane realized he'd admitted he loved her, he immediately retreated.

But Ginger wouldn't allow it. She grabbed handfuls of his shirt and held him in place. "You love me?"

He stared at her with that damnable inscrutable look.

"Answer the question, Mr. McKay. Do you love me?"

"Yes. Goddammit, I'm in love with you. Must you interrogate me about every damn thing?"

"Yes. And I'm not done badgering you. Second question. Do you love me because you care about Hayden so much?"

"No. If it weren't for Hayden, we wouldn't have crossed paths."

"Because we're so different, you and I? Because I wear heels and you wear boots? Because I study the law and you study the land? Because I'm a homebody and you used to be a party animal? Well, here's a newsflash, Kane, I was too intimidated by you to make a move on you. For two years! You were this gorgeous gentleman cowboy and my son worshipped you."

He laughed. "Are you serious? Wanna hear something totally fuckin' sappy? I still remember what you wore the first time we met. A pink and white flowered dress and pink spike heels with the sexiest strap that crossed at the ankle. I acted as tongue-tied as a fourteen-year-old boy. Talk about bein' outta my league."

Her mouth dropped open. Kane recalled that vividly what she'd worn? She'd taken special care not to dress provocatively, and she remembered he'd barely given her a second glance. He'd focused all his attention on her son. And she hadn't minded.

"But these last few months when I've gotten to know you? How I feel about *you* has nothin' to do with Hayden. Besides the fact he's such a great kid because he's got such a great mom."

Tears flooded her eyes. "Kane—"

"Let me finish. Yesterday, as soon as we finished calving, I stopped by Stacy Lynnwood's office and resigned as a mentor in the Big Buddies/Little Buddies program. I didn't give her a specific reason." His eyes narrowed. "I assume Stacy told you about what'd happened with Brandi?"

"Not in detail, just the general gist."

"Then you understand why I didn't want our relationship to be dissected by the organization or anyone else?"

She nodded.

"So I resigned. That wasn't something I was gonna tell you over the phone. I don't want to be in your life only as Hayden's mentor. I want to be in your life as your lover and your partner. I want us to be a family."

"Kane—"

"Don't interrupt." He dropped to his knees and gathered both her hands in his. "I'd hoped to do this differently, but I ain't gonna wait for the right time because I'm tired of wasting time. Ginger Paulson, I love you like crazy. Will you marry me?"

Oh dear God. The man wanted to marry her *before* he knew she was pregnant? She swallowed hard. But the nauseous feeling that'd been building wouldn't go away. Saliva pooled in her mouth and she swallowed over and over, but it was pointless. She said, "I'm going to be sick." She clapped her hand over her mouth and stumbled to the bathroom, barely making it before she puked.

After her stomach emptied the last of the Sprite, she flushed the toilet, wobbled to her feet and rinsed her mouth. Feeling dizzy, she rested against the shower door and slid to the floor, eyes closed in absolute mortification.

She heard Kane enter the bathroom. Water ran. A cool washcloth pressed against her forehead. The warmth of Kane's body and his familiar scent enveloped her as he sat beside her. Without thought, she leaned into him.

Kane said, "So the thought of marryin' me makes you physically ill?"

Her eyes flew open. "No. God no. Don't think that. It's so far from the truth you have no idea."

"Then why don't you tell me what's goin' on?"

Ginger lifted her chin. "I'm pregnant."

Every bit of color drained from Kane's face.

"Evidently you're supposed to use alternative methods of birth control when you're on the pill and taking antibiotics."

Kane slumped back against the shower door. "I'll be goddammed. How far along are you?"

"I guess about two months."

"Guess it ain't a blizzard baby like everyone one else's," he murmured.

"I didn't plan this. I feel like such a freakin' idiot. Another unintended pregnancy? I've had one. You'd think I'd have learned my lesson by now. But no. Here I am. Thirty-seven years old, pregnant again."

"How long have you known?"

"Only since this morning. When I heard from Skylar that you'd been in town for two days, and Daphne said you called her last night...'Hey, you're gonna be a daddy' is not exactly news I wanted to break over the phone."

"So you understand why I wanted to tell you and Hayden in person that I'd resigned from the program?"

"Yes." Ginger looked at him. "I wanted to tell you this in person too. I love you. You're only the third man I've ever said that to in my life, the first two being my son and my father. You're too good to be true, Kane McKay, and why no other woman has snatched you up for herself absolutely boggles my mind. I've probably fucked this up completely by acting neurotic and jealous and needy. Oh, and let's not forget about me accidentally getting pregnant." A small sob escaped.

"Hey. Hey." Kane trapped her face in his hands. "Don't cry. It rips me clean apart. The only way you'll screw this up is if you say no to marryin' me." He kissed her forehead. "I love you too, sugar. And at the risk of soundin' smug, I ain't exactly gonna be cryin' in my beer over the fact that I knocked up the smartest, sexiest, funniest, most beautiful woman I've ever known."

More tears leaked out. "You are so sweet. And not so sweet."

He stared at her.

"I like your rougher edges. Even in bed. It surprised me how much I liked you just taking what you wanted that morning after the snowstorm. I freaked out a little because..."

"Why?"

"Probably because I did like it so much. It scared me to think I could give up everything to you if you asked. But that's the real truth, isn't it? You'll never ask for more than I'm willing to give you and you'll give me what I need even when I'm not exactly sure what that is."

"Ginger—"

"I'm sorry. I never meant to make you think I couldn't handle it. Or you. I like all sides of you, Kane McKay."

"Is that a yes to my marriage proposal?"

Ginger snorted. "Yes. As if there was ever any doubt that I'd marry you."

He beamed a grin that caused her heart to skip a beat. "Wanna know something else?" He laughed a little nervously. "I was busier than you know while I was sneaking around in town yesterday."

"What did you do?"

"Stopped by your house and asked your father for his blessing to marry you. I wasn't gonna ask the ornery bugger for his permission and give him a chance to say no, but I didn't want to spring it on him, either. He's a big part of your life, which means he'll be a big part of mine too."

This sweet, fiery, protective man had thought of everything that was important to her. "Does Hayden know?"

"Nah. I figured we could tell Hayden together if I got you to say yes and had the ring on your finger."

"You already bought a ring?"

His face flushed crimson. "I'm optimistic. But I never thought I'd be showin' it to you in the crapper. Christ Almighty, talk about romantic."

Ginger touched his jaw. "That you want to be with me forever is highly romantic."

He rummaged in his vest pocket, bringing out a small black velvet bag with a gold drawstring.

She reached for it and he moved it out of reach.

"Huh-uh. Close your eyes and give me your left hand."

Cool metal circled her fourth finger.

"Okay. Now you can look."

Even in dim bathroom lighting the ring sparkled. The round emerald was nestled in the middle of silver vines, connected to clusters of small pink stones surrounded by rectangular diamonds that fanned out to create flowers. She gasped and blinked at him. "Oh my God, Kane. This is exquisite."

"The green stone reminded me of your eyes." His thumb swept over the center of the ring. "It wasn't a custom design, but it seemed like fate when I saw it. The pink diamonds reminded me of the dress you wore when we first met, so I just went ahead and bought it."

"When?"

Kane blushed again. "Colt called me a pussy and told me to man up, grow up and marry you. So he and Kade dragged my ass to Spearfish when we had a small break durin' calving."

Ginger brought his hand to her lips and kissed his rough-skinned knuckles. "I'm so going to love being married to you."

"Why? Because I buy you jewelry?"

"No. Because you are the best man, with the biggest heart, that I've ever known, and I am the luckiest woman in the world to have found you. I'd take you to bed to prove it, but I'm still feeling barfy."

His blue eyes clouded with concern. "Is this normal?"

"I think so. It was a blur being pregnant with Hayden, especially those early months."

"Well, sugar, I'll be involved every step of the way this time so don't even think about tryin' to handle any of this on your own."

"I won't. I promise."

"Although havin' a baby is gonna be cool, the bonus is I get Hayden as mine. I want to adopt him, Red. Make him my son in name too."

She'd always suspected Hayden had been Kane's son in his heart. "Come on. Let's go talk to him."

Kane helped her to her feet. He wrapped his fingers around her upper arms and studied her intently. "How do you think he's gonna react?"

"Just like me."

His eyes widened. "He'll throw up?"

Ginger smiled. "Probably. Then he'll strut around like he hit the lottery." She tapped him on the chest. "He's going to take full credit for us getting together."

"Because of the Little Buddies program?"

"No, because of the lucky hat he gave you."

"It worked. I'm unlucky at cards, but I'm damn lucky in love."

Chapter Twenty

Two weeks later...

Kane whistled as he scaled the steps to Ginger's office.

He found himself whistling all the damn time in the last two weeks since Ginger agreed to make him the happiest man alive. So far they'd only hit a few bumps in the road in melding their lives together. They'd decided on a small ceremony at the courthouse, keeping the attendance to immediate family: Hayden and Dash, his folks, Kade and Skylar and their girls. Ginger's best friend, Ava Dumond, was flying in from California to stand up for Ginger and he'd tapped Kade as his best man.

But the after party, held at the Golden Boot, courtesy of his parents and Dash Paulson, would include all his McKay relations, as well as relatives from the West side, and all of Dash's friends and clients over the years. His mother was in hog heaven planning the shindig with his Aunt Carolyn, who'd been through her fair share of McKay wedding receptions. Dash just rolled his eyes and opened his checkbook.

Hayden had taken the news of them becoming a family far better than either he or Ginger anticipated. When Kane mentioned adoption, Hayden immediately stopped calling him Buck and started calling him "Dad", which had been beyond cool in Kane's opinion. But it also drove home the point there was a big difference between being a Big Buddy and being a father. But he couldn't imagine loving any kid more than he did Hayden.

Kane knocked on Ginger's office door. He heard a muffled "Come in," and entered the room.

The redheaded woman of his dreams stood in front of the window behind her desk, her left arm braced across her lower belly, her left hand up by her face.

"Ginger? Everything okay?"

She shook her head and he was by her side instantaneously.

Kane turned her to face him. His heart plummeted at seeing her tear-stained face and red-rimmed eyes. "Do you feel all right?"

"No." Her arms circled his waist. She sobbed against his chest. She cried so hard he couldn't make heads nor tails of the words.

He held her, attempting to soothe her. When her cries faded, he tipped her chin up and wiped her tears. "You're scarin' me. What's goin' on?"

"It's my dad. You know he's supposed to stay at the retirement home temporarily while we're on our honeymoon?"

Kane nodded.

"Well, he told me he's moving in there permanently."

"What?"

"He said he didn't want to get in the way of us becoming a real family and it'd be best all around if he just moved out. Why would he even say that?"

Because the old coot was being a damn fool and still making assumptions.

"I just want to scream at him. Then I think great, if I'm even remotely considering berating a handicapped man...what kind of mother am I going to be to this baby?"

"Ssh. Hey. C'mere." Kane's heart broke with her every stuttered sob. He led her to the couch in the corner of her office. "Sit. Relax. Better yet, lay down."

"I don't have time to lie down. I have to talk to him. Right away, before we get married and go on our honeymoon. I have to make him understand—"

"You need to chill out. Getting all worked up ain't good for you. Now I want you to lay here and think happy thoughts until you've calmed down."

She inhaled and released a long sigh.

"That's my girl. I'll go talk to Dash. See if I can't get to the bottom of it, okay?"

"You'd do that for me?"

"Don't you know by now that I'd do anything for you?" He

pressed his lips to her forehead. "But this isn't just about you. It affects all of us. You don't have to do any of this alone any more, Ginger."

Tears shimmered in her eyes again. "I love you."

"I love you too. Stop cryin', sugar. I'll send Rissa in with some tea before you upset yourself to the point you start barfin' again."

"Too late. Oh God. Hand me the garbage can."

Lightning fast, he had the small garbage can by the edge of the couch. "You want me to stay and hold your hair?" He'd gotten in a lot of practice holding her hair and rubbing her back as she suffered through morning sickness. Although he felt guilty as hell their child was making her the vomit queen, he was so damn excited about this baby he could hardly stand it. But he'd hold off on telling her his mother's suspicions on why Ginger was so sick...at least until after the honeymoon and Doc Monroe confirmed it at their first prenatal appointment.

"No. Go. I'll be fine."

With one last, lingering look, he left and spoke to Rissa before heading outside.

In a town the size of Sundance, it took him about four minutes to walk to the retirement home. He brushed off the snow from his clothes and hat, thinking in three days he and Ginger would be in sunny California enjoying a week at Ava's beach house, just the two of them.

He walked up to the kiosk and recognized the woman manning the desk as a former classmate. "Lucy. How are you?"

"Good. I hear congratulations are in order."

"Thanks."

Lucy leaned closer. "Tell me the truth, wild man McKay. Are you nervous about settling down with just one woman?"

"Nope. Been waiting for her all my life." Kane smiled because the question didn't bother him. "Where have you stashed Dash Paulson?"

"Room twelve."

He skirted wheelchairs and carts until he stood in front of the right door. It was fully open, but he knocked anyway. "Dash? You in here?"

"Where else would I be?"

Kane fought his *Testy much?* response.

"You might as well come in and sit down."

Not exactly a hearty welcome. Kane crossed the tile floor. It was the first time he'd been in this side of the nursing home/assisted living facility. The space had a living area with a big picture window, and a loveseat and a chair. The TV was on an end table, shoved against the wall. A kitchenette consisted of a countertop with stools beneath and a small refrigerator and a microwave on the opposite wall. No stove. A doorway off to the left led to a bedroom and a bathroom. Everything in the place was brand new and handicapped-accessible.

"Did my daughter send you here?"

"Nope. I volunteered." Kane took off his coat and plopped on the couch. He waited for Dash to wheel to the open spot beside the recliner. "So what's this bullshit about you movin' in here permanently?"

Dash straightened in his wheelchair, notching up his stubborn chin. "Not bullshit. It's time I permanently settle in a place like this."

"Why? Is the bed comfier here?"

That gave Dash pause. "No."

"Tastier food?"

"No."

Kane glanced around the room. "It can't be lure of the luxury atmosphere that's makin' you uproot your life. This place is more bland than my trailer." Kane's eyes narrowed. "Is this about sex? Are you knockin' boots with a horny widow and you want privacy to get it on?"

Dash's mouth dropped open. Then snapped shut. "What in the hell is wrong with you, McKay? Even if I was, what business is it of yours?"

"Two days from now, what happens in this family definitely will be my business. So if you ain't upgraded to a place that's better, why would you wanna leave the comforts of the home you've already got?"

When Dash cocked his head and studied him, Kane was glad he'd never stood before this man when he'd been Judge Dash Paulson.

"Since you're a straight shooter, I'll give it to you plain. I never intended to live with Ginger and Hayden forever."

"That so?"

Dash nodded. "My daughter seemed eager to create that happy family vibe she'd been denied growing up and I went along with it to make her happy. I'd always hoped she'd find a good man and settle down. Now that she's about to get married, it's time for me to let her have her own family life."

Kane looked at Dash coolly. "As long as we're bein' honest and all... Have I ever given you the sense that I don't want you around?"

Another confused look. "Well, no. But you've got to admit taking on the responsibility of a wife, a young boy, and soon enough, a baby, is plenty to have on your plate. You'll still be ranching fulltime too."

"And you believe I can't do it all...because I ain't got a college degree? That juggling several roles is beyond my limited capabilities?"

"No."

"Then what's the real reason for you bailin' on your family?"

Dash glared at him. "Blast it, boy, I'm giving you an out."

"How so?"

"By making sure that taking care of an infirm old man isn't on your list of roles. Despite the fact I've hired a male nurse to assist me with personal needs I can no longer do for myself, I'd still be underfoot all the time. I can't imagine you'd be happy about that."

Kane counted to ten. "You think I'm that shallow?"

"Maybe at first I wasn't thrilled when I figured out you two had feelings for each other." He pointed at Kane. "And yes, this was before you volunteered to 'help' out after her accident. I worried about your previous ladies' man reputation and I believed you'd get fed up with her after a spell and Ginger would end up getting hurt."

Her take-charge nature appealed to him, but he appreciated that she was comfortable enough to let him call the shots.

"Since she's established herself here, it's not like she can run away, like she did after that rotten business in California."

Again, he fought the urge to defend himself. "I sense a 'but'."

"But I was wrong to be worried. I'm glad I kept my damn

fool mouth shut and let this play out between you two without my interference. You're a good man and the best thing that's happened to her since she moved to Sundance. You two need a chance to...bond or whatever."

"Trust me, Ginger's mornin' sickness is proof of how well she and I have already bonded," Kane said dryly.

The corners of Dash's mouth twitched.

"What about Hayden? He's always spent so much time with you. Doesn't your grandson get his say about how this move will affect him?"

Sadness flickered in Dash's eyes. "That boy can come and see me a couple of times a week. Besides, you'll need time to build a father bond with Hayden."

"What about the father bond you've finally built with Ginger?" Kane countered. "You just gonna throw that away?"

"Never." Dash placed his gnarled hands on his knees. "But be honest, wouldn't it be better if I wasn't there?"

"Better for who?"

"For all of you."

"Bullshit." Kane gave him a long, measured look. "Did you know that my Grandpa McKay lived with us from my fourth birthday until he passed when I was almost thirteen?"

"I vaguely recall something about that."

"Since Carson was older than my dad by like ten minutes, Grandpop deeded him the family ranch house after my grandma died. Plus, Uncle Carson and Aunt Carolyn kept havin' all them kids and needed the space. Grandpop didn't much like his son Casper, so movin' in with him was out as an option. And he wasn't too fond of my Uncle Charles' wife, Vi, neither. So he came to live with us."

"How'd your mama feel about that? Wasn't there bad blood between the Wests and the McKays?"

"For years. But my Ma never got along with her own father, and Grandpop never had a daughter, so surprisingly, the two of them hit it off like gangbusters."

"It's hard not to like your mama."

"She is something else." Kane smiled. "So Kade and I were raised by both our parents and our grandfather. It didn't cause problems because Ma and Dad handled all the discipline. Grandpop never butted in—at least if he did, it wasn't in front of my brother and me. He taught us everything from how to hunt and fish, to how to rope and ride. How being honest wasn't a character trait to be discarded when it suited."

Dash was quiet for a spell and Kane wasn't sure he'd gotten his point across.

"But that's where I'm back to reminding you that I can't do any of those things with my grandson because I'm in this damn wheelchair."

"As frustrating as that must be to you, who taught Hayden how to play chess? Or to use critical thinking skills? You've passed on your love of history to him. The kid devours books. Just because you're not out on a horse with him or worming a fishhook for him don't mean you're useless to him. Far from it, Dash." When the man opened his mouth to argue, Kane braced himself to fight back with everything he had.

"The McKay family is massive. Now Hayden will have cousins, aunts and uncles and more family than he can shake a stick at."

"But none of them will replace you. I ain't lookin' to replace you either."

Dash frowned.

"Look, havin' my grandpop in my life growin' up didn't seem special or cool because we didn't know any other way. He was always there. Always part of the family. That's where me'n Hayden are alike. It's what I knew. It's what Hayden knows. You've been in his life every day since he moved here. I'd bet he can't remember a day when you weren't around. You are his family. So don't do this to him. Or to Ginger. Or hell, even to me."

"To you?" he repeated skeptically.

"Yeah. I'm a selfish bastard. I want Hayden to continue havin' this same kind of childhood—growin' up in his house surrounded by his family—that I did. His life wouldn't be the same without you in it every day, Dash. Neither would Ginger's. And I don't want you cheatin' this baby out of the same chance to know you because you have some misguided sense of pride. Please. Swallow it and come back home with us where you belong."

Silence floated between them. Kane stood and gazed out the window, allowing Dash time to compose himself. He needed time to get a handle on his emotions too. He hadn't realized how strongly he felt about this until he'd said it out loud.

Finally, Dash spoke. "All right, McKay, you made a very convincing argument. I'll agree to live there, as before, on one condition."

"Damn lawyers and their conditions," Kane muttered. "What's the condition?"

"I'm never getting out of this wheelchair. My body will eventually fail me. The time will come when I'll require fulltime care and I won't put that burden on my daughter, on my grandson, or now, on you. So promise me when that day arrives, you'll back me, despite whatever claim my daughter makes that she'll be happy caring for me in perpetuity. She'll need to let me go. You'll have to side with me, Kane. Against her. It won't be easy, but I deserve to leave the situation with a little dignity."

Kane whirled around and faced him. "Dammit, Dash. I don't even wanna think about that."

"You have to."

"Can't we wait to make that decision until that time comes?"

Dash shook his head. "I need the promise now."

"Why?"

"Because you're a man of your word. To be honest, this has been weighing on me for a while. I knew I'd never get Ginger to stick to it. But you? You will."

He opened his mouth. Found the words stuck in his throat. He swallowed a couple of times. "Okay. You have my word."

Dash was visibly relieved. "Good."

"Now can I tell your daughter you had a change of heart?"

"Absolutely."

Kane skirted the recliner and stopped to place his hand on Dash's shoulder. "Thank you. I mean that."

"I know you do, son." He covered Kane's hand with his. "I look forward to whipping your butt in poker for many years to come, McKay."

"Bring it. And don't cry foul when I end up with a whole pile of your money."

Dash's laughter followed Kane out of the room.

He'd cleared the doorjamb when Ginger launched herself at him. She squeezed him so tightly he could barely breathe.

"Thank you," she whispered. "I thought maybe you'd need backup, so I hung out here, but you did fine on your own. Better than fine actually."

"Good to know," he murmured.

"You'd make a damn good lawyer," she said.

"Bite your tongue," Kane shot back.

Ginger smirked. "Have I told you lately that I love you?"

"Not in the last hour."

She peppered his face with kisses. "I love love love you, Kane McKay."

"I love love love you too, Red."

"I'm feeling much better. How about if we pick Hayden up from school and go out for an early family dinner?"

Kane brushed the curls from her face, wondering if he'd ever get used to the idea that this beautiful, perfect, smart, sexy woman had picked him. "Sounds good. Glad to see you've got your appetite back."

"That's not the only appetite I've got back," she purred.

He chuckled and untangled her arms from his neck. "Hold that thought." He walked the twenty steps back to Dash's room and yelled inside. "Hey, Gramps? Think you can make yourself presentable before I come back to get you in an hour or so? We're all goin' out for supper."

"Does that offer include beer?"

"Yep."

"Then I'll be ready."

Ginger looped his arm through his as they walked past the front desk. "Why an hour? Why don't we just load him up now?"

"Because it's my job as your baby daddy to sate all your appetites. And guess which one will always get priority?"

She blushed. And giggled.

He so was going to love being married to this woman for the rest of his life. "We have an hour, an empty house, and it'd be a damn cryin' shame to let it go to waste."

"Effective time management. Just another thing I love about you, cowboy."

"What can I say? My mama raised me right."

About the Author

To learn more about Lorelei James, please visit www.loreleijames.com. Send an email to lorelei@loreleijames.com or join her Yahoo! group to join in the fun with other readers as well as Lorelei: http://groups.yahoo.com/group/LoreleiJamesGang

Pulling off the ultimate con...
if they can keep from pulling off their clothes.

All Jacked Up
© *2009 Lorelei James*
Rough Riders, Book 8

Keely McKay knows Jack—and Jack Donohue is a certified pain in her Wranglers. The lone girl in the prolific McKay family, Keely needs another man giving her orders like she needs a hole in her boot. What she does need is a restoration specialist so she can open her physical therapy clinic—and prove she's left her wild-child days behind. That means dealing with buttoned-down, uptight Jack.

Jack is this close to securing a career make-or-break project, until he learns his lack of marital status puts him out of contention. When the notoriously hot-tempered and hot-bodied Keely begs him for help, he proposes a crazy idea. He'll oversee her project—if she acts the part of his loving fiancée.

Their sizzling lust makes it all too easy to go from butting heads to knocking boots—but outside the bedroom they're as mismatched as ever. The McKays remind Jack of the humble upbringing he left behind, and cowgirl Keely feels she doesn't measure up to Jack's big-city lifestyle.

When the dust settles, Jack and Keely must face the fact they're not fooling anyone but themselves—or they'll risk losing the real deal.

Warning: This book contains one hot-blooded cowgirl and one cool-headed businessman in a stripped-down, revved-up game of sexual truth or dare.

Available now in ebook and print from Samhain Publishing.

*The truth could make their
one perfect night crumble into dust.*

A Little White Lie
© 2010 Mackenzie McKade

It's Friday night and advertising agent Stella Sinclair's plan to catch the red-eye back to New York is fading with the Montana sunset. She'll do anything to land this western-wear company's account, but what's she going to do all weekend in this Podunk town?

On the way back to the hotel to watch paint peel from the walls, she makes a quick stop in a local bar to answer the call of nature. One slippery spot later, her stiletto heels are flying—and her fall is broken by the most delicious cowboy she's ever laid eyes on.

Heaven just dropped into JD Foster's arms. City girls—and city life—aren't his style, which made it easy to skip out on his grandfather's business meeting earlier today. For this classical beauty, though, he just might make an exception.

A drink, a dance, and their chemistry takes the reins. Then JD remembers why Stella's name seems familiar. She's courting the family business. JD wants her sighing in pleasure tonight, but for the right reasons. And he's not above withholding a vital detail or two in order to seal the deal...

Warning: This book contains lies, explicit sex, and betrayal. All necessary elements to light a fire between two people and lay the foundation for some really hot makeup sex.

Available now in ebook from Samhain Publishing.